Bill Smoot's *San Quentin Exodus* is a thoughtful, deeply humane novel that blends social realism with quiet suspense. Written with restraint and intelligence, the book explores incarceration, identity, and moral courage without resorting to melodrama or easy answers...One of the book's strengths is its moral complexity. Smoot does not frame the story as a simple critique of the justice system, nor does he romanticize escape. James understands the risk clearly: "The greater danger is not that he'll get caught... but that the hope he's allowed himself to feel will die." Hope, not freedom alone, becomes the central currency of the novel.

— Kyle Eaton, *San Francisco Review*

San Quentin Exodus, Bill Smoot's deeply compelling novel, introduces readers to the world of prison but really to the much bigger world of his characters' lives, inviting us to follow the trajectory of each as it unfolds with surprise and mystery, love and loss. Like all good literature, *San Quentin Exodus* ultimately asks us to reconsider everything we believe—or think we believe. Smoot is the consummate storyteller: restrained, wise, compassionate.

— Lori Ostlund, author of *Are You Happy?* and *The Bigness of the World*

In *San Quentin Exodus*, Bill Smoot takes us deeply into the world of incarceration and rehabilitation, with its pitfalls and fragile possibility. Smoot has delivered two unforgettable characters whose encounter alters the trajectory of each of their lives. The social and economic circumstances that lead to the young James's incarceration, and the disturbing story of his long tenure behind bars, suggest the abject limitations of our current penal system, while the well-intentioned Allison, who tutors James in the prison's college program, draws upon the perspective of her own marginalization to risk everything in the story's dramatic final act.

— Angela Pneuman, author of *Lay It on My Heart* and *Home Remedies*

A belief in a "truer kind of justice" powers Smoot's ambitious, engaging novel, which blends coming-of-age story, adult redemption

arc, thoughtful social drama, and an exciting attempted prison break. In a tantalizing prologue, Smoot introduces Allison Anderson, one of his two protagonists, six years after she started volunteering as a prison tutor at San Quentin prison. From her first moments inside the medium-security penitentiary, her problem-solving mind speculates on how a prisoner might escape. In the book's present, she is about to put a real plan in motion to spring James, incarcerated for 30 years. With readers hooked, the narrative flashes back to the 1980s, James's rough-and-tumble California childhood, and two pressing mysteries: how did he wind up in prison, and will Allison's plan succeed?

— *Publishers Weekly*

The power of this book lies in the author's deep compassion for both characters. The characters are so strong, this would be an excellent read even if the book had no plot. Smoot creates complex portraits of emotionally rich lives in short, clear sentences reminiscent of Hemingway. To be able to convey such richness with such simple prose requires instinct and skill. The writing style makes the book easy to read, while the story and characters make it hard to put down.... The world needs more writing like this.

— Andrew Diamond, *Andrew Diamond Blog*

Are you ready for a book to touch your soul? *San Quentin Exodus* delivers blow after blow to the heart... but leaves you jumping for joy in the end.

The book takes places in California, where a young Black man, James, who just wants to do the right thing, gets caught up in a whirlwind of a mess that leaves him behind bars. And it seems like the world just wants to keep him there. There is hope, however, in the shape of a girl from Indiana who formulates a plan to break James out of his prison home for good.

This book deals with themes of race, poverty, sexual orientation, and more. It was wonderful to read about a strong LGBTQ+ female lead, and some pages will leave you screaming at the all-too-familiar failures of the justice system, especially when it relates to race.

Smoot's writing is powerful, yet easy to digest. He is character-driven and intellectual, but far from isolating. The realism is truly believable as he brings us along on the prison ride (and college, and

Covid), and the result is an unforgettable story about two unforgettable people.

— Anna Keibler, author of *Firecrackers*

The narrative tension builds steadily, balancing moments of stark realism with introspective depth. Smoot avoids simplistic portrayals of villainy or sainthood; instead, he presents layered characters grappling with responsibility, consequence, and the hope of reintegration. The institutional setting becomes almost a character in itself unyielding, watchful, and deeply influential in shaping the fates of those within its walls.

San Quentin Exodus appears poised to resonate with readers interested in justice reform, human resilience, and stories of second chances. It promises not only drama but thoughtful engagement with themes of accountability, dignity, and the possibility of renewal beyond confinement.

— Michael Doane

A morally ambiguous redemption story, filled with pain, courage, and hope, that captures and intrigues the reader from the first page... *San Quentin Exodus* is masterfully written and utterly compelling as it captures the stark contrasts between the characters and their environments. Highly recommended!

— Sublime Book Review

San Quentin Exodus

San Quentin Exodus

Bill Smoot

First Edition

Library of Congress Control Number: 2025948870

Hardcover ISBN: 978-1-62720-671-6
Paperback ISBN: 978-1-62720-672-3
Ebook ISBN: 978-1-62720-673-0

Cover Design by Leo Arcelay Christiano
Editorial Development by Kate Tourison
Promotional Development by Chase Lawson

Published by Apprentice House Press

Loyola University Maryland
4501 N. Charles Street, Baltimore, MD 21210
410.617.5265
www.ApprenticeHouse.com / info@ApprenticeHouse.com

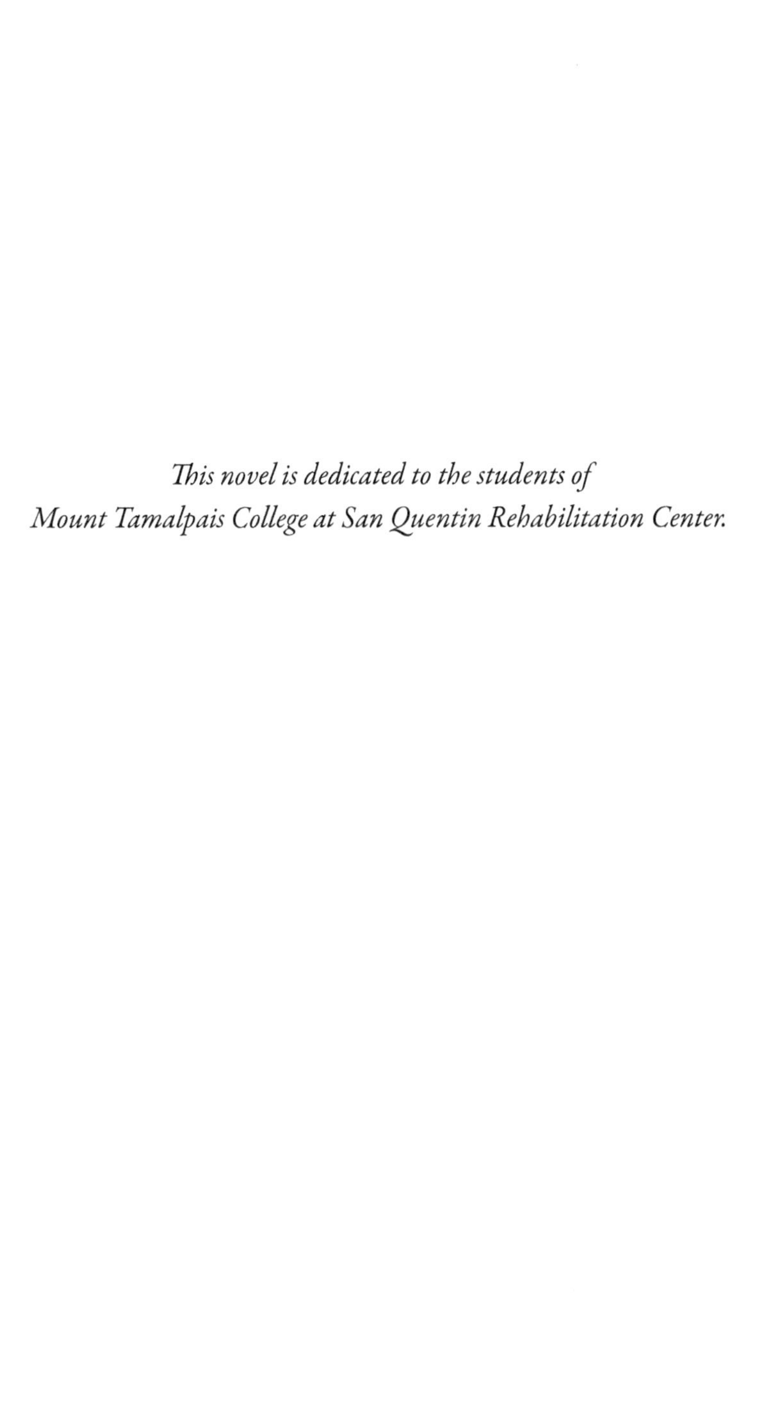

This novel is dedicated to the students of
Mount Tamalpais College at San Quentin Rehabilitation Center.

Novels are political not because writers carry party cards—some do, I do not—but because good fiction is about identifying with and understanding people who are not necessarily like us. By nature all good novels are political because identifying with the other is political. At the heart of "the art of the novel" lies the human capacity to see the world through others' eyes. Compassion is the greatest strength of the novelist.

--Orhan Pamuk

Prologue

Wings

In one week Allison Anderson will commit her first felony: section 4550 of the California Penal Code, helping someone escape from a state prison. Almost everyone who knows her would be stunned with disbelief. For her, it's the ultimate realization of who she is.

One autumn evening six years ago, Allison entered San Quentin Prison as a volunteer tutor. Walking across the prison grounds, she gazed at the forty-foot walls, the spirals of razor-wire, and the imposing guard towers. She wondered how an inmate might escape. It was her first time in a prison, and the question engaged her problem-solving mind. She did not know that one day she would devise an escape plan. She did not know that she would put that plan into action. At the time, it was just a thought experiment, a challenge for a woman whose childhood heroine was Nancy Drew, girl sleuth.

Allison's most vivid memory of entering the prison that evening was the birds. When she and her group rounded the hospital building and walked across the yard, she saw geese and gulls scratching the ground on the baseball field. It was mere minutes before the October sun would set, and their white feathers glowed like gold. A single goose stretched his neck, dipped his thick body, and with a push from his feet and a flapping of his great wings, he rose from the ground and glided across the field, then soared over the wall. Other geese did the same, their necks piercing the air like arrows. Seagulls followed. The walls and guard towers were mere landmarks below them, like trees or outcroppings of rock, obstacles they cleared with ease. They didn't need an escape plan. They had wings.

The First Day and the Last

They say that the two days of prison an inmate remembers most vividly are his first and his last. Everything in between is a blur. James' first day was thirty years ago. His last—maybe—will be in one week. If Hemingway's character could walk away from war, James can declare his separate peace from prison. It's time to move on, regardless of what the parole board has ruled. It's necessary. An absolute must.

For society, James is a statistic, another Black man languishing in prison, costing the state $75,000 a year. His escape—if it succeeds—will save taxpayers money. For himself, it will be his personal exodus, his promised land of another chance at life.

If things go according to plan, no one will know how he did it. He will just disappear, a man become a ghost. Allison is a smart young lady, and he can't find any flaws in her plan, but he is haunted by that old saying: *If it seems too good to be true, then it probably is.*

James is filled with yearning and fear. The greater danger is not that he'll get caught and have time added to his sentence—though that's a real possibility—but that the hope he's allowed himself to feel will die. That's the greater risk. The loss of hope he could not bear.

He lies in his bunk, trying to conjure up positive images. The thought of freedom makes his skin prickle. The shadows of the bars cross his body, spill onto the concrete floor. He listens to the cell block tick with sound, as if the walls are straining to breathe. He imagines a seagull soaring on the wind.

Part One

Sacramento, 1983

It's the summer James turns twelve, and they live on a street of small, well-kept bungalows in Sacramento—Mama, Pops, and James. Their block is mixed: two other Black families, a few White, one Chinese, and one Mexican. Their next-door neighbors are Russian. Pops grows tomatoes in the back yard, and when he wants to make James laugh, he calls their city Sack-a-tomatoes. Mama works as a caretaker at a home for old people. She wants to become a nurse and takes classes at night school. In six years she will have her nursing degree. Pops owns a one-man carpet cleaning business that he started when he got out of the Air Force. He likes having his own business.

"A man should obey only one person—himself," he says. "I took enough orders in the Air Force to last me a lifetime."

Mama is plump and her face is round and soft. Pops is tall with broad shoulders. He holds his chin up as if he's going somewhere. His eyes crinkle when he smiles.

Soon after James was born, Mama required surgery that left her unable to have more children. From this, James draws a heavy sense of responsibility—he is *it.* He has to be everything his brothers and sisters might have been. He minds his parents and teachers, does his homework at school and his chores at home, and strives to do the right thing. A good boy—that's who he is.

In James' room hangs a poster of George Washington Carver, a lab apron over his suit coat and tie, a flower in his lapel. Surrounded by laboratory equipment, he writes in a notebook. He is making discoveries that will help people. He looks pleased. He is James' hero.

The daughter of the Chinese family on their street is in the same home room as James. Her name is Christine Chan. Her porcelain face is the first thing he has been moved to call pretty. Her long black hair glistens in the sun. When he offers to carry her books the eight blocks from school, she presses her lips into a shy smile and says, "No, thank you."

James listens in while Pops tells Mama about a new client opening the door surprised to find a Black man on the porch.

"Has one ever said anything, or canceled an order?" Mama asks, already knowing the answer. She likes to see the glass half full.

"They don't have to say anything. Their face freezes, just long enough for me to see it," Pops says. "Got my red polo shirt that says *A-1 Carpet Cleaning* in white letters. Paid extra for the stitching. Got my red cap, same thing. If it's cold, I'm wearing my red jacket: *A-1 Carpet Cleaning.* Funny how it takes them a minute to notice those white letters on bright red. Guess my big black face just gets in the way. Can be ninety degrees and their face freezes like it's January in Chicago."

Mama narrows her eyes at Pops and jerks her head toward James. She doesn't want him discouraged by these stories.

James wonders if Christine has a frozen face for him. As a test, he gets Kenny, a White boy who lives the next block over, to ask to carry her books. She gives Kenny the same pressed-lips smile, the same "No, thank you."

The church they belong to is mostly Black. Mama takes James to services, but Pops isn't religious and attends only the social events like barbeque picnics. Pops has an old turntable and stereo, and sometimes he puts on his old records—mostly Motown. He sings along to The Temptations, The Four Tops, Jackie Wilson, Smokey Robinson, Aretha Franklin. He dances in the dining room, and though James laughs, he has to admit that Pops' head bobs are fun, his hip rolls rhythmic and smooth. Sometimes Mama joins in, and James dances off to the side, trying to mimic what Mama and Pops are doing. To him, they look like dancers on *Soul Train*.

While Mama cooks dinner, Pops and James walk over to the park to pass baseball or shoot baskets. The park has a lawn kept green in the summer by sprinklers that water the grass at night. There are restrooms in a stone house, a water fountain, and picnic tables. At the far end are two tennis courts, and beyond them, some live oak trees and a large willow tree. Regular park users know one other on sight and wave. Sometimes James sees Christine there with a pink jump rope, her parents sitting on a bench watching her. If someone has a dog at the park, James asks if he can pet it. He hopes to have a dog someday.

After dinner Pops dries the dishes while Mama washes. When James is old enough, he takes over the drying. Pops always compliments Mama on the dinner.

"Your mother is from Georgia," Pops tells him, "and even though they're backward down there—that's just between the two of us—they do some things right, and one of them is being polite. They say please and thank you, yes ma'am and yes sir. You ever hear me get up from dinner and not tell her how good it was?"

"No. No, sir."

"And you should do it, too. People down South might be country, but they have a way of making you feel easy. Women like that kind of thing. Remember that."

James nods.

Watching Mama in the kitchen, James is mesmerized by how she transforms things like dry flour, hard beans, and raw meat into tasty meals. She teaches James how to make chocolate pudding from mix, taking care not to scorch the milk and adding a few drops of vanilla to help the taste. In the garden he learns from Pops how to stake up the tomato plants, how to break off the suckers, how to plant onions between them to repel pests, how not to overwater or the skins will split.

Pops played high school football back in Chicago. A back injury at the beginning of his senior year kept him from getting a college scholarship. A year later his back was good enough to pass the Air Force physical, and he served four years as a maintenance man for jets. He lucked out by not being sent to Vietnam. He married Mama and started his business.

At the end of seventh grade, James has to start wearing glasses. This is the summer Pops' back goes bad. Pushing and pulling the wand of his machine across carpets and lifting the five-gallon tank aggravates his old football injury. Pain spreads like steel tentacles across his back and into his legs. He tries to power through the pain. One morning he can't straighten up. He lies on his side grimacing while James and Mama struggle to pull on his pants for him one leg at a time. He walks to the car bent over, his upper torso parallel to the ground. James has never seen him like this. His new glasses make things clearer than he wants.

Wiping tears from her face, Mama drives Pops to the hospital. After X-rays and MRIs, a specialist says Pops needs expensive and risky surgery on several discs and vertebrae, and he can't guarantee the result. They don't have insurance or money to pay for it. Pops hobbles around the house with a cane, assuring Mama he will get better. He gets on the phone and cancels his upcoming jobs. He mutters that it's going to kill his business. Grimacing, he squirms in his chair as if he's trying to escape from his own back. He calls the doctor for stronger pain pills. He looks for another job, one where he won't have to lift, twist, or bend over.

Weeks become months. His back worsens. Even though Pops hasn't found another job, he sells his carpet cleaning business and his van to a White man for what he calls "pennies on the dollar."

Something is different in the house, and James feels worried. Life has never been like this. Mama looks like she's smiling to keep from crying. Pops sits in his chair with the TV on, swallowing pain pills and washing them down with beer. He uses a cane and walks bent at the waist. His face is scrunched in a permanent grimace.

A year passes, and James is in eighth grade. As if it will make Pops' back better, James studies hard and makes the honor roll. Some days, Pops takes the bus into a bad part of Sacramento. Mama tries to get him back to the doctor, but he won't go. He falls asleep in his chair. His voice trails off when he talks. His eyes look dull, his eyelids heavy. One afternoon James opens the front door after school and sees Pops in his chair injecting his arm with a needle. Looking up, Pops mumbles that it's a new medicine from the doctor. When James says his prayers, he asks God to make Pops better.

One January evening Pops doesn't come home for dinner. Mama looks through the front window at the darkening street. She serves James his dinner. While she is washing and James is drying the dishes, two policemen knock on the door. When they see James, they ask to talk to Mama on the front porch. They tell her that Pops lost consciousness and died on the bus. Mama tells James that it was a heart attack. James feels like he's been watching a burning house that has finally collapsed. A mound of cold, wet ashes remains. He can taste the ashes in his mouth.

A small funeral is held in the church. Neither Mama nor Pops has siblings or living parents, so theirs is the smallest family James knows of. Two women Mama works with at the nursing home attend, as do a dozen people from their church. Christine Chan's family and the Russian family from their block are there. Christine approaches James with short, rapid steps and tells him she is sorry for his loss. He wonders if she'll let him carry her books now. Mama tells everyone it was a heart attack. When they remark that he was so young, she says that it was a massive heart attack, and they nod like that explains it.

It's the first time James has seen a dead person. Lying in the casket, Pops is dressed in a suit and tie, his face waxy and thin. Dark circles surround his eyes and his skin is an unearthly shade of brown. James feels like it's somebody else. Like it's some big joke and Pops will be at home waiting for them. His back will be better and they will have a good laugh. Pops will put on a Motown record and dance.

The minister starts the ceremony and everyone stands up to pray. It's a long prayer, and halfway through, Mama crumples to the carpet. James is paralyzed and fears she's had a heart attack. Mrs. Chan kneels beside Mama and pats her hand. A church woman fans her with a hymnal. The minister sends someone for water. When Mama comes to, she asks where James is. Mrs. Chan points to him and Mama starts to cry. Someone hands her water in a paper cup. She sits for the rest of the ceremony, which the minister seems to cut short.

The next afternoon, the Chans knock on the door. On the porch, they bow and present Mama with a casserole. Christine stands behind her mother, watching James. After they leave, Mama heats the food—fried rice, mushrooms, and bits of duck. James has never eaten Chinese food before but he likes the new tastes. He imagines that if he marries Christine she will make this for dinner.

At school, kids get quiet when James is around. They don't know what to say and neither does he. He avoids the park because he is afraid of how he'll feel when he gets there. Mama talks to him about more things now. Or maybe she just talks to herself while he's there. Money is a big problem. They get social security checks but it isn't enough. Her job doesn't pay much, and their rent is too high. Bills pile up. They owe a large chunk to the funeral parlor.

One Saturday their car is towed away because they've missed three payments. James feels guilty, like he should have done something to help Pops, like he should do something now. He works hard on his homework and tries to be extra polite. He does household chores before he's asked. He reads a biography of George Washington Carver, whose father died when he was an infant. He vows to study and work hard as Carver did. He wonders if he can grow tomatoes like Pops. Maybe he could improve them, like Carver did with peanuts.

Just after James finishes eighth grade, Mama finds a job with the DMV, but it's at the Oakland office. That means they have to move. The first thing James thinks of is Christine. Maybe he can write her letters. A man from their church rents them an apartment in a small building he owns in Oakland. The Russian man who lives next door will drive them to Oakland in his truck. Men from the church help them load their stuff. James and Mama stand on the sidewalk and look at their now empty house. Scenes of their life there play in James' mind. The Chans bring them a paper plate of sweet buns and wish them luck. James and Christine shake hands. It is the first time he has touched her soft skin. He and Mama sit beside the Russian man in the cab of his truck. When they pull away from the curb, James turns and tries to look at their house, but he can't see out the back.

Nancy Drew

One Saturday afternoon in the autumn Allison turns ten, she stops at a yard sale on her block in Indianapolis, mesmerized by a box of old Nancy Drew novels in the neighbor's driveway. These are originals, written in the 1930s, and their titles contain words like *hidden, mystery, secret*, and *clue*. The old-fashioned covers, painted by Russell Tandy, show a steady-eyed Nancy Drew taking a courageous step toward some source of likely danger like an abandoned farmhouse or a hidden staircase.

Allison feels a jolt of kinship, and she spends her saved-up allowance money on the box of books. At home, she arranges the volumes on her bed and studies the covers. Bent forward from the waist, Nancy Drew wears trim slacks or a long skirt and a neat blouse with a fitted blazer. It is the first time Allison notices fashion. Nancy Drew's hair is parted to one side, Lauren Bacall style. The novels call her hair color titian. When Allison is older, she will say the girl on those covers occupies that sweet spot of femme-leaning with a whisper of butch. It's the style she will aspire to, like a sauce with the perfect balance of savory and sweet. When her middle school classmates are taking fashion cues from *Seventeen*, Allison will wonder where to get a blazer or a cloche hat like Nancy Drew's.

As Allison reads her way through the novels, she falls in love with Nancy's way of being in the world—smart, calm under pressure, determined. Purposeful. A problem solver. Nancy's courage doesn't call attention to itself; it's the byproduct of letting nothing stand in her way of solving a mystery, of lending a hand to someone who needs help. Her tools are mental: sharp logic, attention to details, investigations of things most people miss. This is the time of the OJ Simpson trial, and Allison follows it on TV, despite her parents' objections, imaging how Nancy Drew would solve the case. By the time Allison finishes all the novels in the box, Nancy Drew is her imaginary friend and secret crush. She is her model, the person Allison wants to be.

Like Nancy Drew, Allison is an only child. Her family lives in a small brick house on a shady street in residential Indianapolis. It has a screened-in back porch. Though she talks more with her mother, she has a stronger bond with her dad, who spends hours in his basement workshop while Allison sits on the steps above his workbench to watch. She inhales the earthy scent of fresh-sawed wood, the acrid smoke curling up from his soldering gun. She dreams up spy devices that could help Nancy Drew solve mysteries: a radio transmitter concealed in a cuckoo clock, a camera hidden in a doll, a secret compartment in a clothes closet.

Sometimes her dad asks her to hold something and she scampers down the steps to be his third hand. She watches him examine a broken appliance. It is a new mystery. Why did it stop working? How can it be fixed? He selects a screwdriver from the rack and removes the top of Mother's steam iron. He examines the small plastic box behind the dial and brings it to his nose.

"Smells burned out," he says aloud.

"Why did that happen?" Allison asks.

"Usually a mechanical malfunction makes the electrical circuit arc over. Remember to consider all the aspects. Here you have the electrical and the mechanical. Each dimension affects the other."

Allison mouths the words: *Each dimension affects the other.*

He shines a tiny flashlight on the plastic and writes the part number on a sheet of paper. He pulls a thick catalog from his shelf and orders the part.

One by one he teaches Allison to use tools: the soldering gun, the hammer, a plane, a rat tail file, the electric drill.

"You'd be surprised how few people know how to hammer a nail," he tells her. "They grip the handle too tight. They pound too hard. They look at the hammer, not the nail. They smash their fingers."

She tells him about her Nancy Drew novels and how Nancy uses logic and intuition to solve mysteries that baffle the police. He nods and reminds Allison that the ultimate tool is the mind. Sometimes in the middle of a book Allison describes the mystery, and she and her dad try to solve it together.

One day when she's reading under the shade tree in the back yard, her dad comes out to water his vegetable garden.

"Want to learn about electricity?" he asks.

"From the hose?"

"Feel the water," he says.

She runs over and holds her palm in front of the nozzle. He reaches back to turn the faucet higher and then lower.

"Feel the difference in pressure? That's like voltage. Now," he says, bending a kink into the hose. "I've narrowed the hose. That's resistance. So how much water is coming out now, more or less?"

"Less."

"The amount coming out is called current. It's how much electricity flows through."

She nods.

"If I increase resistance, is there more or less current?"

She looks at the hose. "Less."

"And what about the pressure, the voltage?"

"More," she answers.

He grins.

That September she starts sixth grade understanding Ohm's Law and the math required to apply it: current equals voltage divided by resistance. As an adult, the sight of a garden hose will remind her of electricity and of her dad.

Allison is acquiring the habits of thought that twenty-five years later she will employ in planning a prison escape.

Oakland, 1985

James and his mother leave their bright Sacramento bungalow and move into a dingy two-bedroom apartment in Oakland. The dust-washed stucco building has four apartments, two on the first floor and two on the second. Theirs is upstairs. The linoleum on the kitchen floor is faded and cracked, the bathtub is rust-stained, and the caulking around the window glass is brittle and crumbling. James tapes his poster of George Washington Carver on his bedroom wall.

"Whoever lived here before didn't care about *nothing*," Mama says. She is angry that the man at her church didn't tell her how bad it is. They are paying double the rent of their bungalow in Sacramento. James locks his bike to the back stairs of the building. When he goes down to ride it on the third morning, it is gone, the chain cut. Mama says they'll move someplace better after she gets a few paychecks.

The move to Oakland feels like a journey to another planet. Running an errand to the nearest corner store is a minefield of threats and traps: passed-out drunks, glaring cops, invitations to buy dope or get a ten-dollar blow job. There are shootings and muggings. James has never heard of crack, but he hears about it now. It's the new thing—a magnet for money, power, and ruin. Words are spray-painted on walls, the style so jacked it's hard to read. James had never seen a condom but now he sees them lying used on the ground. When the sun gets hot, the alleys stink of shit and the sidewalks reek of piss. Porn tabloids spill from newspaper racks. Young kids—both boys and girls—smoke cigarettes. Women lean against buildings in knee-high boots, hot pants, and tube tops. Most are Black but some are White or Asian. The streets pulse with danger and the dark underside of life. Oakland feels like a place where he was not meant to be.

An old man with a black, wizened face and a big gray Afro leans against the wall of the corner store and talks when people pass, like an announcer at a game without end. People call him Einstein. One day he looks at James and says, "Little man *astonished* by what he see."

Black Snake

Every morning James and Mama walk over to the bus stop on International Boulevard. There is a shared, unspoken sadness between them. She catches her bus to the DMV and he boards his bus to the high school. His bus is crowded with adults going to work and kids going to school. The people are Black, Asian, Brown. Of the few White people, most are homeless.

At school, the classrooms and hallways are crowded and loud. Other students seem not to notice him. In the hall a Black boy tells him he dresses like a Chink. A girl overhears and laughs. He looks down at himself. He is wearing khakis, a white polo shirt, and the expansion band Timex watch Mama gave him for his birthday. He wears his black-framed glasses.

The areas of the school yard are designated Africa, Mexico, Asia, and Europe. Africa is the biggest. Europe, an area next to the main building, has just a few dozen White students. Within each group, students cluster with their grade level. Black freshmen, especially the boys, stand at the outer edges of Africa. Some of the freshmen girls are coaxed to the center.

In the cafeteria he sits by himself. It gives him a stomach ache to eat there. He doesn't know if it's the food or because he feels nervous and eats too fast. He begins taking the lunch off his tray—a sandwich, fruit, cookie, and milk carton—and going outside to eat. He sits against the building at the edge of Africa and listens. Students, especially the older ones, talk about the streets, guns, dope, bling, bitches, and keeping it real. They drop names of gangsters and gangs: Big Fee, Mick Mo, Lil D, The Family, the 69 Mob. Boys compete to show how much they know. They brag about the money they make looking out for cops, delivering dope. Some wear beepers that go off when they are needed to make a delivery. They pull cash from their pockets to show how much they are making. One boy has a hundred-dollar bill. Like bees drawing nectar from flowers, they draw a feeling of power from the gangs. Those who have nothing to say, like James, keep quiet.

One of the older boys pulls his shirt up to show gunshot scars, two pink ovals, one on the dark brown skin of his side and another on his back. They are badges. He tells the story. "This nigger pulls his piece out his waistband, then pop-pop-pop. Next thing I know, I wake up in the emergency room, doctors and nurses running around like crazy." *Nigger:* James blanches at the word, which he has heard more in the first month of school than in his entire life. Mama says it is a vile word of hatred toward Black people, and she'll wash out his mouth with soap if she ever hears him say it.

James feels more at home in the classroom. The teachers are the only ones who know his name. He listens to them and does his assignments. He earns A's on papers and tests. Ninth grade here is easier than eighth grade in Sacramento. He replaces his khaki pants with jeans, his polo shirts with tee shirts.

On the sidewalk after school, kids gather in a circle around boys rapping as they make it up, bouncing to the beat, stabbing their fingers at the ground. Boys carry boom boxes that blast pulsing music, the bass threatening to break the air. They carry them like briefcases or balance them on their shoulders. James feels he should join, but he doesn't know how. He likes Pops' Motown music more.

One evening Mama starts to cry while she's cooking dinner. She wipes her eyes with the insides of her wrists. Her training period at the DMV has ended and she's been working the window for two weeks. People plead, demand, become angry. They owe money they don't have, lack the documentation they need, tell obvious lies while swearing to God that they are telling the truth. They offer to pay a third of what they owe, and then they curse Mama when she tells them they have to pay it all, as if she made the rules. This day a younger woman called her a bitch for not accepting a third-party check.

"It's real hard here," she says, blowing her nose into a tissue. James doesn't know whether by *hard* she means difficult or unfeeling and mean.

One morning as James walks onto the school grounds, a Black boy strides up to him and says with a sneer, "Give me some money, bitch."

The boy is a sophomore named Marvin Mitchell, taller and heavier than James. Everyone calls him Black Snake.

"I don't have any," James says. "Just my bus fare."

As he tries to walk on, the Black Snake blocks his way and drives his hand into the pocket of James' jeans. He pulls out a dollar.

"Give it back," James says, reaching for it.

"What?" the boy says, leaning forward, cupping his hand behind his ear. "Can't hear you."

"Give it back," James says, knowing his voice sounds more like a plea than a demand.

"You my bitch now. I don't give nothing back."

"Give it back," James says, trying to sound more forceful.

"You want me to fuck you up right here in front of everybody?" Black Snake steps closer and slips his finger under the band of James' watch. He gives it a yank and the band breaks, scratching James' wrist. The watch hits the ground and James snatches it from the asphalt.

"Shit," the boy says. "Cheap-ass watch break apart. I don't even want it." He turns and walks away. James' mouth tastes like metal. The face of the watch is scratched but it still runs. He slips it into his pocket.

With no bus money, James walks home that afternoon. It takes him an hour. His encounter with Black Snake plays in his mind like a tormenting video he can't turn off. At home, he sits at the kitchen table to do his homework, but he can't focus. Mama doesn't get home until six. James wishes he could turn back the calendar to Mama cooking dinner in their Sacramento bungalow while he and Pops walk down to the park to shoot baskets. He wonders how Christine Chan is doing.

James keeps seeing Black Snake take his money. He walks into his bedroom and pulls his belt from his pants. He imagines that Black Snake is in front of him. In a fury he whips the mattress with his belt as hard and as fast as he can, spittle flying from his mouth. When he stops, he is sweating and out of breath. He pictures Black Snake cowering on the ground, welts across his face.

Two days later in the school hallway, James feels someone grab his shirt from behind. He is shoved into his locker smashing his lip. A hand dips into the pocket of his jeans and extracts his dollar. It is Black Snake, already walking away.

A girl, tall with a big Afro, says to James, "Did he just take your money?"

James wants to say no, but since she saw it happen, he nods.

"Somebody ought to kick his ass," she says.

James feels shame that she knows he would not be the one to do it. When he gets home that afternoon, he looks at his swollen lip in the mirror. It doesn't look as bad as it feels. In his room he keeps a notebook where he records his thoughts about things. He writes, "I'd like to kill Black Snake. I hate his guts." He takes off his belt and whips his mattress until he's breathless.

Big Mike

In the school yard, Black Snake grabs James' ear and twists it hard until James gives up his bus money. James grimaces and tears fill his eyes. During algebra class his ear rings so loud that he fears his hearing has been damaged. He tries to figure out where Black Snake's classes are so that he can avoid him. He has heard at school that kids who snitch get beat up really bad. One boy got stabbed and had to leave the school.

Walking past a corner store on his way home, James sees a dark-skinned Black guy wearing a celery-green muscle shirt, leaning against the wall drinking a soda. He looks at James and says, "What's wrong with you, little brother? Your head hung so low, looks like you trying to suck your own dick."

James pauses. The guy looks older, out of high school. James starts to walk away.

"Hey!" he calls.

James stops.

"You know who I am?"

James shakes his head.

"Big Mike. You heard of me?"

"I just moved here," James says.

"Where from?"

"Sacramento."

"I asked you a question. What's wrong with you?"

James hesitates, then says, "Somebody took my bus money at school again."

"Again?" Big Mike shakes his head, takes a swig of his soda, then gestures with the can. "You know why that happen?"

James shrugs.

"Cause you let him," Big Mike shouts, raising his arms. "One look at you, he knows you some kind of Lionel on *The Jeffersons* that can't deal with the streets. Sacramento. Shit."

Three older boys walk past and nod to Big Mike. "Whatsup?" they say.

Big Mike nods in return, a gold tooth gleaming. He looks at James and says, "Listen little brother, you want a job?"

"Doing what?"

"Helping with my dogs. Cleaning cages. Taking them on walks."

"I like dogs," James says, raising his head. "Never had one, though."

"You want the job?"

James hesitates.

Big Mike says, like a slow drum beat, "Do-you-want-the-job?"

"I guess."

"Shit. Don't be guessing. 'Guess' is a pussy word. Yes or no?"

James figures he can quit if he doesn't like it. "Yes," he says.

With a jerk of his head, Big Mike says, "Come on."

Big Mike walks fast with long strides. James follows, half afraid he's about to be robbed. He occasionally jogs to keep up. They turn down an alley and stop before a concrete block garage with a padlocked rolling metal door. When Big Mike puts the key in the lock, James hears muffled barking. Big Mike rolls up the door, and the dogs stop barking. The smell of dog shit hits James like a wave. He turns his face away.

"Got to get used to it," Big Mike says.

In the back of the garage sit two large wire cages. A tan pit bull stands in one and a gray pit bull in the other. Both dogs are big and muscle-bound. They look like canine body builders. Their faces are marked with scabs as if they've been rooting in a thicket of thorns. The tan dog has a long, open gash glistening pink on his front shoulder.

Big Mike unlatches the tan dog's cage. James takes a couple of steps back.

"This is Spike," Big Mike says. The dog wags his tail as Big Mike pounds his good shoulder with his open hand. When he stops, Spike walks over to James and smells his feet and legs. James pats his shoulder like Big Mike did, but not as hard. Spike looks up at him and wags his tail.

"Look here," Big Mike says. He shows James the galvanized garbage can filled with kibble, how to measure out two scoops and fill the metal bowls. He hands James a small shovel to lift the large turds out of the cage and put them in a garbage bag.

"Got to keep the bowls in their cages filled with water," Big Mike says. "These dogs are athletes. Need lots of water."

Spike eats his kibble, his chain collar clinking against the bowl.

"You gonna do this, got to come every day. Last kid wasn't dependable. Had to fire his sorry ass."

James points toward Spike. "What happened to his shoulder?"

"These are fighting dogs. Spike won his fight last Saturday night. Made me some good money. Got bit though."

Big Mike shows James how to pour peroxide on the wound and then dab on ointment from a tube.

They put a leash on Spike's chain collar and set off down the street. Big Mike explains that when the dogs are walked, they wear a canvas cape filled with twenty pounds of lead weights. Spike isn't wearing his until his shoulder heals. The two dogs are fed and walked one at a time, never together.

They walk to a park about halfway between the garage and James' apartment. It has neither grass nor trees, just hard ground, cracked asphalt, and gravel. There is a concrete basketball court with netless hoops. The water fountain is missing its hardware and has been turned off. There are restrooms in a concrete block house, but the doors are padlocked. The walls are covered with layers of spray-painted graffiti, mostly gang tags. Cigarette butts and flattened soda cans litter the ground. Weathered paper shreds are caught in the chain link fence.

When they arrive back at the garage, James and Big Mike feed and walk the other dog, Silver Bullet. He wears the weighted cape.

"Got to watch out for other guys with pit bulls," Big Mike says. "Dumb-asses want their dogs to do street fighting. You cross the street to avoid those motherfuckers. My dogs are professionals, can't be doing that shit. You don't see Sugar Ray Leonard getting in no street fights."

Big Mike hands James a duplicate key to the padlock.

"Tomorrow after school," he says. "You know what to do? And don't say 'I guess.' You can't be guessing if you're going to survive on the streets."

James nods and says, "I know what to do."

Real Cool

James' English teacher is Ms. Davis, a young Black woman, tall and thin, with natural hair and a fragile-looking face. From the first day she struggles to keep order in the room.

A boy slides down in his seat until his chin rests on the desk.

"Look, Ms. Davis. My head got chopped off in a guillotine. Can you glue it back on?"

"Not funny," she says. "Let's get focused, class."

The boys taunt and aggravate her. The girls exude aloof indifference. One girl opens a magazine, which Ms. Davis takes from her. Another applies nail polish during class, giving students around her an excuse to cough loudly and fan the air.

One morning students walk into class and see that on the board Ms. Davis has written this:

> We real cool. We
> Left school. We
>
> Lurk late. We
> Strike straight. We
>
> Sing sin. We
> Thin gin. We
>
> Jazz June.

"This is not the entire poem," she says. "There are three more words in the same pattern. I want you to write three words that you think would make a good ending." She gives them five minutes.

When Ms. Davis asks for volunteers to read their endings, a hand shoots up. He is a loud, heavy boy in the back row with an

Afro comb in his hair. He pauses for dramatic effect and reads,

> We real cool. We
> Left school. We
>
> Lurk late. We
> Strike straight. We
>
> Sing sin. We
> Thin gin. We
>
> Jazz June. We
> Fuck the moon.

The room erupts with raucous laughter, hands slapping desk tops, feet stomping the floor. Once Ms. Davis restores order, she asks for others to read. James volunteers his last line: "We spread gloom." Ms. Davis nods and says it's good. But "fuck the moon" still echoes in the air, overpowering the other attempts.

Ms. Davis says, "This is the poet's last line." On the board she writes, *We die soon*. "Think about that. How does that change our reading of the earlier lines?"

The students refuse to take the bait. They don't like the poem. One objects that no one says "cool" any more. Another gets laughs by saying, "We drink Hennessy, not gin."

The disruptive jokes continue. James is unable to join in the hilarity. He likes the poem, wants to talk about it. He sees how deflated Ms. Davis feels. The students broke the lesson and they broke her.

Over the weeks, James has a creeping realization. Kids here want to break everything. They paint graffiti on the walls, shatter bottles in parking lots, smash windows, shoplift at the corner store, undermine their teachers. They want to poison it all.

Spike

James tries out for the school basketball team. He played on his junior high team in Sacramento. He wasn't one of the better players, but he tried to do what the coach wanted. He worked hard. If he made the team here, he would have guys to hang out with. It would make him seem less a nobody in the eyes of others.

The try-out session is a series of scrimmages. The boys are divided into teams and they play games to ten while the coach watches with a clip board. James pretends Pops is in the bleachers watching. James tries hard for him, sprinting as hard as he can up and down the floor. No one passes him the ball, and when he tries to go up for a rebound, he gets knocked out of the way by boys who are taller, heavier, and more aggressive. The next day the list of boys chosen for the freshman team is posted outside the gym, and his name is not among the twelve on the list. He reads it three times to make sure.

James stops at the garage to tend the dogs every day after school. Big Mike pays him ten dollars a week, sometimes fifteen, which seems like a good deal since James likes the work. Silver Bullet is indifferent to James. During the feedings and the walks, he barely looks at James. With Spike, it's different. When James kneels to pet him, Spike licks his face. He learns what Spike likes best—chest rubs and butt scratches. Gentle ear massages. Spike looks into James' eyes as if they know one another. On walks, James talks to him, and Spike seems to like his voice. Of course, Spike doesn't understand what he is saying, but James likes talking to him anyway. On the sidewalk people give them plenty of space. This makes James feel safer and stronger. When James uses his finger to smooth ointment over his wound, Spike looks straight ahead and half closes his eyes. As the days pass, the wound scabs over and begins to shrink. James imagines becoming a veterinarian like George Washington Carver became an agricultural scientist.

One day while walking Spike, James sees Black Snake coming toward them on the other side of the street. Black Snake recognizes him and crosses the street.

"Need me some money, bitch. Got to go to the candy store."

James feels Spike tense up like he does when they see another pit bull.

"No," James says sharply. "I'm not giving you anything more."

Black Snake snaps up in mock shock and announces loudly, "Look at the new attitude on bitch boy." Then in his usual voice, "You ain't giving. I'm taking."

Black Snake reaches for James' pocket. James takes a step back and Black Snake grabs his shirt and gives him a sharp shake.

"No, Motherfucker," James shouts. It's the first time he's called anyone that.

Black Snake draws back his other arm into a cocked fist. Trying to pull away, James stumbles backward. There is a sharp growl as Spike lunges forward. He clamps onto Black Snake's hand with a hard bite and shakes his head violently. Black Snake yells. Spike lets go. Black Snake jerks his hand up to his chest and steps back. Rivulets of blood run down his arm. Spike watches, coiled like a spring.

"You in trouble now, bitch," Black Snake says in a quaking voice, holding his bleeding hand.

"Good dog," James says loudly. He gives Spike a rub on the head.

"If I had my piece, I'd bust a cap in your ass," Black Snake says.

Spike, still tensed, watches Black Snake. Emboldened, James points his finger at Black Snake. "The next time he goes for your face."

Black Snake wheels around and stalks off. He yells something over his shoulder that James can't make out.

James walks back to the garage with Spike trotting at his side.

The next day Big Mike is at the garage when James arrives, and James tells him what happened with Black Snake.

"See," Big Mike says. "Spike knows the ways of the streets. You got to get yourself respected if you're gonna survive."

James looks at Spike waiting in his cage. Spike wags his tail.

"You do your work, and when you done, I got something to show you."

When James returns from the park with Spike, Big Mike is working out on his weight bench. He tells James that he needs to start building himself up.

"Too many these young punks try to get respect from dope, money, guns. Wearing bling. That's bogus respect. Real respect is from what you do, not what you have. Got to start with your own body. You dig?"

He guides James through a workout. He tells James to record in his notebook the exercises, the amount of weight used, and the number of repetitions. Big Mike explains how to increase the weight and the repetitions over time, do three hard workouts a week. At the end of this session, James leaves the garage dizzy and a little nauseous. His arms feel like rubber. But he starts doing the workouts three times a week.

When James sees Black Snake at school, Black Snake glares at him briefly and then looks away. James wonders if Black Snakes really has a gun.

Mama

Every evening after dinner, James helps Mama with the dishes, and then he does his homework while she watches TV. His relationship with her is changing. Mama is moving from a source of strength and comfort to someone he worries about. It's not anything so tangible as a bad back—and that makes it more frightening. She just looks worried and worn, and most of what she talks about are complaints: the dirt on the streets, the loud neighbors, their shabby apartment, drugs and crime in the neighborhood, rude customers at the DMV. Two of her co-workers have been mugged on their way home from work. Several more have come home at the end of the day to find their apartments broken into. Only occasionally, when Mama remembers something about Pops before his back went bad or James when he was young, does her face light up and she seems her old self.

Most of the people Mama works with grew up in Oakland, and they tell her how it used to be. Tidy houses and clean apartments. Friendly people talking over their fences. Respect all around. Winos and dope fiends were small in number and easy to avoid. Then it changed. Guns and dope sprung up. People got mean. Violence everywhere. Criminals with more power than the police. Black people turning on their own kind. No respect.

At night James and Mama hear gunshots. Sometimes it's one or two shots, sometimes six or eight, and sometimes a loud burst too fast to count. The various sounds start to seem familiar—quick pops, sharp bangs, and hollow explosions. This may happen only two or three times a month, but it feels more frequent. In all the years they lived in Sacramento, they never heard a single gunshot. The strangest part is how seldom the gunshots are followed by the sound of sirens. Nor is there anything on the news, as if people firing guns is too common to be newsworthy.

Mama looks for other apartments, but she can't afford them. She hears about a bungalow at a reasonable price, but when she goes to see it, there is a crack house across the street, adult addicts going in and out at all times of the day and night.

James does not mention his job until he's been doing it for a month, and then he tells her he *might* have a job. He describes Big Mike and the dogs.

"No, sir," Mama says, raising her voice and shaking her head. "I don't want you mixed up in that kind of thing. Don't you know what that is? That's dog fighting. It's low class and against the law. People like that end up in jail."

Though her words make his heart thump, the next day he shows up as usual at the garage. The following week he tells her he has a job helping at a Chinese grocery. It will explain where he goes when he takes care of the dogs and how he's earning money. It's the first important thing he's lied to her about.

"That's good," Mama nods. "A little spending money. As long as you do all your homework. School comes first."

One day when he sees Big Mike at the garage, James asks if he has a job.

"The dogs," he answers. "Everybody got to have a hustle. This is mine."

"Isn't it illegal?" James asks.

"Shit. You been here months and you still asking country-ass dumb questions like that? Most hustles are illegal. Dogs ain't no exception."

"Does it make much money?"

"It can. If you do it right. Two ways to make money. One is to bet. I'm good at guessing which dog will win. Sometimes I'm wrong, but more times I'm right. The other way is to have your own dogs and fight them. I just got these two, but I want to get more. You can either buy a fighter, or get a young one and train it. That takes time, and what if the dog got no game? Big waste. You work hard. You take risks. Maybe you come out ahead and maybe you don't—just like owning a store."

Big Mike gets worked up when he talks, stabbing with his hands, making circles with his arms. It's like someone making a speech. At first it intimidated James, but now he's used to it.

"You talk illegal. That's how The Man tries to keep us down. You go to the race track, see White people betting like crazy. That's not illegal. In Florida, they race dogs. I got a cousin there. Same thing—White people, not illegal. Movie stars sit ringside and bet on boxing. Black folks set up dog fights, and that's illegal. What's that tell you?"

Christmas

On his way to the dogs one December afternoon, James sees a poster of a Black Santa in a store window. A light rain is falling. He remembers one Christmas season when he was a little boy, and he asked his parents what color Santa was. He had seen a few images of Black Santas, but most of them were White.

"He's magic that way," Mama said. "Whichever house he visits, that's the color he takes on. Comes in a Black house, he's Black. Goes to the Chans down the block, he's Asian with slanty eyes. Goes to White people's houses, he's White."

"How does he do it?" James asked.

"How does he fly the whole world in a sleigh? People believe. All kind of magic happens when people believe."

James heard Pops say to her, "You a beautiful woman, Margaret Fields."

This will be their first Christmas without Pops. He's been gone eleven months—it seems longer than that. When Mama asks James what he wants for Christmas, he says Air Jordans, the red and white high tops that all the kids at school either have or want. Though James has little interest in fashion and style, he loves these shoes. Besides, the shoes he has now have become too tight. It hurts his toes to walk in them.

Trees are expensive, so Mama buys a cheap one that's about three feet tall, and she sets it on the small table in front of the living room window. From a box they brought from Sacramento, Mama and James lift lights to string and ornaments to hang. When they finish, Mama makes hot chocolate on the stove. They sip it while looking at the tree. Mama gives James a hug, extra long and extra tight.

The next afternoon James does his work with the dogs and then lifts weights, pushing himself as hard as he can. Spike watches him carefully. Walking home, he remembers that Pops always bought a Christmas present for Mama and wrote on the tag, "from Big Sweet and Little Sweet." A year ago, Pops and James took the bus to a department store in Sacramento since Pops' back was too bad to drive. Pops seemed more lively that day, talking to the clerk about what Mama might like and finally deciding on a silky, dark green blouse.

James decides he will get Mama a blouse. At home, he looks into her room and writes down her clothing sizes. Her blouses are an eighteen. He counts his money from Big Mike that he keeps in a shoe in his closet. He's saved eighty-five dollars.

On Saturday he rides the bus to the mall. He decides on a blouse of dark gray with purple grape clusters. It has a built-in bow that ties. The sales clerk, a slim Black lady about Mama's age, thinks she'll like it. She even wraps it for free, winking off the three dollars they are supposed to charge. Smiling, she tells James he's a fine young man. It occurs to him that he gets along better with adults than kids his age. He takes the bus back home feeling that even without Pops, it can still be Christmas.

On Christmas morning James and Mama open their presents. Mama tears up at the card that reads "from Big Sweet and Little Sweet."

"He's still here in spirit," James says, swallowing hard.

Mama loves the blouse, and James is thrilled when he unwraps a pair of Air Jordans. They are a little large, but all the better, since his feet have been growing fast. Mama makes them a dinner of baked chicken, sweet potatoes, and greens. She bakes a chocolate cake, James' favorite. They ignore the elephant in the room—that Pops is gone—and they watch a Christmas special on TV. James feels relieved when the day is over, and the next day he spends a long time with the dogs. He wishes they still had a car and could visit Sacramento. He wonders how Christine celebrated Christmas, whether her mother made rice with duck.

Part Two

Morgan's Autograph

Allison begins seventh grade, and an alum from her school is introduced at a morning assembly. She's in college now and has recently made the U.S. Olympic rowing team. She wears her team warm-up suit, dark blue with red and white piping and the interlocking circles of the Olympic symbol. Her name—*Morgan*—is stitched across the back of her jacket, just above *USA*. Allison wonders if that's her first name or her last.

The principal introduces her—Morgan is her first name—and she talks to the students about pursuing their goals, trying as hard as they can, and never giving up. Morgan has thick, blond hair cut short. She takes off her jacket to reveal a red Olympic tank top. Her shoulders are shaped like a marble sculpture of an athlete. Students line up for autographs, and Morgan's forearm muscles flex as she wields her black marker to autograph notebooks, backpacks, and even the bill of a school cap.

Allison is spellbound. She couldn't be more enthralled if she were six feet away from a lithe cheetah. She steps out of the line and moves to the end so she can look at Morgan longer. Morgan has well-defined biceps, and veins run like rivers under the skin of her hands. She has a strong jawline, white teeth, and full lips. She is tan. She looks at Allison standing fourth in line now, holding her gaze until Allison blushes violently. Morgan's mouth turns up at the corners in a hint of a smile. Dimples crease her cheeks. Where the sun strikes the side of Morgan's face, Allison sees a sprinkling of freckles and fine blond hairs. Morgan exudes an air of accomplishment, a girl who can do things.

When it's Allison's turn, she opens her spiral notebook to a blank page. Morgan pauses and then asks her name. Morgan writes, "Be a champion, Allison. Your friend, Morgan."

Allison feels something new and strange, like bees are making honey between her legs. It's like electricity. Voltage, current, and resistance—an Ohm's law of her body. She investigates what Morgan wrote on the packs and caps of other girls—it was just her name. Did Morgan feel toward Allison something special, or was it just that Allison was the only one who presented Morgan with a blank page? This is a mystery waiting to be solved.

The Rocket Launch

In her first week of high school, Allison attends the activities fair in the gym and signs up for the rocket club, the only one that interests her. At the first meeting there are twelve boys and Allison. They look at her like she's entered the wrong room. The plan is to build rockets and hold a competition to see whose will go the highest. One large, loud boy named Russell says he knows the secret of how to make gunpowder and that his rocket will be the best. No one can beat him. He reminds Allison of the crooks in Nancy Drew novels. Russell says they will use the dues money to buy a chocolate cake for the prize because chocolate is his favorite. He says he can only take three on his crew, and he chooses them from the waving hands. The remaining boys will build a second rocket. The boys snicker when Allison says she will build her own.

That evening Allison asks her dad to teach her how to build a rocket. They sit at the kitchen table with a yellow tablet, and he asks her a series of questions. By answering his questions, she concludes that a good rocket has three qualities: light weight, strong propulsion, and good aerodynamics. Her dad subscribes to several science and hobby magazines, and he scans his basement bookcase until he finds an article he remembers on homemade rockets. Together, they decide on a design. Allison chooses the solid fuel mixture because it's more powerful than the vinegar and baking soda combination.

Her dad smiles. "You might as well make school history."

They decide to make two rockets, one for clubs' day and the other to test in advance. Her dad believes in system redundancy. He helps her decide what to do, but she performs all the tasks herself. They buy one-inch PVC pipe and Allison locks it into the vise. After repeating aloud one of her dad's favorite sayings—*measure twice and cut once*—she puts on her safety glasses and uses a pipe cutter to make two twelve-inch lengths. She makes a nose cone and tail wings by cutting shapes from polycarbonate sheets she buys at a craft shop. She experiments with various wing and nose cone designs by gluing them on an empty length of PVC pipe and sailing it like a paper airplane, recording the results. She makes a launch tube from a length of larger diameter PVC pipe. If the rocket is vertical in its first four feet of flight, it will have a greater chance of staying vertical. She deduces that extra weight at the bottom will help keep the rocket vertical, and her dad breaks into a wide grin when she tells him.

"Brilliant deduction," he says.

She solders a metal ring to the base. For the fuel she follows the article's formula: powdered sugar, potassium nitrate ground superfine in an old blender, and kitty litter. Her dad warns her that once mixed, the combination is flammable, so after it's been tamped into the pipe with a dowel and mallet, she drills the hole in the bottom by hand to avoid the heat that could be generated by the speed of a power drill.

"Safety first," he reminds her.

On an afternoon of autumn drizzle, her dad drives her to a nearby golf course. They carry the test rocket onto a soggy fairway strewn with wet leaves. Allison lights the fuse. It streams skyward to what her father estimates is a thousand feet. Allison is ecstatic.

A week later, the school football field is lined with table displays from the clubs. The weather is cool and sunny. The model train club has set up a track on a piece of plywood in the end zone. The baking club sells cookies, and the knitting club has a table of hats and scarves. The book club displays a poster listing what they have read, and the hiking club posts photos of their trip to

Kentucky. The Irish dancing club puts on a performance, and the Young Republicans and Young Democrats spar in a ten-minute debate about welfare. Immediately after, the three entries of the rocket club are announced.

Four boys have made a vinegar and baking soda powered rocket, but when the operator turns it over and shakes it, the stopper blows off before he can set it on the ground, and it skitters across the field to the screams from students. The operator now reeks of vinegar. With great fanfare Russell and his crew light their rocket, a tube wrapped in aluminum foil to which American flag stickers are adhered. The science teacher stands by with a fire extinguisher. After three attempts, the fuse is successfully lit and the rocket falls on its side, spewing an orange flame three feet long that burns for a half minute and then sizzles. Sulfurous black smoke drifts into the stands. Russell complains loudly that the dampness is to blame.

When Allison carefully positions her rocket in the launch tube, Russell makes fun of its small size.

"It's a pencil rocket," he laughs. "A skinny wiener."

Allison feels her face burning. There must be several hundred people, students and teachers, watching her. She puts on her safety glasses, opens her box of kitchen matches, and lights the fuse. She runs back ten steps. With a sudden whoosh, the rocket streaks upward until it is barely visible in the deep blue sky. Heads tilt skyward with open-mouthed astonishment followed by loud applause. A thousand feet above the field, the rocket completes its climb and gently begins its fall back to the earth. Allison runs to pick it up, a potholder in her hand to guard against burns. When she is awarded the cake, she gives each club member, including Russell, a slice.

Her Secret

Allison grows into her adult body. By the time she turns sixteen, she is slim, taller than average, and small-breasted. She runs on the cross-country team with average speed. While she runs, she looks at the sky, trees, dogs in backyards. She likes to daydream, so she forgets to focus on the coach's advice: lift your knees, relax your hands and shoulders, count your strides. When the coach gives pep talks, Allison watches her closely and remembers Morgan, the Olympic rower.

Everything about romance—in movies, magazine articles, and ads—is clear: it's a boy and a girl. Allison wants to politely raise her hand and say, "What about me?" Sexual activity—the heavy stuff—feels like the Amazon jungle, a place unexplored, scary, enticing. What she finds herself wanting to do is to hold hands with a girl, to touch shoulders as they walk in the woods, or in those same woods, to receive a soft kiss on her lips, to give one in return. She also longs for someone to talk to, someone without judgmental ears. Allison wants to ask a friend, "Do you ever look at a girl in class and think how pretty she is?" And the friend would reply, "Oh, yes. All the time."

Lacking such a friend, Allison feels vulnerable to the judgment of others. She feels it on her skin. Her classmates, to express their dislike of something, comment, "That's so gay." When Ellen DeGeneres comes out on the cover of *Time*, the girls in Allison's class say, "Eww, gross." Their words scald Allison, and she feels the burn. That's why she keeps it secret—from fear of burns.

In the school library, Allison reads the DeGeneres interview multiple times. DeGeneres' phrase "comfortable with myself" sticks in her mind. It's what she admired about Nancy Drew—she was comfortable with herself. It's what she wants to become.

Say No

In 1908 Henry Ford sold the first Model T. His assembly line method of production allowed the price to sink to $250 per car. The theory was that a product sold at a lower price to many people will make more money than a product sold at a higher to a few people. Model T sales skyrocketed, and Henry Ford became very rich.

Eighty years later, the same marketing strategy revolutionizes the intercity drug market. Cocaine, arriving in ever larger quantities from South America, is processed into small hard pieces called rocks. Anyone with five dollars can enjoy the same cocaine-induced euphoria as the Hollywood rich and famous. This new Model T of the drug world is called crack: smokable, highly addictive, and cheap. Free samples are handed out. Markets burgeon in New York, Philadelphia, Baltimore, Miami, Los Angeles, and the San Francisco Bay Area. Among American cities, Oakland ranks seventh highest in crack sales.

At school, James takes the required class in "social living." Students are warned against gangs, guns, teen pregnancy, and dope. In the first class on dope, they are shown a video of a man injecting himself with heroin. James is stunned. It is the exact picture of what he saw Pops doing that afternoon in their house in Sacramento.

A few weeks later, First Lady Nancy Reagan comes to Oakland to speak to an auditorium of elementary school children. James and Mama watch the story on the six o'clock news while they eat. The children, pep-rally style, shout in unison, "Just say no!" Mrs. Reagan, wearing a powder blue suit, smiles and cheers with them.

Mama shakes her head. "I hear about this all the time at work. People's sons, nephews, husbands. Women, too. Drugs ruining people's lives. Nobody sets out to become an addict, but that's what happens. On the streets, young punks drive flashy cars with gold wheels. You know how they get that kind of money? From selling that poison to their own people, that's how. They hurt more Black folks here than the Klan did in Georgia, and that's the Lord's truth. Martin Luther King is turning over in his grave."

After dinner, Mama washes the dishes and James dries. Quietly, he says, "Mama, did Pops take drugs? You know, after his back went out. I saw him using a needle one day."

Mama lifts her hands from the dishwater and wrings water from the dish rag. She pulls the stopper and water gurgles down the drain.

"Just look at this," she says, pressing her fingers against a piece of warped Formica that has come loose from the counter top. She walks to the kitchen table, pulls out a chair and sits heavily. James pauses in drying the dishes and looks at her.

"You saw that?" she asks.

James nods.

"You might as well know," she sighs. "He was in so much pain, and the pills from the doctor didn't help much. He couldn't sleep at night. He started using heroin. I suspected it and he finally confessed. He broke down and cried when he told me. He said the day he tried it was the first time in months he hadn't hurt. Said it was like floating on a cloud in heaven—those were his exact words. Pretty soon he couldn't stop. He mistook heaven for hell."

She wipes her eyes.

"Did he really have a heart attack?" James asks.

She looks at the floor. "He took too much somewhere downtown that day. After he got on the bus, his heart just stopped."

A plate slips in James' hand but he catches it before it falls.

"Just promise me that one thing," Mama says. "You'll never

take drugs. Not ever. Not even once."

"I won't, Mama. I promise."

Spike's Last Fight

On a Monday afternoon, James unlocks the garage and rolls up the door. Spike lies in his cage trembling. He has deep bites on his rear hip and a trail of dried blood down to his paw. There are open wounds on his muzzle. One bloody ear is so badly mangled it looks like a piece of it might fall off. The end of his tail has been chewed up. When James opens the cage door, Spike struggles to stand. He whimpers and licks James' face.

In a panic James grabs the peroxide and the ointment from the shelf and kneels in front of Spike to treat his wounds. Spike leans against James' chest and whines.

"Don't do any of that," Big Mike says as he stalks into the garage, his brow knotted up like a fist, anger flaring in his eyes.

"He's no good anymore. Wouldn't hardly fight back. They stopped the fight."

"Shouldn't he go to the vet?" James asks, still kneeling beside Spike.

"Shit, no. I ain't paying no vet after what I lost yesterday. Besides, some vets call the cops on you." He turns on James, pointing a finger at him. "It's probably your damn fault. You treat him like a teddy bear. Take the fight out of him. Nothing to do now but put him down. I got to go home and get my gun."

"You're going to shoot him?" James cries.

"No choice. Can't feed a dog that's got no game."

"You can't just shoot him," James says.

"He won't feel nothing. I know where to shoot him in the back of the head."

James stands up. "I'll take him."

Big Mike flashes James a look. "Shit. Your mama won't let you have a dog. Besides, he ain't breathing right. Gonna die if he don't get to a vet. Where you get money for that?"

"I'm taking him," James says. He reaches for the leash and clips it to Spike's collar.

His hands on his hips, Big Mike says, "You are one crazy motherfucker."

James coaxes a limping Spike to the garage entrance. He wants out of there before Big Mike tries to stop him.

"Don't tell nobody where he from," Big Mike calls after him. "Cops come poking around this garage, I be looking for your sorry ass."

"Don't worry," James calls over his shoulder.

James remembers passing a vet office up on the avenue, maybe ten blocks away. Spike stands in the middle of the alley whining. He's shivering and can barely walk. James sees an abandoned grocery cart leaning against a fence and runs to retrieve it. He spreads his jacket on the lower tray and coaxes Spike to lie on it. He barely fits. Very carefully, James pushes the cart to the end of the alley and down the sidewalk. Spike raises his head to watch where they are going. James talks to him in a low voice. "Hold on, Spike. I'm going to get you help." People turn to stare. A couple of times he stops to push Spike back toward the center of the tray. They pass the corner store and Einstein calls out, "Young man saving his soul dog."

When at last James reaches the vet office, he helps Spike off of the lower tray and into the office.

The White woman behind the counter looks at Spike and says, "Oh, my."

The vet happens to be standing beside her with a folder in his hands. He is Dr. Carter, a tall, thin man with white hair, a pale face, a trimmed white beard, and a white medical coat. He's the whitest man James has ever seen.

"Please sir, can you help this dog?"

Dr. Carter looks over the top of his half-glasses. "He's your dog?"

"He is now. His owner was going to shoot him. I took him to save his life."

"And just who is this piece of shit owner—if you'll pardon my French, Ann," he says, nodding to the lady at the desk.

"He told me not to tell."

"I bet he said that."

"Please, sir," James says. His glasses have slipped to the end of his nose and he pushes them back into place.

Dr. Carter takes a long look at James. "You may be the only young man within a fifty-block radius who still knows the word *sir*," he mutters. With a toss of his head, he says, "Bring him back."

In the exam room stands the veterinary assistant, a young Black woman, also in a white coat. She smiles at James and pulls on latex gloves. Spike whines when they lift him onto the table. He starts to tremble.

The assistant takes Spike's temperature while Dr. Carter examines the wounds one by one. He listens to his chest with the stethoscope and uses a finger to press on Spike's gums. He pats Spike on the head.

"His wounds are bad, but not as bad as they look. His blood volume is low, and he does have a fever, which indicates infection. Sounds like he's starting a pneumonia. As long as we can control the infection, his wounds will heal. He'll need stitches, an IV, and antibiotics."

James nods.

Dr. Carter says, "You could also put him down. We can give him an injection. He won't feel anything. He'll just go to sleep."

James shakes his head. "No," he says firmly. "I want to save him."

"You have a place to keep him?"

"Yes, sir. Our apartment."

"You know he's a fighting dog, don't you?"

"Yes, sir."

"They can be dangerous, more often to other dogs than to people. How long have you known this dog?"

James counts on his fingers. "Five months. I had a job feeding and walking him."

"He's not going back to the owner?"

"No, sir. The owner says he's lost his drive to fight."

"And you can pay my charges?"

James tries to remember what he has left after buying Mama's Christmas presents. "I've saved some money—maybe forty dollars. I could work for you here. I can clean cages, mop the floors."

The vet and his assistant exchange looks. Dr. Carter tells her to clean Spike's wounds.

James sits in a chair in the corner while the vet and his assistant work. Spike occasionally turns his head to make sure James is there. The assistant starts to put a muzzle on Spike and he yelps.

"He thinks the muzzle means he has to go to a fight," James says. "He won't bite you."

The assistant takes the muzzle away.

"Seems like you understand this dog pretty well," Dr. Carter says.

"Yes, sir," James answers. He walks to the exam table and puts his mouth to Spike's face. He whispers that it's okay. He tells Spike he won't have to fight again.

The assistant cleans his wounds, one by one. She shaves a patch on Spike's front leg and Dr. Carter starts an IV.

"This is to get his blood volume up. It's also an antibiotic and a mild sedative," Dr. Carter says over his shoulder to James. He stitches up the deeper wounds. He does it like Mama mends clothes.

After an hour and a half, they take out the IV and Spike is ready to go. One ear and the tip of his tail are wrapped in white bandages. The long gash in his hip has stiches, and the bites on his muzzle are painted with an orange antiseptic. Dr. Carter gives James a sack with a bottle of antibiotics, pain pills, a tube of ointment, and a dozen packets of dog food samples. He says to bring Spike back in a week. James asks if he can bring the money tomorrow.

"This one's *pro bono*," he sighs.

When James looks puzzled, Dr. Carter says, "That means 'for the good.' No charge. A smart boy like you should be taking Latin."

James thanks him.

The shopping cart is still on the sidewalk. James wheels Spike to their apartment. Spike pulls himself up the stairs to the second floor.

When James opens the door, Mama calls from the kitchen, "You're late. I was worried."

"I'm sorry," James answers.

Mama hears Spike's nails clicking on the wooden floor and wheels around. "Jesus on a mountain!" she cries. "What in hell is that?"

"He's really friendly."

"Friendly? That's your explanation? That he's friendly? Whose dog is that?"

"I'm keeping him for now. Just for a few days."

"Oh, no." Mama says, her hands on her hips. "Not for one minute. No dogs. Especially this one. No."

"You told me you had dogs growing up," James says.

"We had hogs, too, but we had enough sense not to bring them into the house where folks eat and sleep."

"He can sleep on my floor."

"He can't sleep on *my* floor, and I'm the one that pays the rent. I'm disappointed in you, James. Very disappointed," she says, shaking her finger. "Any fool can see this half dead thing is a fighting dog, and I told you to stay away from those no-count people. You disobeyed me. They have a pound here, and as soon as you get home from school tomorrow, I want you to take that dog straight to the pound. Do you understand me?"

"Yes, ma'am." James feels relieved. That means Spike can stay the night.

"Good."

"His name is Spike."

"I don't care if his name is Ezekiel the Prophet. He's going to the pound tomorrow."

"Yes, ma'am."

The Soft Weapon

When James arrives at school the next morning he goes to his first period class for five minutes and then leaves. With his hand over his mouth, he tells the woman in the office that he just threw up and needs to go home. Hurriedly, she signs his slip. James takes the bus back home.

Spike's eyes are bright but his body is stiff and sore. James rubs ointment on his wounds. He fries a couple of eggs and mixes them with the pills and some of the sample kibble from the vet's office. He fills a saucepan with water and puts it on the floor. He is relieved that Spike eats all the food and drinks half a pan of water. James takes him for a walk. Spike moves slow, and he whimpers on the stairs, but they make it around the block. Back in the apartment, James helps Spike onto his bed. Spike rests his chin on the bedspread and rolls his eyes toward James as if to say, injuries or not, he can't believe his luck. His bandaged tail thumps the mattress twice. James rubs his chest, the one place that has no bite wounds.

Though James revels in the feeling of being at home alone on a school day, he must think of a solution for the crisis at hand. Wondering where the dog pound is, he looks it up in the phone book and is relieved to find it's sixty blocks away, on the other side of the freeway. Spike can't walk that far, they don't have a car, and dogs aren't allowed on the bus. This buys him some time.

He wishes he had someone to talk to about this. He can talk to Mama only about an ever-decreasing number of things. Big Mike gave him some advice—like how to lift weights—but he only talks. He doesn't listen. Besides, James will probably never see him again. At school, teachers can explain homework, but that's all. He hasn't really had a personal talk, the kind that occurs in movies and on

TV, with anyone since he left Sacramento.

At midday he walks a half hour to a pet store, and with his dog-tending money he buys a bag of kibble, two dog bowls, and a large rubber bone. He washes out the pan he had used for Spike's breakfast and puts it back in the kitchen cabinet. He does his homework while Spike snores on the bed. A photograph of a family at dinner in his Spanish book gives him an idea.

He walks to the supermarket. In the wine aisle, he slips a bottle of Manischewitz Concord Grape wine under his jacket, the first time in his life he has shoplifted. He picks out a frozen pecan pie, an *Ebony* magazine (Mama's favorite), and a bouquet of flowers. He pays at the checkout, his heart pounding. Mama will be home in an hour. He stops at Kentucky Fried Chicken for a dinner—chicken, mashed potatoes, biscuits, and gravy. At home he lights the oven and puts in the frozen pie. By the time he hears Mama at the door, he has set the table, poured her a glass of grape wine, and put the flowers in a tall glass. The magazine is beside her plate, along with a note that reads, please let me stay. It is signed with a drawing of a paw print. The fried chicken dinner is arranged on a large platter in the center of the table.

When Mama enters, Spike walks out of James' room and Mama's face tightens into a scowl. James blurts out that the pound is sixty blocks away and he has no way to get there.

"I told you—" Mama begins, and then she sees the table. She sees the grape wine, the flowers, her favorite magazine and the note, the chicken piled on the platter. Her face softens. Tears fill her eyes and run down her cheeks.

"Oh, honey," she says. "You did this for your mama?"

"From me and Spike," James says.

Mama wipes the tears from her cheeks.

Halfway through dinner, eating her third piece of chicken and drinking her second glass of wine, Mama looks at Spike and says, "I don't know what *you're* like, but this little man here is a no-good scamp."

The grape wine brings out Mama's Georgia accent. James grins. He knows that Spike will be allowed to stay and that he has brought Mama happiness. Pops would be proud of him.

Spike at Home

A few days after Spike's stitches are removed, he walks into the kitchen and paws the cabinet door where his kibble is kept.

"Spike!" Mama says in a sharp voice. "So that's where those scratch marks came from." She shakes her finger at him and says, "This place looks bad enough without you messing things up. You're on real thin ice in this house, and if I was you, I wouldn't be scratching up people's doors."

Spike cocks his head and looks at her thoughtfully. The next afternoon James is doing math homework at the kitchen table when Spike walks to the cabinet door. Mama sees him and turns in his direction, her hands on her hips. Spike stops in front of the door and begins to lick the handle.

"It's a good thing you're so ugly," Mama says. "Otherwise I might take a liking to you."

James bites his lip to keep from laughing.

One evening a couple of weeks later, there is a knock at their door. Mama is stirring a pan at the stove, and James is setting the table for dinner. Mama walks to the door. Though residents need a key to get in the building, Mama is ever the cautious one and attaches the chain before cracking the door. Someone pushes hard against the door and Mama gasps and takes a step back. The chain holds. A White man's bony hand reaches around the edge of the door and the fingers claw at the chain. Mama screams. Paper napkins and utensils in his hands, James freezes. Spike's nails sound like someone throwing tacks on the linoleum floor as he charges the door growling. He launches toward the hand and snags it in his teeth, jerking the hand side to side. There is loud scream from the other side of the door and the thud of someone falling. Spike jerks the hand a few more times and then releases it. A hand spurting red blood is pulled back. The sound of stumbling footsteps recedes down the hall. Spike tilts his head to listen. Mama gives Spike a hug, and he wags his tail. She uses bleach to wipe away the crimson drops splattered on the door. James dials 911 and is put on hold. After five minutes, he hangs up.

Tomatoes

One day as James walks past the corner market, Einstein looks at him and says, "He becoming a *man*."

It's true that his body is changing. He has grown taller. He needs to shave once or twice a week. Mama buys him deodorant. His voice deepens. He has continued his weight training in the school gym, and his muscles are larger and harder. But being a man is more than that. To him, it means following in Pops' footsteps.

In the spring James takes the bus to the store and buys six tomato plants, just as Pops always did. He has no garden tools, so he uses a pointed stick to dig up the bare ground in front of their building, still soft from the rainy season. Every afternoon he carries a pan of water down and waters the six plants. They begin to grow, and he goes back to the store for stakes, gently tying each plant to a stake. In a month small yellow flowers appear, each one representing the tomato it will become. Pops would be pleased.

One afternoon when James waters the plants, the sharp smell of urine wafts up and he realizes that someone has peed on his plants. It happens twice more over the next few weeks, and then, after tiny green tomatoes have begun to appear in June, he walks out one morning to see that all the plants have been ripped from the ground and thrown onto the sidewalk.

Felix the Cat

The funeral procession of Felix Mitchell, one of Oakland's biggest drug lords, takes place on August 27, 1986. It is the start of James' sophomore year. Mitchell was convicted and sent to Leavenworth Federal Penitentiary in 1985, where he was murdered by another inmate a year later. Because the necessary permits have been procured, the police cannot stop the lavish funeral parade. The coffin is carried in a glass carriage fit for French royalty, pulled by two high-stepping horses driven by a White man in a top hat. Six Rolls-Royces and a long line of cars follow. Huey Newton is said to be in one of them. Crowds line the route. Excited boys follow on their bicycles.

The robber barons of the Gilded Age dealt in steel and railroads, coal and copper, real estate and finance. This is the new gilded age, Oakland style. The lords deal in heroin and cocaine, PCP and marijuana, prostitution, guns. Big Fee, Mick Mo, Lil D, and Hollyrock are the new Mellon, Carnegie, Vanderbilt, and Rockefeller. Ten-year-old boys can make a hundred a week as police spotters. More than that as runners delivering drugs. If a drive-by is needed for somebody who has crossed the organization, a young man with a gun can make money and elevate himself in the hierarchy of the streets. The feds estimate that Felix Mitchell took in a half a million dollars a month selling heroin.

James stands on the sidewalk to watch. Around him people debate the life of Felix the Cat. TV reporters capture some of their comments for the evening news. A woman stuck in the traffic fumes, "Look at the kids out here. What message is this sending them, glorifying a thug?" One man praises Felix Mitchell for donating money to build a park. Another claims Felix Mitchell had been the largest employer in the city. He looks into the camera and challenges the authorities to bring jobs to Oakland. Others praise Felix for having style. Another man says, "It's capitalism, baby."

When the funeral procession approaches, James hears the clopping of the horses' hooves on the pavement. The glass carriage carrying the bronze coffin rolls by. Felix Mitchell was a hero to guys who aspire to cars with gold rim wheels and gold ropes around their necks. James remembers the day he saw Pops injecting himself. People like Felix Mitchell killed Pops. James imagines throwing an egg at the passing carriage, its glass side splattered with bits of white eggshell and slimy yellow yolk. He wishes a TV reporter would point a microphone at him. He'd like to make a speech. He wants to say that he's glad Felix Mitchell is dead.

A couple of Black kids at school have said that James acts White, that he's bougie. James composes speeches in his mind to defend himself. Who is Black, Martin Luther King or an Oakland gang member? Who did more good in the world, George Washington Carver or Felix Mitchell? In social studies their young teacher gives them a list of Black authors, actors, scientists, doctors, and military heroes. When they have a matching test on the list, James gets them all right. Most kids flunk the test. There are no Black veterinarians listed, but maybe James will be one. Meanwhile, his speeches remain in his head, unspoken.

The press and the police had hailed the imprisonment of Felix Mitchell as a victory in the war on drugs. But drug sales did not slow. As for violence, it increased. The demise of the most powerful drug network created a vacuum in which start-up gangs grow. These new gangs are just as violent but less disciplined, so the murder rate goes up. So do drug sales. Criminologists will call this the "Felix Mitchell paradox."

What Spike Knows

Mama's feet hurt from standing at her DMV window all day, so after dinner she fills a plastic dish tub with hot water and Epsom salts and soaks her feet while watching TV. When she gets settled, Spike walks over and lays his chin on her leg while she rubs his ears and talks to him.

Spike sleeps on James' bed. Sometimes when James opens his eyes in the morning, Spike is already awake and watching him. When James moves, Spike's tail thumps on the mattress and he roots his way next to James, licking his face. James wraps his arm around Spike and scratches his chest. Spike's leg pumps as if he's scratching himself.

James gives Spike two walks a day, a short one in the morning and a long one in the afternoon. In the park he does push-ups, pull-ups, and dips while Spike watches him. He throws a ball for Spike. He feels more relaxed when Spike is with him.

Spike is mostly indifferent to other people, but sometimes he stops to look at someone as if he sees inside them. One afternoon coming back from the park, Spike pauses close to two women sitting on a bus stop bench. One looks about the age of Mama, and the other is much older, probably the woman's mother. Thin gray hair rises like wisps of smoke from her dark skin, and she stares straight ahead.

The old woman turns to look at Spike, and he walks toward her. When the daughter tenses up, James says, "He's friendly."

"Penny," the old woman says in a creaky voice.

Her daughter says, "That's not Penny, Mama. Penny was a long time back."

Spike takes a step forward and rests his chin on the old woman's bony knee. She lifts her hand and moves it like a paint brush, front to back, across Spike's big head.

"Penny's a good dog," the old woman says.

Her daughter smiles sadly at James and says, "This is the first time she's talked today."

James starts to ask what's wrong with her, but then he thinks better of it and just nods.

When the old woman stops petting Spike, he lifts his muzzle and looks at her face, which has gone back to staring straight ahead.

Standing, the daughter says, "Our bus is coming, Mama." She helps her mother to her feet, and James leads Spike away.

James doesn't know how, but somewhere in that great head of his, Spike can sense pain and suffering in people. Maybe that's what Einstein means when he calls out one day as James and Spike walk past, "You listen to that dog now. That dog got *knowledge*."

Shakespeare

James' junior English teacher, Ms. Rosenbaum, young and new to the school this year, assigns a composition on the quote, "To thine own self be true." She says it's from Shakespeare.

James feels strongly drawn to the quote, and he gives the topic a lot of thought. What does it mean? Is he true to himself?

They have a week. He writes it the last weekend, and on Monday he hands in his composition.

> *The Dog Who Was True to His Self*
>
> *Two years ago, I got a job from a guy who had a couple of fighting pit bulls. People bet on the dogs like they do horse races or boxing matches. One of the dogs named Spike had won some fights, and when I started the job (cleaning the cages, feeding, and taking the dogs for walks), he was getting over wounds from his last fight. The fights are illegal and I never went to one.*
>
> *Dogs can't talk or do math problems or things like that, but I have learned that they are a lot like people. They like to do some things but not others. Some things they don't really want to do, but they've been trained to do them. I could tell this dog did not want to fight except he was trained that way.*
>
> *When he was put in a ring, if he didn't fight back the other dog would kill him, so he fought just to stay alive. Let's face it, our school is in a high crime area. You see it on the news and you hear about*

it in the halls. There are robberies and shootings everywhere, drugs all around. A couple of our students have been shot just walking down the street. A little girl was killed by a bullet that came through her window while she was watching TV. Do people deep down inside really want to rob and kill and sell drugs? Or are they like pit bulls, just trained to do it even though they really don't want to? In other words, are they not being true to their real selves?

The dog part of my story has a happy ending. After the dog lost his last fight, his owner didn't want him anymore. He said the dog had lost his will to fight. I took him to a nice veterinarian who didn't even charge me, and he saved the dog's life. Now the dog lives with me and my mama and he doesn't have to fight. He can be true to his real self. That's what the quote means to me—to live the way it is our nature to live. I wish we could all be true to ourselves the way Spike is now.

It is only through writing the essay that James fits his feelings into thoughts. He feels anxious and out of place because he *is* out of place, as much as Spike would be in fighting pit. He belongs in a place where there are no Black Snakes, where students listen to the teacher, and where Pops is still alive. He wants to be a good boy and grow into a good person, like George Washington Carver, doing good for humanity. He wants to be true to who he is.

The next Monday Ms. Rosenbaum reads James' composition aloud to the class. She asks the students what they think. They don't have much to say. But afterward, they give James a new name: Shakespeare. It sticks and spreads. People who didn't even know his name is James now call him Shakespeare.

Big Mike Again

James is walking home from the park when Spike comes to an abrupt halt, staring ahead. Big Mike is walking toward them in red basketball shorts and a black muscle shirt. It is spring and James hasn't seen Big Mike in two years.

"Little brother's gotten bigger," Big Mike says with a wide grin. He reaches out and feels James' biceps.

Spike extends his head and wags his tail. Big Mike rubs his face with both hands and then pounds his shoulder. Spike gives his pit bull smile. Fears dart through James. What if Big Mike wants Spike back? What if Spike wants to go with him?

James says, "How's it going, Big Mike?"

Big Mike smiles and says, "It's goin'. It's goin'. You still feeding this dog that lost me big money?"

"He's part of the family."

"Your Mama let you keep him, huh?"

"Yeah. It helped that some man tried to break into our place and Spike nearly tore his hand off."

"Old Spike," Big Mike chuckles. "Fights only if he has to."

"You still doing dog fights?"

"I don't have any dogs now. I still bet, though. Got me a couple of side hustles. Over in West Oakland. What about you? The streets haven't ate you up?"

"Not yet. I don't cross anybody. I'm true to myself."

Big Mike smiles. "True to yourself. I like that," he nods. "That's good." He turns as if he's looking for someone and says, "Gotta motor." He walks away and calls over his shoulder, "Keep working out. Looking good, little brother."

"I will," James answers. He looks down at Spike and sees that

Spike is looking up at him.

That night when James is doing homework, Spike has a dream. Lying on the rug, he growls and yips. His legs twitch and his body jerks. James wonders if he's reliving his fighting days. After a while his tail thumps the floor. James wants to believe that Spike is now dreaming of him.

Where There's a Will, There's a Way

One evening when James is watching Mama cook, she looks at him and says, "You want to learn how to do this?"

He does. Even back in Sacramento, she showed him how to make things like instant pudding. Now she starts teaching him new things—how to make black eyed peas with ham hocks, corn bread, even fried chicken. It's a matter of technique. The right consistency of the batter, the right temperature of the oven, the cooking times that make things like beans just done enough, but not too done. It's a matter of paying close attention and taking good care of the food. He likes that. Sometimes he goes to the market with her so he can carry the groceries home. On some afternoons after Spike's walk to the park, he starts dinner before she gets home from work. If not a veterinarian, maybe he could become a chef.

One night Mama fries up strips of bacon and makes greens with onions and bit of hot sauce. James makes corn bread. He likes it when they cook together. As they eat, Mama comments on how the three foods—greens, cornbread, and bacon—taste better together than any one of them separately. James agrees. The next time he bakes cornbread, he fries some bacon strips, chops them into small crisp pieces, and stirs them into the batter. He loves the outcome and on impulse he wraps up some pieces, puts Spike on his leash, and walks to Dr. Carter's office.

Dr. Carter and his assistant remember James and Spike, greeting them like old friends.

"I hope you like cornbread," James said. "I made it myself."

"I've wondered if I'd ever see you two again," Dr. Carter says thoughtfully.

"I feel so thankful for what you did," James says. "I still

remember what *pro bono* means."

Dr. Carter asks about his studies and his grades.

"Honor roll every semester," James says.

"Congratulations," Dr. Carter says.

"I want to be someone like George Washington Carver," James blurts, surprising himself that he's said it.

Dr. Carter smiles. "The desire is crucial. Where there's a will, there's a way."

"Yes, sir," James says.

He walks home with the words resounding in his head. *Where there's a will, there's a way.*

In media depictions of Oakland, older boys prey on the younger, force them to join gangs, do drugs, and commit crimes. The reality is more complex. On the streets James cultivates a persona of low visibility, the aura of a lone wolf. With a quiet defiance, he ignores the prostitutes, the guys selling dope, the stumbling drunks, the junkies nodding out. He knows which blocks to avoid, when to slip to the other side of the street. He often has Spike at his side. He lets challenges and taunts slide off rather than stick. He keeps his head level and his eyes straight ahead. Like a swimmer who glides through the water without splashing, James masters quietude.

At school, no one bothers him anymore. He hasn't seen Black Snake in three years. Like school athletes, the serious students are often left alone—unless they exude vulnerability, and James no longer does. He's known as Shakespeare, if he's known at all, one of the kids who does his homework and does not matter to those living more dangerous and exciting lives. Weekends and summers, he works as a bag boy at a supermarket and a counter person at McDonald's.

By his senior year, classes aren't as large and classroom

disruptions are fewer. That's because so many have dropped out—the boys sent to juvie or to jail, the gang members, the pregnant girls, the crackheads desperate for their next rock. Some just don't like school.

James hears classmates talk about their futures. Many have no plans. Of those who do, one says he's going to get a basketball scholarship to college, but he's not on the team. He says a scout will see him playing in the park. Another vaguely plans to own a store. Several are going to become rap stars. They plan to make demo tapes so they can be discovered. A California state lottery begins and some plan to win it.

James makes an appointment with the college counselor in his basement office. Mr. Hart is a young White man with red hair and a closely trimmed red beard. It's his first year at the school. Outside his office, military recruitment posters line the walls. There are no chairs in the hall, so James sits against the wall with two other students.

When it's his turn, James takes the chair in front of Mr. Hart's desk. Mr. Hart shifts through a stack of files until he finds James'. He opens it and scans the single page.

"Good grades," he says. "You should apply to Hayward State. Affordable tuition, and you can live at home and take BART." He swivels around in his chair and grabs an application and hands it to James. "I went there."

James looks at the application and then up at Mr. Hart. "What about other places?"

"Like where?" Mr. Hart says.

"Bigger places, like Berkeley."

"You have three thousand dollars a year for tuition and fees?"

"No, but what about scholarships?"

"They never cover it all. Besides, Berkeley would eat you alive,"

Mr. Hart says, loosening his tie. "Don't aim too high." He looks through his glass door to the other student waiting.

"I've been thinking of vet school," James says.

"I knew a girl at Hayward State who went on to med school. Apply to Hayward. You'll feel more at home there."

James feels he has more questions, but he's not sure what they are. "Thanks," he says, standing up.

"Any time," Mr. Hart says.

Keesha

In January of James' senior year, a girl is transferred into his section of English. She's someone he's noticed for a couple of years. She has bright, brown eyes that dance. Her rich, brown skin is smooth, and her hair in cornrows gives her a look of elegance. James imagines an African queen. Her name is Keesha.

One day after class she asks James, "Why do they call you Shakespeare?"

"In sophomore year I wrote a composition on a Shakespeare quote. The teacher liked it and read it to the class."

"What was the quote?" she asks.

He tells her and she asks, "Are you true to yourself?" Her question seems partly sincere, partly a tease.

He answers seriously. "I try to be."

She nods and walks away.

That night he tries to think of ways he can start a conversation with her. He asks Mama what girls like to talk about.

"Themselves," she laughs. "But I can tell you one thing. If you're even asking that question, you're ahead of ninety per cent of the men God put on his earth."

James' confidence ticks upward.

Their history teacher offers extra credit to anyone who writes a movie review of *Mississippi Burning*, so this gives James an excuse to ask Keesha to the movies. She says yes, but her parents have a rule: they have to meet him.

He arrives at her address wearing navy blue slacks and a burgundy sweater Mama gave him for Christmas. Keesha's family lives in a whole house, like James' place in Sacramento, except bigger. She has two younger sisters. The surrounding streets look run-down, but Keesha's block is an island of nice in a sea of not-nice. The houses have clean windows. Leafy trees grow between the sidewalks and the curb. The fence around her house is black iron, not chain link. There is no litter or graffiti in sight.

James makes small talk with her parents, and then he and Keesha take a bus down to the big movie theater near the lake. They find the film riveting, though parts frighten Keesha so badly that she balls up her fists and presses them to her temples. Afterwards, while waiting for the bus, they talk about race. Keesha wonders if there are still White racists like the ones in the movie, and they trade stories of times when their parents felt they'd been discriminated against. They talk about times when they felt Whites had looked at them in a certain way, and Keesha laughs when James tells her about his father's phrase, *the frozen face*. She asks about his father and James says he died of a heart attack.

As his mother instructed, James walks Keesha from the bus stop to her house. A block from home she offers her face for a kiss. Once they get past the awkward phase of not knowing which way to tilt their heads and knocking their teeth together, they lean against a tree and make out. James loves kissing her soft lips and her warm mouth. That night he relives their date by whispering the story to Spike. He basks in the feeling that life is going well for him.

Kelp

In April, Keesha invites James to go to the beach on a Sunday with her and her parents. Her younger sisters are attending a birthday party. Because James doesn't want them to see what his building and his block look like, he offers to walk to her place, but they pick him up anyway.

Mama waits on the sidewalk with James so she can introduce herself to Keesha's parents. Spike is with her on a leash. While the adults make small talk, James notices Spike. Spike looks worried, as if James might be leaving, never to return. He's never seen James get into a car. When they pull away from the curb, James feels a pang of sadness.

When they arrive at Ocean Beach, they park the car and Keesha pulls James by his hand toward the sand. Her mother calls after them, "Come back when you want sandwiches. And don't turn your back on the ocean."

"Why did she say that?" James asks.

"Oh," Keesha says, "she worries about sneaker waves. Undertow. Sharks. Enemy submarines. You know how mothers are."

James laughs. It's sunny and mild, so he slips off his jacket and ties it around his waist. There are some Asian men with long fishing poles mounted on metal holders stuck into the sand. Their barely visible lines slant far into the water. Dogs chase and then run from the waves. James wishes he could have brought Spike.

He and Keesha talk about their families. Her father drives a truck for UPS and her mother is a receptionist for a dentist. He tells her about Spike and says he's like a brother. She giggles. "You say funny things," she says. He smiles but he doesn't understand what was funny about his comment.

He asks Keesha about the long, green, slimy things washing onto the beach. They look like life from outer space.

"Kelp," she answers. "Some kinds of it they eat in Japan." He wonders how she knows that.

They sit on the sand and gaze at the vast ocean. He's mesmerized by the rhythmic succession of the waves. One gathers and churns frothy white as it somersaults over itself with a sonorous rushing sound, spreading into a swirling pond before it's pulled back out. Soon another gathers, and then another.

"You look like someone who's never seen the ocean before," Keesha says.

Watching the waves, he considers laughing it off as the joke she means it to be. But he remembers his mantra. Being true to himself means being true *about* himself.

"I never have," he says.

"You've never seen the ocean?"

James shakes his head. "Never until now."

"Wow," she says.

"I mean, I've seen it on TV. And in movies. But not in person. It's amazing. How it looks. The sound. The smells."

They sit in silence, looking out at the water.

"You're right," she says, resting her head sideways on her knee and looking at James. "It is amazing."

A few days later at school, Keesha walks up to James while he is pulling books from his locker. Bouncing on the balls of her feet, she says, "I got into UCLA. With a scholarship."

James is surprised and impressed. UCLA is famous—for football, for basketball, for everything. She gushes about what it was like when she visited the campus with her parents—the students, the buildings and lawns, the coffee places. They went for a burger and saw Magic Johnson crossing the street. James feels his smile fade.

Beaming, she runs off to class. James has a study hall that period, and after he takes his seat, he feels glum. Keesha is a good student, but her grades are about the same as his. He wonders how she knew about applying to UCLA and he didn't. He remembers how Mr. Hart dismissed his question about colleges other than Hayward State. James feels forlorn, like he is standing on a platform, realizing the train he wants to be on is leaving the station and he has no ticket.

After the last period, he hurries off the school grounds so he won't see Keesha. He feels like he's been betrayed, but he doesn't know how or by whom.

Looking for Home

James knows that Spike would love to go to the ocean, trot along the beach and chase the waves spreading their foam across the sand. James wants to take him, but it doesn't seem possible. Mama doesn't have a car, and buses and BART don't allow dogs. It's a modest desire—to take Spike to the beach—but James is unable to fulfill it. Mama always says they're not poor; they just don't have much money. But maybe they *are* poor. Maybe poor means not being able to do simple things like take your dog to the beach. Maybe poor is not knowing things—like how to apply for a scholarship to UCLA. He remembers what Dr. Carter said, *where there's a will, there's a way*. What if that's wrong? What if there is no way?

When James walks Spike to the park on Monday, it strikes him that he and Spike had something in common when they met—both were in lives they had not chosen, lives they did not like. Spike, gentle by nature, was made to fight against other dogs, and James had to live in a city ruled by the culture of the streets, when all he really wanted was to go to a peaceful neighborhood school, not be preyed upon by bullies, and have a few friends. To ask Christine Chan for a date. To grow tomatoes like Pops. Seeing the ocean reminded James how alien and hostile the world of the streets really is. Everybody on the streets strains for domination, but the powerful ocean is naturally itself and needs nothing more.

James indulges in fantasies in which he and Spike escape to a little shack on the beach or a cabin in the woods. James could chop wood and draw water from a well. Sometimes Keesha is present in these daydreams, but more often it is just he and Spike.

Whenever James begins to feel sorry for himself, he reminds himself to be grateful for what he has. From what he hears at school, he knows that some kids get beat at home. Some have parents—often drunk or addicted—who don't care about them. Some don't go home to a good dinner like James does, but buy—or steal—a soda and a slice of pizza or a bag of chips for dinner. Some drop out of school and end up in juvie or in jail. Some read far below their grade level, whereas James came from his Sacramento school with solid skills. He remembers how much adversity George Washington Carver had to face.

"Count your blessings," Mama tells him, and he does. But he wants more.

Spike's Last Walk

On the afternoon of May 18, 1989, three weeks before graduation and a month after his eighteenth birthday, James walks Spike to the park. A thick fog has rolled in and the cold wind puts a spring into Spike's trot. At the park, James throws the ball, which Spike runs down and brings back at a proud prance. James wonders if chasing the ball is fun for Spike, or if he does it because he thinks it pleases James. They are the only ones in the park, and the fog muffles the sound so that the streets seem peaceful.

After Spike brings the ball back for the last time, James puts it in his jacket pocket. He sees someone walking through the park, a boy in black warm-up suit. James puts his hands on either side of Spike's big head and scratches his face. Spike wags his tail. When James looks up, he recognizes the boy as Black Snake. His heart pounds. He looks older now, and harder. James is now as tall as Black Snake and more muscular. Black Snake takes a long look at James and then at Spike. Abruptly he stops, looking at James.

"Shit," he says. "I know you. That's the motherfucking dog that bit me."

James is about to say it was because Black Snake was trying to rob him. Black Snake reaches into his waistband and pulls out a gun. He points the gun at Spike. Three sharp cracks split the air. Spike yelps and his legs collapse. Blood spurts from three holes in his side. Spike reaches for his side with his mouth, as if to grab what's hurting him, but his strength ebbs and his head falls back to the ground. James sinks to his knees and presses his hands to the wounds. Spike's legs jerk as if he's trying to run, and then they stop. Spike whimpers and looks into James' eyes as if he wants to speak. James leans forward and presses his mouth to Spike's face. Spike gives him two licks, then swallows hard and clenches his teeth. A weak groan comes from deep inside him. His heaving chest goes still. His eyes go dim, and his big tongue slides limp from his mouth. Something of Spike slips away and James can't hold it.

For a long instant James forgets Black Snake is still there, standing over him.

Black Snake snickers. "Look. Dumb dog shit himself." Then he snorts, "He's dead meat now. Go cook him for dinner, motherfucker."

James stands, roiling with rage. He takes a step toward the sneering Black Snake, who points the gun at him. James does not care. His clenched fist explodes into the center of Black Snake's face. Black Snake falls back, his arms flailing. He hits the ground with a thud. The gun bounces off the asphalt and lies at James' feet. James grabs it and pounces on Black Snake, straddling his chest. He jams the gun into Black Snake's mouth. He hears a choking gag. He pulls the trigger and Black Snake's body jerks with the sharp bang. James fires twice more, and then there are just clicks. Black Snake's mouth fills with dark blood. James looks down at the glassed-over eyes, a pool of thick blood spreading beneath the head. He stands and walks away. He can't feel his own body.

James wipes the gun with his shirttail, just as he's seen in movies. Ahead, a bus stops at the corner of the park and two guys get off. James slips the gun into his jacket pocket. When he reaches the end of the park, he looks back. No one is around. He crosses the street, and when he sees a garbage can he pulls the gun from his pocket and tosses it in. He realizes he did not wipe it off again, but he keeps walking.

When James enters the apartment with Spike neither at his side nor waiting inside the door, the realization hits him like a collapsing building. In his room he sits on his bed, a blade of ice lodged in his chest. He sees the look in Spike's eyes as he lay bleeding on the hard ground. He believes it was a look of apology. I'm sorry I'm leaving you.

When Mama comes home, James starts to tell her, but his lips quiver so much he can't speak. What finally comes out is that Spike ran for a squirrel, pulled the leash out of his hand, and was hit by a truck.

Spike's Rug

James lives in a state of anxious agitation. Though what he did felt like self-defense, he knows that if he's identified, he will go to prison. When he hears a siren, his heart pounds. He can't eat or sleep. He worries that someone saw him in the park, or that the police are asking who owned a tan pit bull. Fortunately, there are a lot of tan pit pulls around, and because he always had Spike on a leash, he had never spent the money to buy a tag for his collar. The word on the street is that when a brother is shot, the police don't try that hard to find his killer. James hopes that will help him.

In addition to this constant fear, he lives with searing grief. He dreads the walk home after school when he can't escape the visceral expectation that Spike will be waiting to greet him. At moments, he believes he hears Spike's nails on the floor, hears him shake or scratch himself. In bed at night, he pulls his pillow over his head and sobs. When he sleeps, he dreams about Spike.

One afternoon his classmate Draymond walks with him as he's leaving school and says at the corner, "Come down this way, I want to see something."

"What?" asks James.

"Black Snake's house. Remember him? He got popped."

James' face goes prickly and his chest tightens.

"Who shot him?" James asks.

"Don't know. These days, motherfuckers get killed for nothing. It's a cold game out there."

They reach a dingy bungalow where a memorial is piling up. A couple of mylar balloons are tied to the chain link fence. Bunches of carnations lie on the packed dirt in front of the steps to the porch. Black Snake's cap and his black silky jacket are spread out like they're waiting for him to put them on. Beside some empty bottles of Hennessy lies a 5x7 school photo, Black Snake smiling into the camera. It takes James a moment to recognize this boyish face as the person who killed Spike. He looks much younger, so it would have been taken before he was sent to juvie, maybe the year he first stole from James. The photographer must have said something to make him laugh.

"Didn't he quit school?" James asks.

"Yeah," Draymond says. "Got sent to juvie. Ran with the 77 group, I heard."

When James passes the corner store, Einstein sees him and says, "Got to wash away them troubles, young man. But not too soon. Everything in time."

At home, James does something he hasn't done since his freshman year. He whips off his belt and begins beating his mattress, harder and harder, making guttural animal sounds until he is out of breath and slobbering on himself. He feels full of poison. He uses the belt so hard and for so long that the sheet on his bed splits. He sinks to all fours and pulls from under his bed Spike's rug. He lies on his side, pulls the rug into his chest, and sobs. Relieved at being alone in the apartment, he allows himself to wail.

He sits up and walks to the bathroom. Tears and snot cover his face. There are tan dog hairs on his T-shirt. He rinses his face, returns to his bedroom. He sits on his bed and looks at the rug. He wants to talk to Pops.

He begins to have nightmares. What wakes him is the physical sensation of Black Snake's body jerking when James fires the gun into his mouth. In some of the dreams, the body keeps jerking, even after he stops firing.

At school James tells Keesha that Spike was run over. He wants to tell her the real story— all of it—but he's afraid. She might tell her parents, who would call the police. She might freak out and think he's a terrible person, even call the cops herself. She's never had a dog, and she does not realize what a loss it is for James.

Near the end of May, James takes Keesha to the prom. He buys a ticket for forty dollars, rents his tux, and buys her a corsage. He chips in for his share of the limousine her friends have rented. He spends most of what is in his shoebox in the closet.

On prom night, Keesha looks very pretty in her red dress, and she bubbles with happiness and affection toward James. She tells him he looks handsome. Thus prompted, he tells her she looks very pretty. They dance, but he has trouble moving. He feels tired. The drums in the music sound like gunfire. Halfway through the evening she pulls him into a corner and asks him what is wrong. Isn't he having a good time?

Her question makes him feel trapped. He doesn't know what to say. All he knows is that he wants to run screaming from the prom, from Oakland, from himself. Keesha's parents have given her a curfew of midnight, so they skip the after-prom parties. The limousine takes them to her house and he walks her to the door. She tells him what a wonderful evening it was. He can't tell if she means it.

At graduation James and Keesha receive certificates for graduating in the top fifth of their class. After the ceremony, Mama, beaming with pride, says that she thought the commencement speaker was great. James vacantly agrees, realizing he did not hear a word of what was said.

Summer begins and nothing feels right. James has more bad feelings than he has names for. To make money for college, he works thirty hours a week at the supermarket and twenty-four hours a week at MacDonald's. All the better—the two jobs make him tired and occupy his mind. Both pay minimum wage, \$3.35

an hour before taxes. He is saving for his tuition at Hayward State.

Keesha works as a restaurant hostess, and they have little time off in common. When they are together, Keesha complains that he seems distant. She asks if he's seeing someone else. When she brings him a 5x7 print of their prom photo, he is stunned. Keesha is smiling radiantly and really does look beautiful. He appears haunted. His smile is a grimace. He looks like someone who has killed a person. He again considers telling her, but he can't. At first, she reacts to his distance by trying harder, but then she drifts away.

In mid-July Keesha leaves for UCLA. She has a special six-week program for incoming minority students. James had expected to feel relieved when she left, but instead he feels more empty. The distance in their relationship was his fault, though he suspects she will soon find a new boyfriend at UCLA.

Textbooks

A week before Hayward State classes begin, James takes BART down to the campus. He has brought a cashier's check for his tuition, and he turns it in at the administration building. He walks to the bookstore, and with his schedule in hand he wanders the aisles looking for his required texts. The economics book, a six-hundred-page hardback containing abundant colored graphs, tables, and photos, is $240. Used copies are $175. He did not know a book could cost that much. He fills his basket, losing track of the total. When the clerk tallies them up, the cost is over $600. He hands her his debit card, unsure of its balance. The card is refused, so she hands it back to him. His face burns.

"I'll get the cash and come back," he says.

"No problem," she says, lifting his basket and setting it behind the counter.

Outside the store, he sits on the curb. He feels like he's been duped. He calculates the price of the econ book in terms of his take-home pay from his jobs. A used copy costs 80 hours of bagging groceries or filling burger orders. When he estimated college expenses, no one warned him about the cost of textbooks. Pops used to say that the economy was stacked against the average man. He believes it.

He feels a rising panic. Classes start in three days, and he's got the have the textbooks. He slips back inside the bookstore and walks the aisles. The shelves are full of books, stacks of them. He's sure there will be leftovers after all the students have bought their books. All he needs are single copies. He selects his books again. This time it's faster since he remembers where they are. The store is crowded. Students are coming and going. Holding the books in the crook of his arm, he walks out the door, his mouth dry and his throat tight. It's the only thing he's stolen since shoplifting the bottle of grape wine for his mother three and a half years ago. He starts down the sidewalk and hears someone trot up beside him, then a second.

"Store security," says an Asian guy. He points to a badge attached to the belt of his jeans. The other is a big Black guy wearing a security officer jacket. He looks like a football player. They are not much older than James. They walk James back to the store, and the same cashier gives him a long look. They walk down the aisle and the Asian guy opens an unmarked door. Inside are a metal desk and wall shelves containing six TV monitors showing various parts of the store. The big guy moves a metal folding chair against the door and sits down.

"Have a seat," the Asian guy says. "Just put the books on the desk." He picks up the receiver of a wall phone and requests an officer for a 459.5.

"I'm really sorry," James says.

The Asian guy fiddles with a bank of switches and controls. Finally he says, "Here" and he points to one of the screens. The video shows James walking out the door with the books under his arm. The guy pushes a button and the video cassette pops out. He writes something on a label and presses it to the cassette. Then he goes through the stack of books, copying the titles and prices on a sheet of paper. He punches the figures into a calculator to get the total cost.

"Can I just pay for them?" James asks.

"Too late for that," the big guy says from his chair.

"It's store policy," the Asian guy says. "We have to bring in the cops, whether we want to or not."

Bands tighten around James' chest. The two security guards

watch the monitors until there is a knock on the door. A uniformed Hayward policeman enters. The Asian guy hands him the list and says they've got it on video. The policeman handcuffs James and leads him through a rear entrance. At the police station James is fingerprinted and photographed, then released. The cost of the books makes the charge felony shoplifting. He will have a court date in a month.

On the first day of classes, James notes which books he will need immediately, and unfortunately the econ book is one of them. It's already been checked out of the library. He waits in a long line at the financial aid office to apply for an emergency loan. They will let him know in a few days. That night he tells Mama not about the shoplifting but about the price of the econ book. She gives him the money that she had set aside for the electric bill.

The Poppy Plant

The knock on the apartment door makes James' heart pound. Something about the sound—authoritative, insistent, loud. In the depths of his fear, he knows who it is. He attaches the chain and cracks the door. A White man wearing a coat and tie holds up a badge. Two uniformed policemen, one Black and one White, stand behind him.

"Oakland PD," the man says. "Open the door."

James unhooks the chain and opens the door.

"Are you James Fields?" the man with the badge asks.

"Yes, sir," James answers.

The two uniformed police take him firmly by each arm, turn him around, and cuff his hands behind his back. They pat him down.

"Is anyone else here?"

"No, sir," James says. "My mother gets home around six."

"Let me do this now," the man says to the two uniformed officers. He pulls a card from his shirt pocket and reads James his rights.

"I don't understand," James says, grasping for a last strand of hope. "My court date isn't until next month."

When the man in the suit tells him he's under arrest for the murder of Marvin Mitchell, James recognizes Black Snake's real name. He feels like the bottom has dropped out of the world and he's falling through space. As they walk down the stairs, he feels dizzy. A squad car sits in front of the building. The White patrolman seems indifferent. The Black patrolman looks at James like he wants to hit him. The White officer says to the man in the suit, "Another 187 bust. The second this week, isn't it?"

The man nods.

The officer chuckles. "At this rate, you'll make captain soon."

When they pause to unlock the car door, James looks back at his building. Just inside the chain link fence, where he tried to grow tomato plants, stands a single California poppy, its lacy green leaves surrounding the flowers that look like delicate yellow-orange cups. The glowing beauty seems to James the last pretty thing he will ever see, and he is still looking at it when the White uniformed officer places his palm on the top of James' head and steers him into the back seat.

Riding in the car, James thinks of Mama. He wishes he had known he was going to be arrested today so that he could have stepped in front of a bus and died as a good son who was just starting college.

Part Three

Math Camp

The summer before her senior year of high school, Allison attends a week-long math camp on the campus of Purdue University. Two hundred high school students—most of them boys—stay in dorm rooms and sit in lectures with Purdue math professors. They are put into groups and challenged to solve problems. There are competitions. The emphasis is applied math and real-world problems.

The camp begins on a Sunday evening, where Allison notes that it is a convention of nerds. Awkward, gawky, badly dressed, ill at ease, mostly male. On Monday morning she notices a participant in her geometry group who doesn't fit the mold. She's wearing cut-offs, a black tank top, and combat boots. She has a small dolphin tattoo above her ankle, spikey blond hair, and eyeliner that looks like it was applied with a marking pen. Her name is Starburst and she has come all the way from LA, where she attends a private school. Her parents know rock singers and movie stars. She walks with long, slouchy strides. There is a mischievous glint in her eye. She is adventurous and irreverent.

After dinner one night, Starburst asks if Allison likes to bowl. There is a bowling alley on the lower level of the student union building. Having bowled a few times with her dad, Allison says sure. It's the first night of after-dinner bowling in a series of three. They laugh, they are silly. Starburst's squeals of delight and groans of disappointment are infectious. She invents bowling styles. Her back to the pins, she rolls the ball backwards through her legs like a football player hiking the ball. Using both arms, she rolls two balls at once. She swears like a sailor. On the second night, they stop in Starburst's room and Allison complains that her shoulder is sore from bowling.

"You ever had a massage?" Starburst asks.

Allison shakes her head. She is sitting in the chair and Starburst is perched on the desk. "Then you're overdue," Starburst says, jumping off the desk. "I'll get my oil."

Allison is not sure what's about to happen, but she thinks of herself as a bold individualist, and this seems like something a bold individualist would not refuse.

Starburst tells Allison to lie on the bed in her panties and bra. "Since this is Indiana," Starburst says. "In California, everyone gets massages in the nude."

Allison lies on her stomach and Starburst straddles her back, pressing on the sore spots with her thumbs.

"Ouch," Allison says.

"I'm releasing your blockages," Starburst says. "It's supposed to hurt."

Allison giggles.

Starburst kneads the muscles with her thumbs, the heels of her hands, and even her elbows. Allison's nervousness melts like soft candle wax. Starburst undoes Allison's bra and takes off her own shirt. She isn't wearing a bra.

"So we'll be equal," she says. Allison's fear of what's coming gives way to desire. Starburst takes the lead and the massage becomes a seduction.

Sex after bowling. Allison feels she's getting a crash course in the erotic arts. She is willing in part because Starburst does everything in a matter-of-fact manner, as if new and varied sex acts are new styles of bowling, all innocence and irreverent fun. Starburst says that nerdy librarian types like Allison turn her on. When Allison asks Starburst how she got an all-over tan, Starburst says, "How do you think? Being nude in the sun."

"Do people in California just walk around naked?" Allison

asks.

"Except when we're skateboarding," Starburst replies.

While Allison is thinking about this, Starburst breaks out laughing and hits Allison over the head with a pillow.

On their last night, under Starburst's tutelage, Allison smokes her first joint. They are sitting cross-legged on the bed. After a coughing fit, Allison asks, "So are you a lesbian?"

"Bi, I guess. I just like sex. My theory is, everything in the world is either pro-sex or anti-sex. Labels are anti-sex."

Starburst rattles off a long list of celebrities who are lesbian or bi: singers, movie stars, artists, writers.

"I wonder if Nancy Drew was," Allison says.

"Definitely," Starburst says. "Buffy, too. Straight people are boring."

When Allison's parents pick her up on Saturday, she feels dizzy. Her body pulses with some new kind of life.

For weeks, memories of Starburst fill Allison's mind. They talked about what was around them: the eccentric professors, the math problems, the awkward boys, their bowling, the dorm food. Back home in Indianapolis, she keeps thinking of things she wants to say to Starburst. She wishes they had talked about more—about their parents, what it's like to live in LA, where they want to go to college. She misses Starburst for the talks they might have had.

Allison writes Starburst a couple of letters and brings herself to say she misses her. She says the week was very special to her. Allison waits for a return letter, and two weeks later, she receives a card of Garfield bowling. Stars have been drawn in purple ink inside the card. There are no words. Allison looks at the card in search of a hidden meaning. She finds none. She aches to realize that she liked Starburst in a way that Starburst did not like her.

Allison's instant crush on the Olympic athlete Morgan, her

lingering looks at pretty girls at school, even her fascination with Nancy Drew—all of those take on a new meeting after her sex with Starburst. Still, she can't bring herself to accept the word: *lesbian*. Lesbian is what others are; she wants a different word for herself. In the privacy of her mind, she calls it her secret. She envies Starburst's brash and unapologetic ability to be herself, the opinions of others be damned. One of Starburst's favorite sayings, something she said when she rolled a gutter ball or missed her check-in curfew, was, "If they can't take a joke, fuck 'em." It's an attitude Allison wishes she could have.

The following autumn Allison returns to Purdue with her parents for a campus tour. It is six weeks after 9/11, and everywhere the mood seems solemn, watchful, and on edge—but determined. Allison's dad points out that Purdue is a great school with in-state tuition, the best bang for the buck. His eyes brighten when the tour leader takes them past the engineering buildings, citing impressive inventions and statistics. Her mother is wary of the huge size, but likes the autumn leaves falling on the green lawns. She worries about Allison's lack of friends, and she is not looking forward to the empty nest. Allison notices the girls and wonders how many of them like other girls. She keeps expecting to see Starburst, even though she knows she's in California.

They peek into a massive lecture hall where Allison imagines herself seated in the front row, diligently taking notes. She does not know what to expect of college life outside the lecture hall. Will she walk the campus alone for four years, hiding her secret?

When her parents drop her off at the dorm in September of 2002, the prospect of living in a structure of steel, concrete, and glass makes her uneasy. The alien dorm is eight floors of hard synthetic surfaces. All the chairs are plastic. Not even the food tastes real. She cannot imagine a sterile dorm like this on the cover of a

Nancy Drew novel.

When rush begins, Allison joins a sorority—first, because it's a physical house with thick rugs, drapes, couches, and a wood-burning fireplace, and second, because she believes it will prevent her from sliding into lonely isolation. The sorority that wants her is known as a plain girls' house that caters to bookish types. She figures it's a good fit.

On the day the sororities announce bids, the selected girls are brought to the house, given roses, and serenaded on the lawn. It suggests a group marriage proposal. Girls cry tears of joy, and while Allison feels excited and a little anxious, she can't understand the tears or what outpouring of feeling they represent. She accepts her rose with dry-eyed poise and a polite smile.

Poised and polite—these are the pillars of the style with which she emerges from adolescence. The style allows her to overcome her introversion to pursue her goals while protecting her secret. She greets people with a handshake but avoids a hug.

Poetry and Math

At the end of her freshman year, Allison declares a double major in English and math.

Both involve sleuthing. Math analyzes problems and creates solutions. It's an abstract version of her dad's workbench. Literature has meanings to be unearthed and understood, mysteries requiring close attention. It's food for the soul.

Each is beautiful in its own way. Math embodies order and harmony. A straight line is the shortest distance between two points, and nothing could be more elegant in its precision, more precise in its simplicity. Math is the beauty of her rocket soaring into the sky, perfectly obedient to scientific law.

Poetry is the beauty of water, earth, and fire. Poetry is seamless, free in its movement, wetting all it touches—here a trickle, there a mighty wave, at one moment creating life and in another taking life away. Poetry is vast and weightless. Poetry can both burn the skin and provide the balm to heal it. Poetry is her stormy nights with Starburst. Poetry is watching snow melt on her windowsill. Poetry is the dream she feels but can't remember. It's a cocoon into which she can crawl. It's an enchanted land where girls fall in love with one another.

A Friend

Allison is comfortable in her sorority. The house and her room are homey. Thick drapes frame the windows, lamps bathe the living room in soft yellow light, and the plush couches are comfortable. She imagines Nancy Drew sitting in one of the leather chairs, wearing a red beret and reading a book. The bathrooms sparkle, smelling of herbal shampoos. The cook prepares good, homey food. Her sorority sisters are friendly and helpful to one another, and that goes a long way toward making everyday life pleasant. Occasionally a sister will offer to set her up with a blind date, but Allison cheerfully declines. No one suspects.

Allison comes to enjoy Saturday nights with a few dateless sisters eating popcorn and watching a movie in the pine-paneled TV room. Her time in the sorority makes her more socially at ease with people, but no more ready to share her secret. There is a gay pride organization on campus, and at the beginning of her sophomore year, the lesbian part of the group hosts an open house in a meeting room of the student union building. Allison makes herself go, but after pausing at the door and seeing a dozen girls leaning awkwardly against the walls with Styrofoam cups of punch, she slips away, her face burning.

In her junior year, Allison becomes friends with a movie-star handsome boy in her poetry class. His name is Gene, and the class is a seminar on Emily Dickinson and Walt Whitman. They often walk to the sweet shop for coffee after class.

One day they sit over coffee talking about the poems they discussed in class. They are both in love with Emily Dickinson. Walt Whitman, not as much.

"But some of his lines are exquisite," Allison says. "Like, 'When lilacs last in the dooryard bloom'd.' So simple and elegiac."

"I like him, too," Gene nods. "At his best, he's very musical. But sometimes he hits a little too close to home. I have to take a walk and breathe."

Allison tilts her head. "How do you mean?"

Gene lowers his chin and stares into his coffee, and then he looks up at her with a wry smile. "I think you and I share similar secrets, Allison."

She shifts her weight. "What secrets?"

"We-ell," he says, drawing out the word. "The truth is...I like boys."

A blurred image is dialed into sharp focus. Of course—he's gay. It makes sense.

Then he adds, "And I have a sneaky suspicion that you like girls."

Allison's face glows red. Gene laughs warmly and says, "And you're cute when you blush."

She fans her face with her hand and says, "I've had this problem since I was a kid. My dad used to call me Glow Worm."

"Am I right?" Gene asks.

"Yes," she sighs. "I am...a lesbian, I guess. It's ridiculous how I have trouble picking a word and saying it. I'm an idiot. But yes, I like girls." An image of Starburst flashes in her mind. "How did you know?" It frightens her to think that people can tell.

"Gaydar. My sixth sense."

She chuckles and turns her coffee cup in her hands.

"It's not easy," she says.

"No, it's not." He reaches across the table and squeezes her hand. "What's the not-easy part for you?"

She sighs. "Living with a secret. Of course, there's a simple solution. I could come out, and then it wouldn't be a secret. But I haven't. I don't know why."

"The judgment of others?"

"That's most of it, I guess. Over the years, they add up—all those snarky anti-gay remarks, mostly from people I don't like or respect or even know. It's like being told everybody hates your voice, so you just don't sing."

"It *is* hard," Gene says. "Indiana—and Purdue included—is not exactly ground zero for the gay liberation movement. Yes, I know it's 2005, but here we're in some weird time warp."

"But our marching band has the world's largest drum," she says.

"Yes, it does," Gene laughs. He hums the first bars of the school song.

"Sis, boom, bah," Allison laughs.

"Now that the air is cleared, I have a question for you. I'm a Sigma Chi, you know." He wiggles his hand to show his ring.

"Really?" she says. "You never mentioned that."

"It doesn't have a lot of relevance."

"And you don't wear a pin."

"The ring is enough, thank you. But our spring formal is coming up. I would like to ask you to be my date. We could be the two secrets of Sigma Chi."

"You're not out, either?"

"Ha! I don't think the Sig house is ready for that."

"I'd love to," she says, blushing again.

Allison said yes before she thought. She didn't even go to her high school prom, so she's not sure she knows how to act. She does own a black cocktail dress, knee length, so that's what she wears for her first college date. One of her sorority sisters does her make-up, clean and natural. Gene picks her up wearing a dark blue suit, impeccably tailored. A crisp white shirt and a pink tie. He looks like he's on his way to a photoshoot for *GQ*. He pins a gardenia to her dress. He is so loquacious and effusive that she can relax and listen to him and not feel pressured or awkward.

The Sigma Chi house looks like an English hunting lodge, and Allison loves its exposed beams and tall leaded windows. The fireplace is so large a person could stand in it. Allison and Gene forgo the high-alcohol punch and drink champagne from a bottle Gene has entrusted to the bartender. Gene turns out to be a great dancer, and she can tell he tones down his style for her, like a tennis pro hitting easy balls to a novice. A couple of her sorority sisters are there, and they give Allison conspiratorial winks. After her second glass of champagne, she thinks to herself, *Here I am, Plain-Jane Allison Anderson, at the best fraternity on campus with the handsomest guy in the room. To channel Mrs. Dalloway, "What a lark!"*

At the end of the evening, when the DJ packs up and people drift off, they go to Gene's room for a last glass of champagne.

"I had fun," Allison exclaims. "My first college date!"

Gene looks at her and says, "I have to ask—I hope I'm not prying—if you've ever had a girlfriend."

She tells him about math camp with Starburst. "When we did 'Wild Nights' in class, I was thinking of her the whole time."

"Done with the Compass," he quotes.

"Done with the Charts," she responds.

"That's a great story," he laughs. "Mothers! Protect your daughters from the lavender menace. Don't send them to math camp!"

Allison bursts out laughing, and then raises her glass. "Lesbian math nerds of the world unite." Then she adds, "I'm terrible. I have trouble spitting out the word. But the champagne helps."

"Champagne always helps," he says.

"What about you?" she says. "Boyfriends?"

"Tragically, no. Flings, for sure. Brief encounters, too many. But never a boyfriend. That's what I want, though. My fond fantasy. It's hard here. People stay closeted."

"I want that, too," she says. "A girlfriend, I mean."

Gene stands up and holds out his hand. "A last dance?" She stands. He walks across the room and puts on Celine Dion, "My Heart Will Go On."

"Not too cheesy?" he asks.

Smiling, she shakes her head and leans into him. It occurs to her that he is her first true friend.

The next morning at the sorority house breakfast table, the sisters in their PJs and fuzzy slippers, Allison is asked about her movie-star date.

"Did he ask you out again?" they want to know.

"We're just friends," Allison says. "He's in my poetry class."

"Poetry," they coo. "Sounds romantic."

They lean forward, like puppies waiting to be fed. Allison smiles politely, enjoying the unintended ruse. She has an impulse to tell them she's gay, but that's a line she's not quite ready to cross.

The friendship between Allison and Gene deepens. With him, her skin feels safe from burns. Sharing their secrets cements their bond. They arrange to have a class together the following semester.

One day over coffee in the student union, Gene asks if she ever hears from her math camp fling. She shakes her head.

Gene smiles with sympathy and says, "A cloud just passed over your face."

"You're very observant."

"And?"

"Our week together was thrilling and sexy and all that, but back in Indianapolis, I kept thinking about her. I doubt she thought much about me. I wrote her a couple of times, but she only sent back a card. With no writing on it. Her LA life sounded wild and exciting. I think I was just nerd *du jour* for her."

"Nerd?"

"She told me she found nerds sexy."

Gene laughs. "To each his own when it comes to fetishes." His smile disappears. "You felt hurt?"

"Yeah, I did."

"You're not the one-night stand type. Or even one-week stand."

"No, I'm not."

"You're not attracted to anyone in your house? Which could be a disaster, of course."

Allison shakes her head. "But there's one girl in our seminar, Amanda, who has caught my eye. I saw her at the house dance."

"Oh, God," Gene says. "She's pinned—to one of my fraternity brothers. Stence. I think he's going to pop the question soon."

"Unlike you, I have no gaydar," she says, resting the side of her face glumly on her palm. "None whatsoever."

"I'm not so sure. There *is* a vibe about Amanda. But if she's gay, she doesn't know it—yet."

"It's hopeless," Allison sighs.

"It's not, though. You just need to get out of Indiana. It will happen. For both of us. Trust me."

What Next?

In Allison's senior year, there is rampant worry among her sorority classmates about what they will do after graduation. That winter, a pledge whom Allison has been helping with calculus says to her, "You're so much better at explaining things than my professor. You should be a teacher."

The remark plants a seed. Allison stops by the education office of the career center. She would need a teaching credential for public school, but she is surprised to learn that private schools do not require them. Some of her sorority sisters attended private schools, and they sound like places she would like to teach. She collects a list of private schools that offer internships for starting teachers and sends off applications.

In March she is offered an internship at a New England boarding school. Her *what next?* question has an answer.

"That's wonderful," Gene beams when they meet for lunch. "I can totally see you as a teacher. Private school will be perfect. Students are serious about learning—most of them, anyway."

"You went to private school, right?"

"Oh, yes. Lakeside Country Day. Doesn't that sound *so* J. Crew?" He strikes a pose and says with drama, "Gene—in deck shoes and pastel cotton sweater, born to sail."

"What about you? Still planning to go to San Francisco?"

He nods. "It's toxic around here. I find myself thinking, 'I *can't* be a stockbroker; they're all straight. Or, 'I *can't* be a real estate agent; they're all straight.' I need to breathe some gay air. Expand my horizons. I'm tired of feeling I have to censor my bodily movements so I won't look swishy. I want to have my own apartment. Maybe just wait tables for a while. See what comes my way."

Graduation

When people line up for graduation, sweating under their black gowns, Allison spots Gene and asks someone to save her place in line so she can skip over and say hello. Jauntily, she starts to tell him she's never seen him wear anything so ill-fitting, but his face is flushed, his mouth is twisted in anguish, and his eyes are full of tears. The sight stops Allison mid-sentence.

"What's wrong?" she asks.

"I'm a stupid ass," he says. "I came out to my parents at my graduation brunch. How could I be so stupid?"

She hooks her arm in his and walks him over to the shade of a tree. "How did they react?"

"Just great. My mother said she felt pity for me, and my father said I was not his true son. A wonderful graduation present."

"Oh God, I'm so sorry," she says. She gives him a long hug.

"I feel so diminished. Like a five-year-old who's told he's a changeling."

Allison put her hands on his shoulders.

"Listen to me," she says firmly. "You're...you're you. Gene. You're great and wonderful and I know this really, really hurts, but it doesn't take away how great you are. And you're the best friend I ever had." She blushes and chokes up.

Gene takes out a tissue and blots his eyes. "Good thing I didn't wear mascara," he says, laughing and crying at once.

Gene's parents leave immediately after the ceremony so Allison insists he come to dinner with her and her parents. Gene meets them at the restaurant wearing a crisp yellow shirt and a navy blazer. Allison's mother is mesmerized by his good looks and his smooth, charming manners. Though Allison has explained that Gene is a platonic friend, her mother keeps looking back and forth between them as if trying to push them together with her eyes. Allison sees the sadness beneath Gene's warm and charming demeanor, but her parents do not. She wonders what it will be like when at some future time she comes out to them.

The next morning, Gene stops by her sorority house, now empty except for a handful of seniors. His car is packed for the cross-country drive to San Francisco. They walk up to The Hill, a large grassy slope empty during the day but dotted with couples on blankets at night. They sit in the shade of a tree near the top. Allison takes his arm.

"My dad says I'm not his son," Gene says, squinting into the distance, "but I realized last night, as I was on my fourth cognac in my room, that I was never his son."

Gene's eyes are not tearing today. His jaw is set. He seems determined and calm.

"I doubt he even loved me. How could he? He didn't *know* me. He just wanted me to fit some model in his mind: athletic, successful, and straight. That's who he loved—a model that I never was."

Allison says, "Maybe he'll come around. Maybe that was just his first reaction."

Gene shakes his head. "No, it's who he is. Here's an example. My prep school had a summer program, and one of the offerings was art. This was the summer before my senior year. I didn't ask Father. I just signed up. It was a watercolor class, because I had fallen in love with an exhibit I saw at the museum. I loved how the boundaries were imprecise. Edges were soft. Colors desaturated. Subtle. In watercolors, everything gently bleeds into its neighbor. An Apollonian orgy."

Gene looks out over the campus.

"He pulled me out of the program. Said it was not what I

should be doing."

"What did he have against watercolor?"

"Good question. I think that at some hidden level of his narrow, brittle mind he knew I was gay. *Don't do watercolor* was proxy for don't be gay. Or even, don't have a feminine side."

"I'm really sorry," Allison says, squeezing his arm.

"Don't be. It's dawning on me that when he said, 'You're not my son,' the bastard did me a favor. Now I'm rid of him. On to San Francisco."

Back at her sorority house, they embrace.

"Promise me we'll keep in close touch," he says.

"I promise," she says.

When someone is in need, Allison's instinct is to be a fixer, a problem solver. Her dad used the expression "bent wheel" for something damaged beyond fixing. Allison hates bent wheels, and Gene's problem with his father is a bent wheel. Her inability to help smacks up against her very nature, makes her feel like a fish unable to swim. When he drives away from her sorority house, she realizes she is waving so hard because she absurdly hopes it will somehow help.

Part Four

The Deal

After his arrest, James is transferred to Santa Rita jail, where he sits in a one-man cell with a cot, a steel sink, and a toilet. The metal door has a small square window at eye level and a horizontal slot at the bottom. There is nothing to look at but the yellow cinder block walls and the door. Meals are passed through the slot in the bottom of the door, and the food is so bad he can't choke down more than a few bites. He shivers without being cold. The inside of his mouth is coated with film. His heart races even in his sleep. He does push-ups and knee bends. He tries to take deep breaths, but he feels like he's suffocating. He wants to cry but can't. To occupy his mind, he counts from one to a thousand. He talks in desperate whispers to Spike. His mind feels like it's swirling in a panic without end. He would sell his soul for a cyanide capsule.

One afternoon a guard puts James in handcuffs and a belly chain and walks him to a small conference room for his second meeting with his public defender, a White guy named Gary Turner. Gary is young and looks like the president of a college fraternity. During their first meeting, he told James that the new computer system had matched the fingerprints lifted from the gun found in the garbage can with James' prints taken after his shoplifting arrest. James admitted to killing Black Snake at his first police interrogation. It seems to him that shooting Black Snake is a case of self-defense.

"You doing okay, James?" Gary asks.

James shakes his head. "Not really. It's like being in a coffin. I feel like I'm going crazy. But what about my case? I don't understand what's going on."

Gary opens his folder. "Look, James. I'm a straight shooter."

He pauses and lets out a breath. "Since I last saw you, I tried to get bail reduced, but nothing doing. I met with a lawyer from the prosecutor's office. I read the police file. I have to tell you—it doesn't look good. There's no question about guilt for the murder. Your prints are on the gun, the recovered bullets match the gun, and a jacket they took from your apartment tested positive for the victim's blood on the cuffs. And you confessed, even after they read you your rights—is that correct?"

James nods.

"Then there's the shots fired into the house several weeks before the murder. I know you say you didn't do it, but the recovered bullets match that same gun."

James puts his elbows on the table, leans his forehead on his cuffed hands.

Gary continues. "The way these things work is the prosecutor's office makes an offer, and I make a counter-offer. We negotiate—in his case, we negotiate both the charges and the sentence. It's like buying a car. We bicker. Ninety per cent of criminal cases are decided by plea bargain."

He looks down at a page of notes. "In my meeting with the prosecutor's office, they said they're charging first-degree murder, gang enhancement, and firing into an occupied dwelling. They want life without possibility of parole."

James' head jerks up and his mouth falls open.

Gary says, "That could be a bluff, but they've got big things on their side. One is the nature of the shooting. The gun in the victim's mouth. Three shots that blew out the back of his head."

James winces.

Gary says, "Believe me, you don't ever want to face a jury that is shown those photos."

He thumbs the pages in his file. "You say you picked up the

gun after the victim fired it and then shot him with it. If that's true, some of the prints on the gun should have been his. None are. We could never sell that story to a jury."

James remembers that he wiped the gun off and then held it to drop it into the trash can. How could he have been so stupid?

"If you had called the cops right away, that would have helped. But you ran. You had three months to come clean and you didn't."

Gary shuffles his papers. "They also think they can establish gang affiliation. Which means gang enhancement in sentencing."

James shakes his head. "I've never been in a gang."

Gary says, "They got a search warrant and went through your room. They recovered clothes in gang colors. They've also got someone in jail now willing to testify to your gang affiliation. It's probably someone willing to lie to score a better deal, but unfortunately this happens, and it's hard to counter. The house that was shot up had a gang resident. Not only that, but your victim had gang affiliation, and the park where the shooting took place is contested gang territory. The prosecution will argue that these things fit together like pieces of a puzzle."

Gary rubs his face. "They also have your journal from your room. They found a reference to wanting to kill Black Snake. That's huge. It establishes malice aforethought."

James slumps in his chair and says in a low voice, "I wrote that three years ago. When I was a freshman. It didn't mean I was going to do anything. I was mad. He stole money from me. He broke my watch. Besides, he pointed his gun at me after he shot my dog. Isn't that self-defense?"

Gary continues. "The dog aspect we can't use. After you told me about it, I checked. There is nothing about a dog in the police report. I checked with animal control—I called them myself—and they don't keep records of dead animals they pick up. Unless the dog has a tag."

"But Black Snake shot Spike. Spike was right there, dead. It's the truth."

"I can't use truth. I can only use evidence. There's no evidence of a dog."

Tears roll down James' face and he wipes them away with the heels of his cuffed hands.

"You admitted to your interrogator that the boy was flat on his back, stunned from having been hit in the face. Even if we could show that Marvin Mitchell had pointed the gun, any self-defense plea ends when he's unarmed, lying on his back, no longer holding the gun. Add in your journal entry, and prosecution has an easy walk to first-degree murder—premeditation and malice aforethought."

James drops his cuffed hands to the table. Gary looks him square in the eye and says, "You see where I'm going with this."

"Can't I just tell the jury what really happened? You know, the whole truth and nothing but the truth. I'll take a lie detector test."

"No jury is going to believe that those are just the colors you like, that the kid testifying to your gang affiliation is lying, that Mitchell pointed the gun at you without leaving his prints, and that the entry in your journal is something you didn't really mean. Not when you stuck a gun in Marvin Mitchell's mouth and blew his head off." He lifts another paper. "With three shots. And lie detector tests are not admissible in court."

Gary shakes his head. "The other thing we have to face is that this is 1989. People have had it up to here"—Gary lifts the blade of his hand to his chin—"with crime. Especially violent crime. Especially in Oakland. That would be the mindset of your jury—both the White jurors and the Black jurors."

Gary leans back in his chair and says, "Bottom line. In a jury trial, the prosecution will ask for life without possibility of parole and it's likely they'll get it. If we plea bargain, I think we can do better."

James lays his forehead on the table and covers his head in his arms.

"Look James, my job is to get the best for you that's possible. I'll try for twenty-five to life. I'll try to get the gang affiliation dropped. The reason for that—let's face it, James. You're going to prison. You'll start in a maximum-security prison, but they vary in California. Some are more dangerous than others. With gang affiliation, they'll send you someplace like Pelican Bay. It's a hell hole—gang-infested and violent. White supremacists. Psycho skinheads. A real nightmare. If I can get the gang enhancement dropped, you'll enter the prison system with fewer points and go to a less dangerous facility."

Gary adjusts his tie. "I meet with the guy from the prosecutor's office next week, and I'll bring you the best deal I can get. Then it's your decision. You can reject their offer and demand a jury trial. That's your right. Nobody can take that away from you. Our office will defend you to the best of our ability. But in my opinion, you'd be taking a hell of a gamble. All the odds would be against you."

Gary closes the folder. He seems like he's in a hurry. "Any questions?"

James shakes his head. He feels like he's trapped in a nightmare from which he cannot awaken.

Mama's Visit

As much as James wants to see Mama, he wishes she wouldn't visit him. He doesn't want to face her. When she enters the visiting room at the jail and sees him in his orange jumpsuit, her eyes well up. They had not been apart for a single day since James was born, but now they haven't seen each other since his arrest. What hurts James most is the look that crosses her face after she sits down. It lasts no more than two seconds, but it's as clear as print on a page. She is afraid of this stranger who murdered a boy his own age. She wonders if she really knows him. The look pierces James like a poisoned spear, and though she quickly puts on a smile and asks how he is, his anguish lingers. If Mama thinks he's a monster, maybe he *is* a monster.

She asks about the food. He says it's so bad he can't believe it, but as soon as the words are out of his mouth, he regrets giving her more to worry about. He can't bear the pained look on her face. He can tell she wants to know what happened, so he tells her about the day in the park, how Black Snake shot Spike and then he grabbed the gun and shot Black Snake. He doesn't tell her that he shoved the gun in Black Snake's mouth. She jumps to James' defense.

"Why, he started the whole thing," she says. "He would have shot you next." She wants to see a lawyer, so she copies down everything James tells her about the case.

"Keesha called me on the phone," Mama says suddenly.

"Yeah? What did she say," James asks, though he's not sure he wants to know.

"She said to tell you she's sorry, and that she'd like to write you but she can't."

"Why can't she?"

Reluctantly, Mama says, "Her parents won't let her."

This is his new reality. He has been exiled. He must seem like a terrible person to everyone who hears the story. He wonders if his former teachers know, if Dr. Carter knows, if the Chans back in Sacramento will find out.

When it is time for her to leave, Mama says, "You're still my boy." The molten lump in his throat prevents him from saying anything in return.

The Lawyer's Office

From her co-workers at the DMV, Mama hears of a good criminal defense lawyer. She makes an appointment and takes the bus to a downtown Oakland office building. She's heard his fee is two hundred dollars for a half hour consultation, so she brings the money in cash. She talks to a White woman, a younger member of the firm. Reading from her notes, she tells her everything James told her, including what the public defender said.

The woman has a kind face. She looks at Mama with sympathy and concern. "Do you know if the public defender checked the search warrant and the details of the interrogation for coercion or failure to inform your son of his rights?"

"My son mentioned those things. He said the public defender's office checked it all."

The woman nods. "I haven't seen the police report, so what I have to say should be taken with a grain of salt. Unless we were able to uncover something unexpected, I doubt we could do any better than the public defender. Like him, we'd want to avoid a jury trial. The details of this case make a jury trial risky. And to be honest, full legal representation by a private attorney would cost many tens of thousands of dollars."

Mama goes silent. After a moment, she unsnaps her purse.

The woman presses her lips and says, "We're not going to charge you for this consultation. I think the public defender will do all that is possible for your son, given the circumstances. I wish you all the best."

The Prison Van

Gary brings James a deal. First-degree murder. No firing a gun into an occupied dwelling. No gang enhancement. The prosecutor would not agree to twenty-five, so Gary settles for thirty-five years to life, parole possible when 85% of the sentence is served. It's a terrible outcome, but James feels he has no choice. He appears before the judge and accepts the deal.

On the day James leaves jail for the state prison at Tehachapi, the guard tosses a plastic platform onto the asphalt and slides open the van door. James carefully lifts his foot onto the step. The chain on his leg irons limits his stride to eighteen inches. The guard places his hand on James' elbow to steady him. It's a cool, sunny morning in February following three days of rain, and the air is fresh and crisp. James lifts his head to take in the blue sky, pauses to inhale a last breath. The guard allows this. James stoops through the van door and into the steel cage. The guard follows and fastens James' seat belt, then hands him a water bottle, a plastic jug if he has to pee, and a barf bag in case he gets carsick. The guard locks the cage door and settles into his own seat outside it. James wonders how they got the cage into the van. It's like those model ships in a bottle.

The van drives away from the parking lot and onto the interstate. The heater is turned up and James is sweating. He looks at his handcuffs and sees a name engraved in the metal—Smith & Wesson. He snorts a sharp laugh. The guard glances at him. According to the police report, the gun he shot Black Snake with was a Smith & Wesson.

James looks out the windows at the hills turning green from the winter rains. A few early poppies dot the hillsides with yellow-orange flowers, and he remembers the single poppy he saw in his yard the day the was arrested for murder. The hills are lovely, and he realizes that in the four years he's lived in Oakland, very little was pretty to look at. He knows prison will be worse.

For the past months, jail has seemed like a terrible mistake that would soon be corrected, even when he knew better. The van ride feels like the coffin lid is closing. He's going to spend most of his life, maybe all of it, in prison.

As he watches the landscape of the interstate pass, James seethes with anger. He feels angry at Pops for becoming an addict and dying, angry at Mama for moving them to Oakland and never having enough money. He feels anger at his school for being substandard, angry at every kid trying to be a gangsta, angry at the politicians and police for doing nothing to make Oakland safe, disgust at the fools who idolized Felix Mitchell, and rage at the whole court system that failed to sentence him on the basis of what really happened. He's enraged that Keesha will not write him. He hopes she flunks out of UCLA. He hates Black Snake. Only Spike is spared his anger, and Spike is dead. In the slow freeway traffic, people in cars look at James in his orange jumpsuit, especially truckers who can see down into the van. He'd like to lunge for the steering wheel and crash the van into one of them.

Tehachapi

After going through intake, James is led to his cell. A man is sitting on the upper bunk watching a tiny TV. He is short, Black, and very stout. His neck and face look like a tree trunk with features chiseled in. He has unusually small ears.

As the guard closes the cell door, James introduces himself. James can't understand what the man says and asks him to repeat it.

"I'm Lonny," the man says loudly and with irritation. He hardly moves his mouth or lips when he talks, so he's hard to understand.

"You know how things work?" he asks.

"They told me the prison rules at intake," James says.

"I don't mean that shit," Lonny says. "How they work in here."

Canned laughter comes from the TV.

James shakes his head.

Lonny tells him to clean the sink and toilet after he uses them. "Hang a towel in front of you when you sit on the can," he says, nodding to a clothesline in front of the toilet. "Use mercy flushes. Don't touch none of my stuff."

James nods and sits on his bunk. He empties his net bag of state-issued soap, toothpaste, toothbrush, towel, toilet paper, and two paper cups. His hands are trembling.

"This your first time?" Lonny asks. "You look like a kid."

"Yes," James says. "But I was in county jail for five months."

"You got a fish, Lonny?" It is a voice from the next cell.

"Yeah," Lonny calls back. "Young one, too."

"Don't let anybody fuck with you," Lonny says. "Not even once." Then he turns up the volume on his TV.

A Cold Wind

A cold wind blows dust and sand across the yard. James sits on the asphalt, just short of the out-of-bounds line. A piece of grit lodges in his eye. The pain is searing. In agony, he turns his back to the wind and removes his glasses. He lets his eye tear. He spits on the ground to rid his mouth of the sand between his teeth. At last he can open his eye. The painful particle has washed out.

Above, spirals of razor wire loop along the top of the wall. Anyone attempting escape would shred his own flesh grasping for freedom. Two Sureños walk past, one with three teardrops tattooed beneath an eye. Their caps are pulled low to their ears and the bills are flipped up. They are heading for their part of the yard. James learned the racial geography of the yard on the first day when he sauntered through the white zone and was gruffly told, "You're in the wrong place, fish. Better figure it out. Fast."

James learns the rules, formal and informal. The inmates run some things and the correctional officers run others, like hostile nations observing the terms of a cease-fire. Inmates wear blue, the COs wear green. Both sides know what rules must be followed. Both sides know what work-arounds are allowed.

Like in high school, every person is identified by his racial group. There are penalties for crossing lines. James learns which is the Black side of the showers, the Black area of the yard, the Black tables at chow. He knows who his shot caller is, but they have never talked. He's a dark-skinned Black man named Dwight, middle-aged, tall and bulky, with a shaved head. James sees him looking over the yard like a land baron. Guys approach him, talk for a few minutes. Dwight nods, says a few words. He attained his position not through violence, but through leadership. The shot caller is a negotiator, measured, strong. He regards fighting as a last resort. The shot caller wants order, not disorder.

The approach that James adopted on the streets of Oakland also works in prison. Being a watchful introvert serves him well. He can spot the guys looking for confrontation, the psychopaths, the snitches, the leaders. He doesn't avoid anyone's eyes, but neither does he challenge their gaze. He never crosses anyone. He is respectful to all, submissive to none. He has nothing to do with drugs and sex, the main sources of conflict in prison. He doesn't gamble. He respects people's privacy. When he rounds a corner and sees a man with his pants around his ankles, another man pounding him in the ass, he turns his head and walks quietly away. When he passes a cell where a man is injecting himself with a needle, he keeps his eyes straight ahead, remembering that terrible afternoon in Sacramento when he walked into his house and saw Pops doing the same thing. When he glimpses contraband changing hands, he pretends not to see it. He never tells anyone what he sees. He never repeats rumors. His vibe is one of self-containment. He ignores the subtle challenges, the pokes in the ribs, the elbow in the back, the muttered insults. If it's racial, he could report it to his shot caller, but he would rather avoid trouble. Stories about having to join a prison gang are a myth, at least at Tehachapi. Without tattoos, it is evident that James has come in unaffiliated, a first timer. Because he reads on the yard, his high school nickname of Shakespeare is resurrected. Other inmates let him be. It gets around that he's a lifer, so guys figure he's in for murder. Because his crime did not involve a woman or a child, he's not a target. An inmate who attacked James without a reason would lose respect, and losing respect can be fatal. The inmate population has its own ethic.

James learns which COs to avoid, which blind spots on the grounds are blood alley. It's in his interest to respect and obey the guards, but not to chat them up—that would make guys wonder if he's a snitch. He runs the track and does exercises: pull-ups, push-ups, dips, and crunches. In the five years since Big Mike showed him how to work out with weights, he has developed a lean, toned physique. With his black-framed glasses, he looks like a young Arthur Ashe.

There is a small library from which he checks out magazines and books. He reads issues of *Time* magazine, all several years old, to catch up on the current events he ignored while he was in high school. In one of them, he sees an article on Felix Mitchel's funeral. He finds his only solace in reading novels. Maybe because it's an escape, the fictional world seems more vital and real than the gray prisonscape in which he spends his long days. He gravitates to authors he's heard of: Hemingway, Fitzgerald, Dickens, Camus, Steinbeck, Baldwin. He identifies with the characters that seem ultimately alone: Pip, Gatsby, Meursault, Frederick Henry, John Grimes. When he really likes a novel, he reads it a second time, and sometimes a third. He starts counting the number of books he's read. It gives him a goal.

Chow is served on plastic trays that supposedly cannot be splintered into weapons. Drinks are held in rubber cups that smell bad. The kitchen serves chicken baloney on white bread with yellow mustard, apple sauce, green beans swimming in warm water, chicken patties with a strange off-taste, colored juices in containers with peel-off tops, beans, noodles, white rice, hash dumped over a slice of white bread, and gray noodle casseroles containing bits of meat or chunks of soy product.

Every inmate has a job, and James is assigned to work in the kitchen. He likes the kitchen job because he works under civilians, people from outside who come in to prepare three meals a day for the inmates. Much of the food arrives in government boxes, some in huge cans. When James unloads, it reminds him of working in the Oakland supermarket. There are boxes of powdered eggs, powdered cheese, dried potatoes. The fruit is usually bananas or apples. He learns that oranges are prized as an ingredient in making pruno, homemade prison wine, and for that reason they are rare. Occasionally, fresh produce arrives, surplus of some sort from the area, packed in waxed cardboard boxes or wooden crates. The fruit is often bruised or blemished, but the taste does not suffer. The vegetables are wilted but look and taste the same after they are cooked. One of the inmates who worked in a San Francisco hotel kitchen shows him how to blanch vegetables. The man will occasionally whip up something tasty for the kitchen crew. The basic life skills of being on time, doing what you're told, and not being a problem serve James here as they did at the supermarket, at McDonald's, and in high school.

The high point of the day in James' prison life is standing in the line to receive mail. Mama writes him a couple of times a week. She mentions work, how crime in Oakland is getting worse. She says it like he is not a criminal himself. She talks with other women at the DMV whose sons, husbands, cousins, or nephews are incarcerated. These talks seem to make her feel less ashamed and help her accept what has happened.

For inmates, the world is divided into the inside and the outside. Inside is a realm of exile, and everyone fears that the outside world will forget them. Even the guards are regarded with envy for their ability to walk to the parking lot at the end of their shift and rejoin the outside world.

Mama's First Visit

James feels apprehensive about his mother's first visit. He doesn't want her to see him like this. It will be like the times she visited the county jail, except worse, since Tehachapi is so starkly what it is—a long-term prison for serious felons. It takes her a full day to travel by bus, and then she checks into a motel a couple of miles from the prison.

On Sunday, James' name is called on the PA system, and he is processed through to the visitors' center. When he hugs Mama, she weeps. They sit at a small table. The rules require James to sit facing the guard station.

"I told myself I wasn't going to cry," Mama says, dabbing her eyes with a tissue. She is wearing the blouse he gave her for Christmas his freshman year in high school, gray with clusters of purple grapes.

"Nice blouse," he smiles.

"My wonderful son gave me this," she says.

He drops his eyes and shakes his head. "I'm not wonderful, Mama. I let you down. Let you down bad."

"Oh, honey. I blame myself every day. I never should have moved us to Oakland. None of this would have happened if we stayed on our nice little block in Sacramento."

She tells him that he can't give up hope. She has written a letter to a defense lawyer she's heard of to see if he'll file an appeal on a pro bono basis. She's making regular deposits into the bank account James opened after he graduated high school so that it will remain active.

"I changed it over to a savings account so it pays interest," she says. "A couple of women at the DMV have sons in prison, and they give me tips, like about the savings account. I got a life insurance policy through work. In case anything ever happens to me."

When Mama turns her head to glance at the guard station, James notices some gray in her hair. He feels a pang of guilt, certain those gray hairs were caused by him. He tells her about working in the kitchen and about his inmate co-worker who worked in a fancy hotel in San Francisco. She says she might try to get a smaller apartment in a better neighborhood. Three times she says she wants to send him cornbread in the mail, and three times he tells her it's not allowed. He feels awkward with her, and he strains to think of things to say. When they lived together at home, conversation came naturally. They watched TV together, and Spike gave them something to talk about. Sitting across from each another in this crowded visitors' room makes their conversation unnatural and strained. When their time is up, James walks back to his cellblock feeling broken and blue.

Home Movies of the Mind

Even in his second year in prison, James awakens every morning stunned that he is here. Some deep part of him cannot accept that this is where he is supposed to be. He feels like an ex-pat in a foreign country, awaiting a flight out that never arrives. He has lucid dreams that he's in prison, but he knows that he's dreaming so all he has to do is wait until he awakens a free man. When he wakes up and realizes he's trapped in prison, he feels soulsick.

James thinks of Mama, of Keesha, of Pops. He remembers Einstein at the corner store. Most of all, he misses Spike. Every night at lights out, he silently talks to Spike, a secret prayer. Sometimes he imagines Spike at his side. One evening at chow he slips a piece of meat into his pocket for Spike. He doesn't know why he did it. He wonders if he is going crazy.

On the yard, he listens to an inmate talking about prison suicides. What James takes away is that hanging yourself with an electrical cord is the best method. It cuts off blood flow to the brain, so the victim loses consciousness in seconds. It helps to jam your hands tightly inside your belt so they can't reflexively go to your neck to loosen the cord. All you have to do is stay determined and count to ten. You'll probably lose consciousness before you reach seven. It's a relief to know this—not because he's planning suicide, but it helps to know that if he can't bear it, there's a way out.

On the yard, guys say, "Do the time, but don't let the time do you." He's not sure what this means.

The worst time of the day for James is lights out. Though he's often tired, it's hard to fall asleep. The mattress is thin and his cell is either too hot or too cold. Noises resound from around the cellblock. Men cough, yell, drop things. The guards walk the tiers in their hard-soled boots. There are strange creaks and snaps, as if the prison bars are straining in the night. Lonny snores. Toilets flush with a loud roar. One of his regular purchases at the canteen is ear plugs. They help the noise, but they do not remedy the feeling he doesn't have a name for, a sense of being trapped in a world that is pressing in on him.

He creates a game. At lights out, he chooses one good memory from his past and lets it play like a movie in his mind until he sleeps. He remembers Pops at the park. He and James are throwing a baseball, and James has the only glove. He worries about Pops' bare hand, but Pops is so strong and his hands so big that the hard ball doesn't bother him. He favorite memories are of Spike, his pittie smile, his tail wagging while he dreams, running to the door when James picks up the leash, tilting his head to listen to noises in the hall, licking James' face, making a sound like a purr when his chest is scratched. He sees Mama at the stove, stirring a kettle of bean soup with ham hocks, Mama opening her Christmas present, Mama telling stories about the farm in Georgia. He remembers a couple of his high school teachers telling him that a piece of his writing was good. He remembers the day he first saw the ocean with Keesha, the time they made out after their movie date.

When he finally dozes off, his sleep is light, more like a nap than deep sleep, and he awakens several times during the night. Most inmates have this problem. Good food, sex, and sound sleep are the most talked about deprivations.

Lonny's Story

One day during a lockdown following a fight in the chow hall, Lonny asks, "What you in for?"

James is getting more accustomed to Lonny's mushy-mouthed speech.

"Murder," James says.

"You do it?'

"Yeah."

"First offense?"

"Second. I shoplifted some books."

Lonny laughs out loud. "Books? That why they call you Shakespeare? Man, you a piece of work."

"What about you?" James asks.

"Murder—which I didn't do. And a lot of robberies, which I did do. Did so many I can't even remember them all."

"How did you get convicted for the murder?"

"A guy got shot dead on my street just before I drove up. Ambulance hadn't even got there yet. Cop pulls me out my car and slaps on handcuffs. Says I did it. In the patrol car I say, 'How come you say I did it when you know I didn't?' He says, 'To protect my wife and kids from niggers like you.'"

Stunned, James asks, "There was no other evidence, besides his word?"

"The gun laying in the street. Cop says he saw me wipe off the prints and drop it."

"How long you been in?"

"Seventeen years."

"What's your sentence?"

"A hundred and twenty-five years. That was my third strike."

The whole story seems too outrageous to believe. James wonders if Lonny is telling the truth. But why would he lie?

Summer

During the summer, daytime temperatures hover around one-hundred. Everyone moves with effort. Tempers grow short. The buildings and the concrete absorb heat during the day and emit it like a brick oven after sundown. Lonny keeps a stack of paper towels on his bunk to wipe his sweating face.

The best time of day is 4:45 AM when James walks to the kitchen to start work. The sky is still dark, the air is cool, and the stars shine like silver pepper sprinkled on a black velvet sky. Night insects chirp from their hiding places.

One morning in July, James is told to peel and slice peaches. They are ripe, so to prevent spoilage it needs to be done today. Then they will be frozen. James sits on a low stool wearing his long plastic apron, working with a paring knife. James slips some slices into his mouth and savors the juicy explosion of sweet flavor. The taste and smell transport him back to Sacramento when he is eight or nine and Mama and Pops take him to an orchard outside of town. They walk rows of fruit trees with a basket, picking their own peaches, nectarines, and plums. Pops laughs at Mama jumping around like a young girl, chattering about her girlhood on the farm in Georgia. When they arrive at home that afternoon, Mama makes a peach pie.

James barely realizes that tears have overflowed his eyes and are running down his checks.

Flo, a very large Black civilian worker with breasts the size of soccer balls, stops, puts her hands on her hips, and says, "Lordy, boy, you going to do that, we may as well have you peel onions."

James clears his throat and laughs, wipes his face with his forearm.

“You’ll get used to it, honey,” she says, patting his shoulder, something that’s not allowed. “Peoples get used to a lot worse.”

Lonny and the GED

Lonny is sitting on his bunk with a practice GED booklet and a pencil.

"Going to take the GED?" James asks.

"I already took it but never passed. Eight times. Still trying."

James is stunned. "You took it eight times?"

"Yeah. It's hard."

"Why don't you sign up for the GED class here?" James asks.

"I did. Eight times. You take the test at the end."

"How far did you go in school?" James asks.

"Seventh grade."

"You quit that young? No one made you go?"

Lonny shakes his head. "Not in Watts. Nobody cares."

"Why'd you drop out?"

"Went to work."

"Doing what?"

"Robbing."

"You couldn't find a job?"

"That *was* my job."

James nods.

"Listen to this," Lonny begins. His reading is slow and laborious. "A red car travels fifty-five miles per hour for five hours, and a green car travels sixty-five miles an hour for three hours. How many more miles does the red car travel? Who the fuck can figure that out?"

Papers rattle on Lonny's bunk.

"Want me to show you?" James asks.

"Yeah," Lonny says.

James stands up and leans on Lonny's bunk. He tries to lead

Lonny through the solution but is stunned when he realizes Lonny doesn't know how to multiply.

"You've got to learn your times tables first," James says.

"That's what my GED teacher says," Lonny answers, "but it's too big for my head."

The Sky

James is reading in a wedge of sunlight against the wall. It's November, late afternoon, and the spot where he's sitting is protected from a cold wind whipping dust and sand around the yard. He's been at Tehachapi for three years and read seventy-six books. Their titles are listed on a sheet of paper taped to the wall of his cell.

An older Black man with gray dreads stands at the far end of the yard looking toward the sky. James follows the man's gaze to a wondrous cloud formation. Covering the north half of the sky are pillows of billowing clouds in colors of dark purple and gray shading into a sulfurous yellow. The setting sun gilds the edges of the clouds with golden light. The colors are beautiful, the slow-motion roiling of the clouds mesmerizing. James' gaze sweeps the yard. No one else has noticed. Only he and the old man are watching the clouds. The man notices James and nods, then turns his face back to the sky.

He has heard the phrase *live in the moment*, but never understood what it means. Now he knows, at least as it applies to himself. It means focusing on whatever he has that makes staying alive better than being dead—Mama, his books, an occasional fresh peach from the kitchen, the sky. Maybe this is what it means to do the time, rather than having the time do you.

The loudspeaker barks that the yard is closing, and James falls in with the men shuffling toward the gate. Over his shoulder, he takes one last look at the sky, now fading into dusk. It strikes him that he had not really looked at the sky for a while—maybe weeks or even months. He is stunned by the realization. His eyes have been on what's in front of him. Or on the ground. He may have the cracks in the asphalt memorized by now. Sometimes guys talk about how prison is affecting them, but he's never heard anyone say that it makes you stop watching the sky. Of course, the sky is just air, water vapor, and light. No big deal. But when seen by a human, those elements become beauty, and if no one is there to drink it in, the beauty never comes to life. To see and appreciate is a duty owed to beauty.

As a kid in Sacramento, James would lie on the grass with other kids, pointing out what animals the puffy clouds resembled. He never did it after he moved to Oakland. He vows he will once again notice things. He will pause and see the sky.

BZ

One day on the yard James sees BZ sitting at the steel picnic table, before him two sheets of notebook paper, his thick fingers gripping a stubby yellow pencil. BZ lives on the same tier as James. He's a middle-aged brother built like a linebacker. He has a gray goatee.

"What's up, BZ?" James says.

BZ looks up. "Hey, Shakespeare. Got you a book again?"

James nods. He is carrying a copy of *A Tale of Two Cities* from the library. This is book number 112.

"You know about them things, reading and all that?"

"Some," James says.

BZ wipes his mouth on the back of his hand. James asks what he's writing.

"I got to write a personal statement. For the Board. I come up next month. Thing is, I don't know how."

James sits down.

"You ever gone before the Board?" BZ says.

James shakes his head. "I'm doing thirty-five to life."

"That's cold," BZ says.

"What have you got so far?" James nods at the paper.

BZ shows him two blank pages. He unfolds a printed sheet from the front pocket of his blue shirt. He smooths out the paper on the steel table. "This is what it 'posed to be."

BZ looks vulnerable. That's a rare expression on an inmate's face that usually looks as blank as stone. James reads over the Department of Corrections page, which describes what the personal statement should include.

James says, "If we're just sitting here kickin it, and I ask how you grew up, and what led to your crimes, what would you say?"

"I don't know how to write, man."

"You know how to talk. It's basically the same thing. Where'd you grow up?"

"Born in Watts, grew up in South Central."

"Parents?"

"Never knew my dad. My mama did drugs so my grandmother raised me. That's when I moved to South Central."

"How old?"

"First grade."

"There you go. Exactly what you just said to me—write it down."

BZ pauses. He picks up the pencil and begins to write, slowly, laboriously, his tongue pressed to one corner of his mouth.

James picks it up and reads it. "Good. See, you're writing."

"Yeah?" BZ says, smiling.

When he finishes, James says, "First grade. What happened then?"

"My grandmother was sick a lot." He looks at James and then looks away. "I didn't have nobody to make me behave."

James points at BZ. "Write it."

BZ bends over the paper and writes.

James and BZ meet every afternoon for a week. On the last day, BZ arrives angry.

"I thought you knew how to write. My cellie says this has spelling mistakes. Bad grammar, too. All fucked up."

"He's right," James says, "but it doesn't matter. Think about your purpose. The parole board wants to know you're real and sincere. They don't give a shit how you spell. They know you didn't finish high school—it's in your record. Tell me this: Is what you wrote honest? Is it from your heart?"

BZ pauses to think about this. "Yeah," he says.

"Take this to the Board and stand behind it," James says. "It's you."

A month later, BZ walks out of his hearing approved for parole.

Soon inmates are approaching James to help with their personal statements for parole, appeals to the Captain, letters to girlfriends and family members. He never writes *for* them; he helps them to write for themselves. When a Hispanic guy asks for help, James knows the rules well enough to get permission from Dwight to help a guy of another race. Dwight confers with the Brown shot caller. Permission is granted. A few months later, a White guy wants help writing a letter to his lawyer. James approaches Dwight, who listens and then tells James he'll think about it. The next day Dwight tells him it's okay. He explains, "It's an investment. I'll collect a payback someday. With interest."

Pruno

It's a Sunday afternoon on the yard, and James sits on the asphalt off to himself, reading in the cool winter sun. The year is 1993, James' fourth year at Tehachapi. Another inmate walks up and sits beside him. James nods and returns to his book. The inmate, a brother, is heavily tatted, but not gang tats. James is not happy that someone is sitting beside him.

"Shakespeare, right?" the brother says.

"Right," James says.

"I'm Mister B," he says.

They bump fists. As if in the middle of a conversation, Mister B says, "Yeah, need things from the kitchen." He says he needs oranges, big cans of fruit cocktail, five pounds of sugar, and yeast.

"Don't say no yet. Just know that I asked you." He walks away.

James' stomach churns. These are ingredients for pruno. No way does he want to be mixed up in this.

That evening James starts his weekly letter to Mama. He always plans so they will be in her mailbox when she gets home from work on Friday. She likes to read them several times over the weekend. For four years she has saved every letter.

The next afternoon James is reading in his regular spot when Dwight, shot-caller for the Blacks, walks up and squats—not sits—beside him.

"I hear Mister B asked you for some things," Dwight says.

"Yes, he did," James says. He closes the book, his index finger marking his place. He knows to give Dwight his full attention.

Dwight squints, gazes out over the yard. A flock of crows are scratching in the dirt at the far end. James looks in that direction, too.

Dwight says, "You a lone wolf, Shakespeare. You don't disrespect nobody, don't make noise. Read your books, mind your own business. Help guys write things. Never make a mess that has to be cleaned up."

James looks him in the eye and nods.

"I'd never tell you to put a shank in somebody or nothing like that. We just need supplies. You do it quiet-like, COs look the other way."

Dwight picks up a few pebbles and rattles them in his fist like dice. James waits to see if he's going to say more. He doesn't.

"For sure?" James asks, realizing he is drifting in a direction he doesn't want to go. "I don't want a 115 write-up. Or a month in the hole."

"No, you don't. You have a clean record."

James nods. "Which is why I can't risk a 115."

"I feel you. Did you ever hear of Dwight getting somebody fucked up?"

James shakes his head.

"COs are cool on this," Dwight says. "That's a fact." The word "fact" lands like a hand clap. Without waiting for an answer, Dwight slips an index card between the pages of James' book.

"Bring this to your cell tomorrow when you get off. Civilians that work in the kitchen are cool, too. Use your laundry bag. Push it under your bunk. COs don't want to see nothing when they walk by."

When Dwight stands, his knees crack. Word on the yard is that Dwight shoots straight. Still. James opens his book but does not read.

Dwight did not ask James whether he would do it. James will deliver the items or not deliver the items. That will be his answer. If he decides no, it is unlikely he will be targeted. That's his best guess.

But his status will slip from respected lone wolf to loner without respect. Without protection. Word will get around. In prison, you don't know the value of what you have until you lose it.

The next day when James finishes his shift in the kitchen, he fills his canvas laundry bag with the items on the index card. Flo turns her back to write inventory on a clipboard. James carries the bag to his cell and stuffs it under his bunk. Just before chow, Mister B stops by and without a word reaches under the bunk and pulls out the bag. He slings it over his shoulder and tosses two contraband gourmet chocolate bars on James' bunk.

This will repeat itself several times a year for as long as James is at Tehachapi. It never brings him any trouble.

Lonny's Girlfriend

One night when James is reading, Lonny leans off the top bunk with a sheet of notebook paper and says, "Is this spell right?"

He points to the word *prety*.

"It has two *t*'s," James says.

"Writing my girlfriend a letter," Lonny says. "Lives in Tulsa."

"You knew her before you got locked up?"

"Naw. Met her by mail—through my church. You give your name and address and some lady can write you. We've been writing for two years."

"You have her picture?"

"She won't send it. She's got low self-esteem, see. Says she's too fat. I tell her she's pretty to me and I don't care if she's fat, but she won't believe me. I keep writing, though."

James nods.

"In the next letter, I'm sending her my picture. It's almost finished."

"What do you mean, 'finished'?"

"Can't have a camera, so I had to draw myself. Look."

Lonny shuffles through some papers on his shelf and leans over to hand a page to James. Expecting the worst, James takes it. He is astounded. It is a pencil drawing that looks like the work of a professional sketch artist: life-like, shaded in realistic tones, a soulful vitality dancing in Lonny's eyes.

"Damn, Lonny. This is amazing. You're a hell of a drawer."

Lonny reaches out his hand and takes the drawing.

"How did you do this? Looking in the mirror?"

"Yeah," Lonny says. "Plus my ID photo."

"This is super. You're a real artist, my man. You did that just with pencil?"

"Yeah. Number one and number two. Have to whittle off the wood with a spoon to get me a long piece of lead. Then hold it different ways for different effects. Wish I had me a nice set of colored pencils."

James rises from his bunk and asks to see the drawing again. It looks at any moment like the face on the paper might wink.

OJ

When James walks out of the chow hall on June 17, 1994, his fifth year at Tehachapi, men are yelling and speed-walking—running is forbidden—toward the cellblocks. Is it a riot? A fight? It takes him a few minutes to understand that the cops are chasing OJ Simpson on live TV. Five days earlier OJ's ex-wife and a friend were found murdered in front of her condo, and today a warrant was issued for OJ's arrest.

Inmates crowd the TV room, the White and Brown men mostly silent while the Black inmates cheer as if it's the Super Bowl. Several hours later the slow speed chase of the Ford Bronco ends at OJ's home, where he is taken into custody. The Black inmates are on his side, whether he's innocent or guilty. Lonny says, "Seem like every time a Black man make it big, Whitey tries to cut him down. To the Man, OJ guilty of being Black. OJ Black all right, but that nothing to be guilty of. That's my view."

Months later the trial begins. The inmates watch as much of the trial as their schedules allow. They seize onto little victories, like OJ being unable to pull on the murderer's gloves, and they believe he is innocent. They predict an uprising if he's found guilty.

When OJ Simpson is acquitted, it creates jubilation among the Black inmates, some Hispanic inmates, and even a few Whites. The army of police and prosecutors has been bested. OJ has juked them like he did defenders on the football field. The Black inmates high-step on the yard, exchanging high fives. "OJ stuck it to the *man*," they say. The guards look on nervously.

James feels divided. He's been in prison for five years now, and in his gut, it's not a fate he would wish on anyone. But he doesn't doubt OJ's guilt. He thinks about his own arrest and wonders what the outcome would have been if he could have afforded his own attorney, let alone a team of top attorneys. On TV it is said that OJ's legal defense has cost five million dollars. With a law team like OJ's, James believes he would never have been convicted. He would have stood before the jury in a suit and tie and been pronounced not guilty.

Fight

Midmorning, while James is still working his kitchen shift, a fight breaks out on the yard. Homemade weapons appear, suggesting this is a planned attack, Whites against Hispanics. The alarm sounds, and guards in the towers fire rubber bullets. James and the other kitchen staff watch as the civilian workers lock the doors. When the fighting moves into the cell blocks, the riot squad rushes in with pepper spray and batons. The Hispanics move into the showers and turn on the water to escape the effects of the pepper spray. Several inmates are hospitalized, and a select group, both Whites and Hispanics, are sent to the hole. No one is killed and no fires are set. No one knows how the fight started. It is best for the brothers that Dwight directed them to a corner of the yard and kept them out of it. It seems he knew it was coming

In the wake of the fight, James' cellblock is put on lockdown. Meals of turkey baloney on white bread and a fruit cup are delivered to cells on carts pushed through the cell blocks. The fight is reported on the 11:00 news that night as a prison riot. Dwight sends out word for all the brothers to stay chill. It takes the guards a full week to complete a weapons search in the cellblocks.

Mama's Last Words

James is in his eighth year at Tehachapi when a guard comes to his cell one evening to tell him that he has a phone call. He follows the CO, his mind racing. It's past phone time, and the guards don't come get you for a call. Is this a trick? Do they know about the kitchen supplies? Is he being taken to the hole?

At the phone bank James picks up the receiver and waits through the usual recording about the call being monitored. A man's voice identifies himself as Reverend Jones, the minister from Mama's church. Reverend Jones tells James that his mother is in the hospital. She had a seizure at work two days ago, and tests show an inoperable brain tumor. James doesn't even need to hear the words. The tone of Reverend Jones' voice tells him everything. Scans show that the cancer has spread. There is nothing they can do.

James lies in his bunk, awash in desperation and panic. He is consumed by the sense that he must do something. He can't sleep. The next morning, he files for a seventy-two hour emergency leave. He finds Dwight on the yard and asks if he can help.

Dwight shakes his head. "Emergency pass is on the books, but they haven't never granted one that anybody knows of. The Governor hisself couldn't get you one."

Late that afternoon James reaches a hospice nurse in Mama's room, and she holds the phone to Mama's ear. Though groggy and weak, Mama tells James she loves him.

"I love you, too, Mama," he says.

She asks when he's coming home to walk Spike. The question knocks the air from his chest. There is silence, and then the nurse comes back on and says Mama is sleeping. She tells James that his mother is on morphine and will not suffer. James wants to ask how long it will be, but he can't form the words.

Words from Flo

A week later a CO comes for James after chow and walks him to the chapel. The prison chaplain tells him that Mama has passed away. The chaplain offers to pray with James, and to be polite James stops and bows his head. He doesn't listen.

James doesn't tell Lonny. He lies awake on his bunk until 4:30 when he gets up for work. When he walks into the florescent-flooded kitchen, Flo says, "What's wrong, Shakespeare?"

He shrugs.

She says, "I *know* when something is wrong, so you may as well tell me."

"Mama died," he says.

Flo puts her arms around him, something not allowed, and pulls him into her ample bosoms. James stiffens, then relaxes enough to accept her hug.

She releases him and says, "Sit down."

They each sit on upturned twenty-five-gallon plastic buckets. Flo puts her hands on her knees.

"How many childrens your mama got?" she asks.

"Just me."

"You have a poppa?"

"He died."

She tilts her head and looks at him.

"Well, honey, I understand how being in prison makes it worse. You let your mama down. You know it, and I know it. She knowed it. You messed up and done whatever it was that got you in here. You weren't with her at the hospital, and you won't be at her funeral. Thems are facts."

Flo blows a strand of hair away from her face and pushes it up under her hairnet. James stares at the floor.

"Here's what else I know. She might have passed, but she's *not* gone. Don't you let me hear you say she gone. She's *here*, and she will always be here. Cause one thing matters the most to her. You. Am I right?"

James looks at her and nods.

"The only way to repay all she done for you is to be like she want you to be. Keep out of trouble and get out of here as soon as you can. And don't come back. Do good for others. Whether you out there or in here, you can do good either way. There's always room to do good. Always room to fall down, too. Wherever you is, stand tall and be good as you can."

Flo heaves a deep sigh.

"You a loner, Shakespeare. I see that. Them walls around this place ain't nothing like the walls you built inside. Open yourself up to peoples. That's what your mama would want."

She looks into James, her face expressing authority and care. She pats his knee and then pushes on her thighs to stand.

"You get on to work now," she says. "We got to slop food on they trays come six o'clock."

A Funeral Drink

One of the deprivations of prison is that there is no private place to weep. After his mother dies, James has moments when tears run down his cheeks but he wipes them away and holds back. He holds back so much that he develops headaches, as if his grief has knotted itself into a hard hemp rope behind his eyes.

On the day of his mother's funeral, James walks the perimeter of the yard. Along the wall, a path has been worn smooth. In halting phrases, he talks to Mama in a low voice, barely moving his lips. It's not that he thinks she can hear him. Nor does he believe in heaven or an afterlife. He talks to her because he has to.

What emerges is a whisper chant: "I'm sorry, Mama. Mama, I'm so, so sorry." Over and over, he repeats this mantra. Lap after lap, the words become automatic, like his breathing or his heartbeat. "I'm sorry, Mama. Mama, I'm so, so sorry."

The afternoon wears on. James' throat is parched from whispering and he aches behind his eyes. Two inmates cross the yard at a diagonal to cut him off. One is Mister B, for whom he pilfers kitchen supplies, and the other is Jimmy K, an older White man who works with him in the kitchen.

"Come on with us," Mister B says, looking a little embarrassed.

Mister B and Jimmy K lead James to a space behind the laundry, one of the blood alleys, invisible to the cat walks and guard towers. When they turn the corner, Dwight is there, leaning against the building. An acrid soap odor wafts from the laundry. James wonders if he's about to be dealt with for something.

Dwight motions for them to sit. When Mister B reaches into his loose prison coat, James expects to see a shank. What Mister B pulls out is a one-liter plastic jug filled with orange-brown pruno.

Dwight reaches out and claps James on the shoulder. "I'm sorry, man," he says. Mister B and Jimmy K nod and mumble their assent.

Mister B unscrews the cap lifts the bottle. "To your mama's memory," he says.

"May she rest in peace," Dwight says.

Mister B takes a swig and grimaces, then passes the bottle to Jimmy K, who pinches his nostrils while swallowing. James takes a small drink and shivers. It smells like a garbage can and leaves the sour taste of vomit on his tongue.

Dwight lifts the bottle without drinking. "I don't drink, but I honor your mother's memory."

The bottle is passed around quietly, a sacrament of sorrow.

"Happened to me with my dad," Jimmy K sighs. "Nobody even called me. I got a letter. A week after he went."

By the third time around the circle, the pruno doesn't taste as foul. James thinks about the risk and effort that went into making it, how it's a condolence for Mama's passing, a balm given for his grief. A gift.

Mister B takes a long swig of the pruno and closes his eyes. He begins to hum, sonorous and deep, the sound morphing into song. "Sometimes I feel like a motherless child," he sings. The sound is like warm honey oozing over rough rocks, the lyrics plaintive yet accepting. "A long, long way from home."

The men close their eyes and rock back and forth to the song. They pass the jug, and when it is empty, they stand. One by one, Jimmy K, Mister B, and Dwight shake James' hand. They do it the old-fashioned way, not a fist bump or a slide, but a firm grip. It feels good.

James stays behind. The hard stone behind his eyes slides into his throat. He leans against the wall of the laundry, lifts his hands to his face, and releases the buried tears that have been building for days, if not years.

Dead Inside

Like many introverts, James has long been a person who observes himself. He kept a journal in high school, and only because he could never be sure of its confidentiality, has he not kept one in prison. What he observes now is that as the months pass, the piercing grief about Mama's death and the gripping guilt that he couldn't be with her fade, replaced by a feeling of numbness. He's not sure which is worse. Even the stress of being in prison has abated, and he feels like a robot, going to work in the kitchen, eating dinner in the chow hall, exercising on the yard, reading on his bunk. Sometimes when he's alone in his cell he tries to masturbate but can't even get hard. The novels he reads don't move him. Twice he forgets what day it is and shows up for work in the kitchen on his day off. With no letters from Mama, there is nothing to look forward to in his week. He wonders if the rest of his life will be like this.

James receives a letter from Reverend Jones asking if the contents of Mama's apartment may be donated to charity. James writes back that they may. Mama's life insurance money is paid to James' savings account, and Reverend Jones sends him a small box of photographs from Mama's apartment.

James waits until he is alone in his cell to look though the pictures—Pops in his Air Force uniform, Mama and Pops at their wedding, Christmas and birthdays in the little house in Sacramento, James' school pictures. He expects to feel moved, but they are a disappointment. They look like nothing more than what they are—photographs—and not the real people in them. He returns them to the box and tucks them onto his shelf. He feels dead inside.

Part Five

Meagan

Allison flies to the Northeast to begin her teaching intern position at a boarding school. During the first day of faculty meetings, she finds herself staring at Meagan, one of the other teaching fellows. She has the same titian hair as Nancy Drew, the muscle tone of an athlete like Morgan, and a tomboyish slouch like Starburst.

Meagan catches Allison staring at her, and Allison turns crimson. Cursing whatever facial capillaries make her vulnerable to violent blushing, she stares at the floor. When she looks up, Meagan is smiling warmly at her, and Allison blushes again. *I haven't changed since I was twelve*, Allison thinks.

As the interns walk across the green after their day of marathon meetings, Meagan bumps shoulders with Allison and asks if she wants to get pizza and a beer. "I know a good place," she says.

"Now?" Allison asks. She is thinking she should shower and change clothes.

"Sure," Meagan says. "My two greatest needs at this moment are beer and pizza. In that order."

Meagan has a car and Allison doesn't, so Meagan drives them to a pizza place in the village. They sit at a table for two at the far end of the patio under a tree. Meagan has dimples in her cheeks and a scattering of freckles across the bridge of her nose. The beer is served in tall, frosted glasses, and they agree on a margherita pizza.

"Simple and basic," Meagan says.

"Integrity," Allison adds.

They clink their glasses.

Meagan says, "When I think that my first class is a week from today, I feel slightly terrified."

"Same here," Allison says.

"Have you ever taught a single class?" Meagan asks. "Because I haven't."

"No. The closest was tutoring a few of my sorority sisters in math."

"Holy crap. You were in a sorority?"

Allison nods. "I was."

They trade personal mini-histories. Meagan grew up on a farm in Wisconsin and just graduated from the University of Wisconsin, majoring in history. She played varsity softball and spent the past two summers in Milwaukee working in a sports program for inter-city girls.

After the first beer on an empty stomach, a slightly tipsy Allison looks at Meagan and says, "Your hair is the color of Nancy Drew's."

"The titian-haired young sleuth!" Meagan says so loudly that people at other tables turn.

"Oh my God," Allison says. "You, too? When I was ten, I wanted to *be* Nancy Drew. Actually, I still do."

"When I was twelve, I wanted to *marry* Nancy Drew," Meagan says. "And I still do."

The waiter sets down the pizza and Meagan pulls a slice from the tray. Allison takes a slice and blows on it. The crust is thin and crispy. The salty tomato taste is the perfect complement to the beer.

"So is this a date?" Meagan says, as casually as if she's asking the time.

Allison blushes violently.

Meagan nods toward Allison's face and says, "I love that you do that."

"What?" Allison asks. "Turn so red it looks like my head is going to explode?"

Meagan laughs and covers her mouth with her hand.

"It's cute," Meagan said. "I bet it lets you get away with anything."

"I feel like a dork," Allison says. "Plus, not only do I blush, but I'm embarrassed that I'm blushing so I blush more. I probably have high blood pressure."

"So is it?" Meagan asks. "Am I being too blunt? I do that sometimes."

"You're the one who invited me to pizza," Allison says. "What do you think?"

"Slick move," Meagan says.

"I suppose it is a date. It's just..."

"Wait. You're not straight, are you?" Meagan asks.

"No, I'm not," Allison says, feeling lighter as soon as she says it. "But—"

"You're not attached, are you?"

Something plaintive in Meagan's voice touches Allison's heart.

"No, not at all," she says. "It's just that I've never really dated."

"Never?"

"In high school, I had a fling, I guess you'd call it, with a girl in math camp."

Meagan bursts out laughing and abruptly stops. "Sorry. It's just...math camp. Why haven't you gone out with girls?"

Allison shrugs. "I didn't know how. At Purdue I didn't see it around me. I was in a sorority, and I let everyone think I was straight. I guess the term is *closeted*."

"Wait. The first time you said sorority I thought I'd heard wrong. I'm going to need another beer." She signals the waiter and holds up two fingers.

"You don't like sororities?" Allison asks.

"It's just that at Madison, sororities were things out of a fifties

TV show. Like saddle shoes. Historical relics."

"You're making fun of me," Allison says.

"I am. But in a fun way." She dips her head and looks at Allison. "Okay?"

Allison smiles. "Okay."

Meagan says, "I can't believe we're having"—she makes finger quotation marks— "*The Talk*." She reaches for another slice of pizza and says, "Tell me if I should lighten up. We could make fun of the people at the meeting."

The waiter sets two beers on the table and takes away the empty glasses. Meagan takes another slice of pizza.

"What about you?" Allison asks. "Have you dated much?"

"Yes and no. Madison's different. Too casual for what you'd call dating. We call ourselves the Berkeley of the Midwest. But girls with girls was fairly common. Plus, my softball team leaned lezzie. When Cris Williamson gave a sell-out concert last year, it seemed like the whole campus was lesbian."

Allison shakes her head. "Don't know who that is."

"Lesbian singer. Made a big splash in the seventies, but she's still good. Just to prove that historical relics can still be relevant. Are you out to your parents?"

Allison shakes her head. "You?"

"Never made a grand announcement, but they know. My dad caught me making out with a girl in eighth grade. In the hayloft. Classic, huh? And I never went out with boys. He used to make jokes, like saying at least he didn't have to worry I'd get pregnant. Plus, my aunt's gay. My parents are pretty cool about things like that. They were Wisconsin hippies when they were young."

"My parents were Hoosier nerds when they were young. I guess I take after them."

Meagan laughs and points to the last slice. "That's yours," she says.

"You take it," Allison says, and Meagan does.

They finish their beers and walk through the village, stopping for ice cream. When Meagan parks the car back at the campus, she leans across the console and kisses Allison softly on the lips.

Then she says, "See you tomorrow."

Allison welcomes the kiss but worries someone might have seen them. She goes to bed that night remembering Meagan's remark that she wanted to marry Nancy Drew.

Teaching

Allison's first month of school feels like teacher boot camp—preparing lessons, observing classes, and conferencing with her master teacher. She teaches two classes of her own, one freshman English and one freshman math. There are essays to read, homework to correct, and dorm duty. It is both exhausting and exhilarating. She is energized by being in the classroom, where she feels more comfortable by the day. In math, when a student seems confused, she says, "Let's back up." At this, boys in the class imitate the beeping noise made by a delivery truck put in reverse. After a few seconds, without being prompted, they stop and listen to what Allison says. Allison believes that methodical step-by-step problem solving is key. She often responds to questions with more questions, leading students to supply their own answers. She feels she is channeling her dad. In her English class, she asks questions, and from student comments she generates further questions. She tells them that reading is like blazing a trail through the forest, paying careful attention to the plants and animals along the path.

When her master teacher observes her class, Allison's students perform at their best, the opposite of what she feared. They want to see her succeed. The feedback from her master teacher is very good. Gene was right in saying that private school would be a good fit.

Meagan's courses are two sections of U.S. history, and after a month she says to Allison over dinner in the dining hall, "I'm hooked. I feel like this is my calling."

Allison nods. "I love it, too. But I'm not sure about calling."

Meagan cocks her head. "Why not?"

"Good question." She pauses. "Teaching is great. I really like it. Love it, even. But there's a voice in my head whispering that I should do more."

"More how?"

"You're going to laugh."

"Maybe, but what do you have to lose?"

"When I was ten I wanted to be Nancy Drew," Allison begins.

"You've mentioned that. I was a fan, too."

"And even though I'm supposedly on the cusp of being a grown-up, I still do. Maybe I'm being silly, but there's something about solving problems to help people. Being a fixer. It's the mission in the marrow of my bones."

"You could become an FBI agent. Do they take women?"

"I'm not sure. But no to the FBI idea. I don't think I'm much of a team player. I liked that Nancy Drew was independent."

Meagan says, "I don't think it's silly at all, though. I hear a voice like that."

"What does yours say?"

The dining hall starts to thin out, but Meagan and Allison stay.

"The summer sports program I worked in," Meagan begins. "For underserved girls. The first summer I had this epiphany. Sociologists search for solutions. What if it's simple? If kids only have school they don't like and jobs they can't get hired for, what do they do? The girls get pregnant. And take drugs. The boys join gangs and commit crimes. And take drugs. And get the girls pregnant. In the sports program, girls learned to swim, to play softball and basketball. They learned to try hard, to cooperate. It made them feel more alive. More in control. It changed them. I saw it. We were making a difference." Meagan frowns. "If those girls hadn't been in the sports program they would have had nothing to do during the summer except veg out. Or get pregnant. So the Meagan answer is, give them something they like to do. That's all the sociology you need."

Meagan sweeps her hand around the dining hall. "Here, kids like my class. I love teaching them. They're doing great with me, but truth is, they'd do just as great without me. Last summer they traveled the world, had internships, went to high level sports camps. I've got a boy in my history class who interned on Capitol Hill. Connections. So why am I here, not there?"

"Why are you?"

Meagan shrugs. "This came along. Which is not a good reason."

Allison reaches across the table to squeeze Meagan's hand. Remembering that they are in the dining hall, she pulls her hand back. Meagan looks crestfallen.

Holly Near

With an impish look in her eye, Meagan invites Allison to a Holly Near concert. They have been secretly dating—though Allison is not sure that's the right word—for a month. They have been lovers—another word that makes her uneasy—for two weeks. Allison has never heard of Holly Near, but she is excited to go. On Saturday afternoon, dressed and ready a half hour early, Allison sits in her room checking her watch and waiting for the knock on her door. She applies lipstick and then wipes it off. She sits by the window.

When Meagan steps inside, she shoves her butt against the door to close it and says, "I forgot something."

"Forgot what?"

"To kiss you," Meagan says, wrapping her arms around Allison and giving her a long, warm kiss.

They drive forty-five minutes to the college campus in Meagan's Corolla. A crowd, largely female, is streaming into the auditorium. The air is charged with excitement. Young women are holding hands. Some are skipping, others are walking with long, easy strides.

Meagan giggles. "Is your gaydar blinking lavender alert?"

Allison answers, "I'm in sleuth mode. Eyes open. Curious."

They find their seats. Allison feels like a child at the circus. Meagan's eyes twinkle, and looking into them, Allison feels a wave of ineffable love. She feels on the edge of something terrible and wondrous.

The performance begins. Holly Near is much older than Allison expected, her body squishy and plump, her face weathered, her sunrise red hair frosted with gray. She could be Allison's mother. The band members are middle-aged women, dressed for comfort. Allison, who through high school and college listened by default to the music of those around her, can't pinpoint what she is hearing, but she likes it, this blend of folk, country, bluegrass, gospel, and rock. The lyrics speak of sisterhood and peace, care of the earth, an end to racism, the rights of gays and lesbians. It sounds not preachy, but aspirational. Women in the audience hug and hold hands, kiss one another, and dance in the aisles.

Allison lets the music wash over her, seep inside. She and Meagan intertwine their arms and sway to the rhythms. Some songs bounce like a pogo stick, others sway like a porch swing in a summer breeze, some dip and soar like a bird in flight. A song begins with piano notes, and Allison at first thinks it is "Amazing Grace." Then Holly Near's voice swells. "I am open and I am willing..." The sound of her voice is soft but powerful, resonant, sometimes with a bright edge of country twang. Its tone conveys question and answer, hope and appeal. Allison stands at the edge of a precipice, the music inviting her to take a step. She has been closed and closeted since she was twelve, and now she wants to open herself, to follow the strip of golden light shining under the door.

The audience joins in the singing. Allison and Meagan look at each another, their mouths filling with song, "I am open and I am willing." For Allison the words are a vow, the feeling momentous.

The last song of the evening is one the audience knows. Everyone sings along, and on the refrain, "We are a gay and lesbian people, singing, singing for our lives," the volume swells. Allison and Meagan join in the singing. Allison remembers how Gene's parents acted at his graduation. Thinking about how she has hidden her own nature in a closed fist, she expands her chest and sings, "We are a gay and lesbian people..."

As Meagan starts the car, Allison says, "I feel like I've just been baptized."

Meagan turns in her seat and she and Allison embrace in a long hug. For the rest of the ride, they sit in peaceful silence. Allison unfastens her seat belt so she can sit closer to Meagan, her hand on her shoulder.

When they arrive back at their campus, Meagan parks in the faculty lot and they walk across the green toward the dorm. A couple of girls see them.

"Oh my God," one of them calls out. "We think we saw you at the Holly Near concert."

It is Allison who answers. "Yes," she calls out. "That was us."

The Announcement

Allison will always remember the concert as an epiphany, a glimpse into a welcoming world where she can be who she is and love whom she loves. In the weeks following the concert, Allison and Meagan say to one another, "I love you." They have a couple of spats and make up, work out a system for spending nights in one another's dorm rooms. Allison writes Gene in San Francisco telling him about Meagan. He writes back, "I am so very, very happy for you. I can't wait to meet her. And I love that as everyone turns to email, you still write letters!"

Among the students there are whispers about Meagan and Allison, but they seem born of curiosity, not condemnation. Allison is overcoming her fear of having her skin burned.

On her first evening at home for Christmas break, Allison's dad celebrates by cooking steaks on the outdoor grill. It is starting to sleet, so he holds an umbrella high above the glowing coals. When the three of them sit down to dinner, Allison takes a silent deep breath and says, "You know how I've mentioned Meagan?"

"Uh-huh," her mother says.

"Wisconsin," her dad adds.

"Right. She's my girlfriend," Allison says, her heart pounding.

"That's good," her mother says. "I've always wanted you to have more friends."

"Do you think I left the steaks on too long?" her dad says.

"They're just right," her mother answers.

"I didn't mean that kind of friend," Allison says, a little more loudly. "We're lovers."

"What do you mean?" her mother asks.

"I'm a lesbian, I guess. Not 'I guess.' I'm a lesbian."

Her dad stops cutting his steak. Her mother stops chewing and winces, as if the word pushes her over the threshold into physical pain.

Her dad clears his throat. "Well, you're your own person."

"When did this happen?" her mother asks.

"Probably when I was born."

"What about that nice boy we met at your graduation?" her mother asks.

"Gene's a friend. A good friend. He's gay, too. Like me."

It feels good to invoke his name. And his gayness. It makes her feel less alone.

"Okay with me," her dad says, trying to smile. "You're still our girl."

Her mother sighs. "If you decide to do this, I hope you don't start dressing mannish."

Her dad clears his throat again. "I got a new cordless drill. The old one is still good. You want to take it with you? Handy to have around an apartment."

Allison smiles sadly. "Thanks, Dad."

Allison is disappointed. She wishes they could be excited and happy, not merely tolerant. At least they're better than Gene's parents. She tells herself that in time they will warm to the reality.

Next Steps

In January, the program director meets with the teaching fellows and outlines how to find a teaching position in a private school. He distributes a handout about the process. The hiring season begins in February with a national convention, this year in Washington, D.C. Many schools are reluctant to hire complete rookies, he tells them, so their year as teaching fellows should give them a leg up. During his presentation Allison and Meagan exchange long, anxious looks.

Walking across the snow-covered lawn after the meeting, Meagan says, "When I think about us separating in June, I want to puke my guts out."

"Me too," Allison says, "though I was going to say bawl my eyes out."

"Same thing," Meagan says.

The bare trees cast long shadows in the low winter sun. Meagan and Allison skip the dining hall and drive into town for dinner. They go to a lesbian-owned diner called Annie's Place. At a small table in the corner, Allison orders the daisy chain chicken noodle soup, Meagan the cowgirl chili.

"What are the chances we could get hired at the same school?" Allison asks as she sips her glass of wine.

"Probably slim," Meagan sighs.

"Schools in the same city?"

"Less slim," Meagan says. Then she adds, "Want to try?"

"Actually, I do," Allison nods. "I really do."

They clink their glasses in a toast and smile, though Allison fears their cheer is whistling in the dark.

Meagan seems to know it, too, and says, "We could have a

plan B. If one of us gets a good job, the other could tag along. Be a barista or something."

Allison frowns.

"I'd come with you," Meagan says, looking expectantly at Allison.

"But—you'd be giving up teaching," Allison says.

"Not forever. Just for that first year."

"You said it was your calling," Allison says.

"It is, but you're my calling, too. What are you saying—you wouldn't come with me if I got a job?"

"I don't know."

"You don't know?" Meagan says, her voice rising in pitch and her eyes filling with tears. "Damn. I thought—"

Allison doesn't know. She loves Meagan, and the past five months have brought her a happiness never before known. The thought of being without Meagan frightens her. But she is also driven by her mission—to solve problems, to help people in need. Teaching might not satisfy that entirely, but it comes much closer than pouring espresso drinks. She can no more turn away from her mission than an autumn flock of geese could fly in any direction except south.

On the ride back to the dorm, Allison says, "I love you to pieces. It's just that we both have missions."

"I wish you had stopped talking after you said you love me to pieces. The 'it's just' part killed me."

They drive back to the campus in silence. When they arrive, they go to their separate rooms.

The conflict hangs over them in February when they travel to Washington for interviews at the independent school convention. Since Allison can teach English or math, she has more interviews, but Meagan has promising ones as well. Allison tries to imagine following Meagan and "playing house," as Meagan calls it. The house part sounds warm and wonderful, but not having a meaningful job would be a descent into something like death. And if Meagan followed her to a job, Allison would feel guilty.

In March they fly west for interviews. Meagan is thrilled to receive an offer at a private school in San Francisco to teach American history and coach girls' softball. It's a dream job. Allison receives an offer to teach math at a good private school in Portland. They talk it over. It takes some of the sting out that they will both be on the West Coast, a ninety-minute plane ride apart. They accept their offers.

Heading West

Allison and Meagan decide to drive west and live together in Berkeley for the summer. When school starts, Allison will move up to Portland. Allison believes their summer will serve as a test, allow them to be sure. It will be the lifestyle equivalent of measuring twice and cutting once.

When school ends, they set off in Meagan's car. In Ohio the engine begins to sputter, and the smell of gasoline wafts into the front seat. They exit the freeway just past Columbus and drive to a service station. The mechanic puts the car on the lift and uses a flashlight to show Meagan and Allison a leak in the fuel line. While he explains to Meagan how it could have caused a dangerous car fire, Allison slips out the door and opens her flip phone. When she returns, the mechanic has written out the estimate on a clip board. The repairs will cost twelve hundred dollars.

Smiling brightly, Allison says, "I just talked to my dad, who is a lawyer for the Ohio Department of Consumer Affairs. He says it will take about a half hour and cost no more than two hundred dollars."

The mechanic's face colors.

"Can you do that for us or should we try another place?" Allison asks. "I told Dad I'd let him know how it turns out."

In a half hour they drive out of town with a repaired fuel line for which they have paid two hundred dollars. It is Allison's turn to drive. Meagan slips off her sandals and rests her bare feet on the dash. Allison feels triumphant.

"Did you really call your dad?" Meagan asks.

Allison nods. "He has files in his basement workshop. Beside his wall phone. He looked up the cost. The part about the Ohio

Department of Consumer Affairs was my own embellishment."

"So he said the cost should be two hundred?"

"Actually, three hundred. I lowered it in case we had to bargain."

"Beneath your nerdy librarian persona lurks a dangerous person," Meagan says.

"But on the side of good," Allison says. "Like the girl sleuth."

They arrive at Allison's place in Indianapolis in time for dinner. Allison's dad fires up his grill for steaks. Allison's parents seem like they're walking on egg shells, asking polite questions about the intern program. Allison's dad shows Meagan his shop in the basement. Having been told that they plan to live together for the summer in Berkeley, he has made them a spice cabinet from some mahogany he had. He eagerly describes how he made the box joints and applied two layers of linseed oil when it was finished.

The next morning they drive to Wisconsin, arriving in the late afternoon. Meagan's mother welcomes Allison as if she's a neighbor from down the road. She tells Meagan that her dad and brothers are still milking, so Meagan takes Allison's hand and leads her to the barn.

"Just in time to help," her dad says, and he lifts Meagan off the ground in a hug.

"Real nice to meet you," he smiles to Allison. "I'd shake your hand if mine was clean."

Meagan's two brothers, one older and one younger, walk awkwardly forward and say hi to Allison. It is the older one—Rob—who turns beet red. *Someone like me*, Allison thinks.

"Okay, boys," the dad says, "let's get this finished up."

Allison has never been in a milking barn, or even on a farm. She looks at the two rows of black and white cows standing in their stanchions, chewing grain while machines pump milk from their teats. She is astounded by the size of their large udders. She stares with fascination at the silicone cups attached their teats. Transparent tubes carry the milk the length of the barn.

"Where does the milk go?" Allison asks.

"Cooling tank in the next room," Meagan says, motioning with her head. "If you're not grossed out, can you help me with this?"

Meagan is pressing down on the base of a cow's tail, and she guides Allison's hand there.

"Just press down," she says, grabbing a flat blade shovel.

"It won't kick?"

"No." Meagan pulls the shovel from the manure cart and holds it under the cow's tail. "Okay, let go." The cow's tail rises and its manure plops onto the shovel. Meagan dumps it into the cart. "Our new job."

"Beats grading papers," Allison says.

"Kind of the same thing," Meagan responds, and they burst out laughing. Meagan's dad glances at them and smiles. The two boys stare with wonder.

Allison is about to ask how you know a cow has to poop when one starts to raise its tail and Meagan quickly slips to its side to hold the tail down. This time Allison picks up the shovel to receive the manure. She is surprised by how much the manure increases the weight of the already heavy shovel.

"Good teamwork," Meagan says.

Allison says, "We're the cow shit sisters."

Walking back to the house, Meagan puts her arm around Allison's shoulders and gives a warm squeeze. "You didn't mind too much?"

"Not at all. But looking at them makes me feel flat-chested."

Meagan bursts out laughing.

"It's interesting to see how everything is done," Allison continues. "My dad would love the milking machine. It's ingenious."

"Maybe they'll come and visit sometime," Meagan says.

"Plus, all that milk," Allison adds. "My ovaries really snapped to attention."

"I love how you talk sexy and make it sound scientific," Meagan says.

After dinner Meagan and Allison play Scrabble with Meagan's mom and dad. The younger brother plays video games in the next room. Rob has driven the pickup to town to meet friends.

Meagan has twin beds in her old room, so each of them takes a bed. Thunder rumbles outside and a breeze blows the curtains. They lie in the dark and gaze out the window, watching the lightning show above the dark fields.

"I can't believe you're wearing long pajamas," Meagan says. "You look like a society lady in a 1940s movie."

"It's the proper thing for a young lady who is a house guest," Allison teases. "What are you wearing?"

"Come over and find out."

"You're a seductive little minx," Allison says.

"It just seems that way because you're so easy," Meagan says, skipping nude across the room to jump onto Allison's bed.

The morning milking starts at 5:30, but Meagan's dad lets the girls sleep. After breakfast, Rob sits beside Allison on the front porch. It has rained during the night, and the air smells fresh. The suitcases have been put in the car, and Meagan and her mom are in the kitchen making sandwiches for the road.

Rob lifts his cap and scratches his head. He turns his head and looks at Allison. "I don't know how I feel about you two, Meagan being my sister and all."

Allison thinks a minute. "You'd rather Meagan came home with some nice young man?"

Rob looks at her and says, "Truth be told, I reckon I do."

Allison says, "Suppose Meagan said that she wished you were gay and brought home some handsome boy. What would you say?"

"I'd say she was crazy."

"She would be asking you to be something you're not, right?"

"That's right."

"Which is what you're asking of her," Allison says, looking him in the eye.

Even with his sunburned face, Allison can see that he's blushing again.

Meagan appears at the screen door. "Ready?"

Rob stands up. "I'll check your oil before you go," he says, and walks out to the driveway. Meagan's dad is out on the tractor. Meagan's mom hugs her and Allison, and tells them to drive carefully. Rob calls out that the oil's okay.

Meagan and Allison climb in the car and drive down the gravel road out to the highway. Allison looks back and sees Rob waving.

Allison and Meagan watch the changing countryside slip past the windows. They drive down through Iowa and then Nebraska, passing hundreds of miles of corn and wheat fields.

"Holy crap," Meagan says late that afternoon. "I never realized how big this country is. We've been driving at seventy miles per hour for nine hours and it still looks the same. What if we're caught in an infinity loop?"

"I know what you mean," Allison says. "But I like that it's gradual. Airplane trips always seem surreal. You slog to the airport in snowy Indianapolis, and two hours later you deplane in sunny Florida with no sense of having traveled. It's disconcerting."

Beneath the enormous sky, the earth seems sparsely populated. Through the windshield Meagan is the first to see the snowcapped Rockies, at first so faint she's unsure whether they are clouds or mountains. As their car climbs, the air becomes cool and fresh. They inhale the smell of pine. They spend a couple of days car camping and hiking in Colorado, and then the mountains fade in the rearview mirror.

They cross the flat, ochre landscape of Utah and Nevada, and then climb again, this time into the Sierras. At the higher elevations, snow still blankets the ground. Near Donner Pass they get out of the car and make snow angels. They hike around Lake Tahoe. Except for their interview trips that spring, neither has been west of the Rockies before, and they are astonished at the extremes of the landscape—the drama of the gigantic mountains, the dry desolation of the desert, the lush beauty of the forests, snow on the ground in June. On the last day they cross the California valley where temperatures rise to a hundred. As they dip into the Bay Area, the temperature rapidly drops. It's seventy when they arrive in Berkeley in the mid-afternoon.

"We just did in a few days' car ride what it took people months to do in wagons a century and a half ago," Meagan says. "I feel like a pioneer."

"Me, too," Allison says.

Berkeley

In Berkeley, Allison and Meagan find a small house to rent, even though Allison will be there for only a couple of months before moving to Portland. Allison insists they hang her dad's spice rack in the kitchen. It's a gesture of faith that she will return there to live in a year.

They each get waitressing jobs at a local restaurant for the summer. Allison calls Gene, and he invites them to his apartment in San Francisco for dinner. He is working as a waiter at a high-end restaurant and taking a real estate course. He wants to do residential sales.

His apartment is a one-bedroom in a charming Victorian. His refined taste shows everywhere. One wall is painted a medium gray and the adjoining wall an offsetting mint green, the bedspread picking up tones from both. Framed black and white photographs make his study look like a tasteful gallery. Delicate ferns hang in his shower. Comfortable cushions in vibrant colors fill the couch. The back door opens onto a covered redwood deck with plants, tasteful porch furniture, and a tiny grill on which he prepares salmon.

"Your place looks like a museum," Allison tells him.

"And my credit card balance looks like the national debt," he says, rolling his eyes.

They sit down to dinner and Gene pours a sauvignon blanc and offers a toast.

"You get my nomination for cute lesbian couple of the year," he says with a warm smile. "I am so very happy for you both."

"Wow," Meagan says, tasting the wine.

"What about you?" Allison says. "Hasn't anyone snagged you yet?"

He shakes his head. "It's not easy," he says. "I know I said that back at Purdue, but here it's not easy for a different reason. There are thousands of gay men everywhere you look, but many of them—especially the twenty-somethings—are like kids in a candy store, sampling everything that looks delicious. I did that for maybe a month—okay, three months—but then I realized that what I really want is a steady boyfriend, a white picket fence, and a basset hound in the yard. Which is *not* what most gay men around here want. Must be my midwestern roots."

Megan lifts her glass. "Here's to midwestern roots."

Riding back to Berkeley, Meagan says, "Holy crap. He's so good-looking I'm surprised you didn't convert."

Allison laughs. "When we'd walk together on campus, heads definitely turned. He was a good friend. And he's a good soul. I hope he finds someone."

On their days off, Meagan and Allison explore the city of San Francisco or the woods and beaches of Marin County. They visit museums, stroll through Golden Gate Park, sip cappuccinos in North Beach, and browse Lawrence Ferlinghetti's bookstore. Allison entertains Meagan by reciting one of his poems from memory. One Sunday in June, they march in the Gay Pride Parade. They have their first experience at a nude beach, Allison counting to ten and then stepping out of her one-piece bathing suit, marveling at the feel of the cool wind and hot sun on her skin. She recalls Starburst's all-over tan. They spend a day in the wine country. On their first drive over the bridge to Marin County, Meagan wonders what the huge expanse of fortress-like buildings is. "San Quentin Prison," Allison says. "I saw a sign."

"Looks so depressing," Meagan says.

Allison turns in her seat to look.

Portland

Sometimes Allison feels like pinching herself to make sure she's not dreaming. In her solitary and closeted years of high school and college, she wondered if she would be alone her entire life. *Lezzie old maid* was the phrase she privately used to torment herself. Only her math camp fling with Starburst suggested anything else was possible, and that seemed unreal—a wild, exotic dream that ended as soon as it began. Then one day she found herself mesmerized by a young woman in a teachers' meeting, and her whole life changed.

Allison begins to dread living alone in Portland. When she made the decision, it seemed the smart option. Her newfound teaching profession was important, and compromising it for a relationship a few months old seemed unwise. The person who formed those mature and rational thoughts now seems like someone else. But she made the decision. She signed the contract. She can't go back on it now.

In Portland, Allison finds a studio apartment over a two-car garage in a peaceful suburban neighborhood close to her new school. Like her teaching intern school in New England, the school in Portland is full of respectful, hardworking students and welcoming colleagues. She teaches freshman math, four sections. She loves the course, but she misses teaching English. When she chats with students, she asks them what they are reading in their English class. She talks with them about Odysseus, Holden, and Othello.

Allison suspects that her parents are relieved that she and Meagan are separated by six hundred miles. They probably hope this is a phase that will pass. On the phone her mother asks if she's still in touch with Gene. Her dad asks if she's hung her spice rack in her kitchen. She tells him it's hanging in the kitchen in Berkeley, where she hopes to be next year.

During her busy weeks, Allison is buoyed by a sense of purpose, energized by the classroom. What ought to be the best time of her week—arriving home on Friday afternoon—is the worst. She feels a hole in her chest as soon as she enters her empty apartment. She peruses the local movie listings but rarely goes. She reads a few pages of a novel. On her laptop she scrolls through photos of Meagan, reliving their drive west and their summer in Berkeley. Finally, she calls Meagan, and sometimes they talk while they're eating, a way to have long-distance dinner together.

Once or twice a month she talks to Gene on the phone. He has a heart like a sponge and soaks up whatever feelings she expresses. He has finished his real estate course and is studying for the license exam. He's also trying an internet site for gay dating.

In mid-October Allison flies down to Berkeley for a weekend visit. To the colleagues who ask about her weekend plans, she says she's visiting her girlfriend in Berkeley. Everyone takes the remark in stride.

At the Oakland Airport she and Meagan fall into one another's arms, hugging tightly. That evening they cook dinner together, eat by candlelight, and then make love. On Saturday they hike on Mount Tamalpais. The trail is dusty, the weeds so dry they crackle in the wind. The hard, baked ground is awaiting the winter rains. The air is hot, but the October light is different—softer, more golden. At one point on the trail, they pause to look down at the Richmond Bridge and the bay.

"Look," Meagan says, "there's San Quentin."

Allison squints into the distance and says, "Oh, yes." From five miles away, it looks still, like an egg shell hiding what's inside, waiting to be broken open.

On Sunday morning Allision awakens with a sense of doom. Her plane leaves a little past noon. They make a big breakfast of French toast, bacon, fresh squeezed orange juice, and fruit. They read the *Times* on the sofa, their legs intertwined. Meagan talks about her classes, describes some of her students. Allison says she misses teaching English.

On the ride to the airport, Meagan sighs and says to Allison, "Do you think we should be seeing other people?"

Allison whips her head toward Meagan. "You mean date? Why?"

Meagan shrugs. "I don't know. Just for something to do. Instead of wasting away at home."

Allison feels the blood draining from her face. She turns and stares out the window. At first, she feels like she's broken and dying. Then she fills with rage.

After a few minutes, Meagan says, "Alli? Are you angry?"

Allison can't talk. Hot tears fill her eyes.

"Alli?"

They pull up in front of the terminal. Allison yanks her bag from the backseat and slams the car door. She stalks into the terminal without looking back.

On the plane, thoughts screech through Allison's mind like frantic crows. Has Meagan fallen out of love? Has she met someone else? Is this how breakups begin? At one point during the flight, she thinks she's going to be airsick. Later, she feels she can't breathe, and she fears the air supply to the cabin is failing. The two-hour flight seems to last forever.

She unlocks her apartment door and dials Gene's number with her jacket still on. She gets his answering machine. She soaks a wash cloth in hot water and lays it over her face like a shroud. She lies on her bed. She is so terrified, she can't cry.

When the phone rings, she feels a wild surge of hope that Meagan is calling. It's Gene. She tells him what happened, her voice periodically cracking. "I just love her so much," Allison says.

"You need hugs," Gene says. "I wish I were there."

"I need wisdom," Allison says.

"I'm better at hugs," Gene says.

"I need both. Seriously—what do you think? This is my first girlfriend. I need an instruction manual."

"Did she seem distant over the weekend?" Gene asks.

"No. Our weekend was great. That's why I feel so slammed by what she said."

"There are two possibilities," Gene says. "Actually, three."

There is a long pause. Allison carries the phone to the bathroom and runs more hot water over the washcloth. She wrings it out and then returns to bed, laying it across her face. She remembers that Gene sometimes does this in serious talks—pauses between the introduction and the body of what he has to say. She waits.

"The first possibility—which I don't believe—is that this is the beginning of a break-up. Step one with more to follow."

"That's my fear. Why don't you believe it?" Allison says.

"Because I've watched you two together. I believe you love each other. Deeply. In a way that doesn't just evaporate."

"I'm nodding," Allison says. "And hoping to God that you're right."

"Two, she's angry you chose to go to Portland, and she's lashing out."

Allison sighs. "I thought of that, too. It doesn't seem like her."

"Don't be so sure. But the third is, you just told me you love her so much. You said it because of what happened today. That may be why she did it. Unconsciously. So you'd realize how much you love her."

"The third is the one I want to believe," Allison says. "What should I do? I want to call in sick and fly down there tomorrow."

"Communicate, definitely. But not yet. Did I ever tell you about the turtle I had when I was a kid?"

"Gene, you're the only person in the world who can pull off a *non sequitur* like that and not sound schizophrenic."

"I found him on our street after a summer rain. Beautiful yellow markings on his dark shell. Naturally, Gene chooses a pet based on aesthetics. I brought him home and he wouldn't open his shell. I kept tapping on it, as if to say 'Can Mister Turtle come out and play?' Well, eventually I learned that the only way to get him to open his shell was to back off and wait. Don't tap on Meagan's shell. Wait for her."

There is a pause and then Allison says, "Slamming the car door like I did was the act of a two-year-old."

"Immature of her to say what she did driving to the airport and, yes, immature of you to slam the door. But it's *okay*. You're allowed to act like two fools. That's what love does to you."

"This is out of character for me," Allison says.

"I know it is. And I'm impressed."

Relief, and a New Fear

With only a couple of hours of fitful sleep, Allison steps in front of her class the next morning. Her face is puffy and her eyes red. One of her students asks if she has a cold. "Just allergies," she tells him. The anxiety monster hovers just behind her, but she manages to teach a good class. Four good classes by the end of the day. Every minute that she's not teaching is torture, and when she arrives in her apartment late that afternoon she feels an anguished terror. In all the years she longed for a girlfriend, she had no inkling of the searing pain love could bring. No wonder most love songs are sad.

She is walking in circles in her kitchen when the phone rings. It's Gene.

He says, "Oh, Allison, sweetie. You thought it might be Meagan. I heard the hope in your voice when you said hello."

She sinks onto her mattress. She admits it's true and says, "But I'm glad to hear your voice. You're such a good friend to me."

She describes her painfully long day and how, now that she's home, every minute lasts an hour.

"You still think I shouldn't call her?"

"I thought about you all day, and that's my one piece of advice I'm not sure about."

"So what do I do?"

"Give it one more day. Call her tomorrow night."

"Talk about yourself. I'm sick of me. How's San Francisco?"

"Crazy. Halloween is next week. I went last year and it's like Mardi Gras, New Year's Eve, and the Gay Pride Parade all rolled into one. And some years, apparently, a smattering of thugs. Let's hope that doesn't happen. I'm trying to decide on my costume. I'm thinking about Zorro. So dashing."

Allison laughs. "I can totally see you as Zorro."

"You dressing up?"

"Hadn't thought about it. Maybe I'll be Nancy Drew."

"It supposed to be a costume, not your real self."

"I'm smiling, even though you can't see it through the phone."

"I know you are, sweetheart."

The next afternoon Allison is wondering what time she should call Meagan when the phone rings. It's Meagan. Allison has thoroughly planned how she will begin this conversation, but she blurts out, "I'm sorry I slammed the door."

"Oh, Alli. I'm sorry I was a butthead."

"Do you want to date other people?" Allison asks. "Have you met someone?" This is not her planned speech.

"No, babe. That's the thing. We had a great weekend, but then on the way to the airport, it hit me that you were going back to Portland, and that we probably wouldn't see each other until Thanksgiving, and—I don't know. I suddenly felt mad, or confused, or frustrated, and...it just flew out of my mouth. About seeing other people—which I don't want to do. I don't understand why I said it. Can I plead temporary insanity?"

For joy, Allison cradles the phone like it's a sacred talisman.

"Let's don't fight anymore, okay?" Allison says. "I almost lost my mind."

"Me, too. I'm sorry," Meagan says.

After Allison hangs up the phone, she feels like someone whose doctor said she has six weeks to live, only to be told later that the x-rays got mislabeled and she's fine. She goes to bed after dinner and sleeps ten hours.

The next day she feels buoyant. The student who asked about her allergies says, "Ms. Anderson, you look like your old self again. Your allergies must be better."

The crisis is over, but Allison's relief isn't total. That patient who suffered through the mistaken x-ray episode, after dancing with happiness and relief, may find herself left with a lingering fear. It wasn't true this time, but it could still happen in the future. A fatal diagnosis could arrive next year, or in five years, or in ten. What if her faith in abiding love proves false?

Prop 8

Meagan is more interested and active in politics than Allison, and in the weeks leading up to the 2008 election, Meagan volunteers to work phone banks for the Obama campaign. Studying the polls, his backers are increasingly optimistic. When the votes are counted, Obama wins and Allison and Meagan are elated. But their joy is undercut by the passage of California's Proposition 8, a ballot measure banning same-sex marriage. Though Meagan believes that court challenges to Prop 8 will ultimately succeed, the voice of the state's voters feels like a kick in the stomach. On the phone, Meagan tells Allison, "This morning on BART, I looked around and thought, which of you evil fuckers voted for Prop 8? The whole thing leaves a shitty taste in my mouth."

That ten percent of the people in California oppose gay marriage would be something Allison could live with. But fifty-two percent is crushing, even if the proposition was defeated in the Bay Area. She wonders if the prejudice will ever end. Have she and Megan been branded as less than legitimate citizens? How could there be so many heartless people? She has flashbacks to the days when her skin felt vulnerable to the burn of others' judgment.

A New Job

Allison begins writing Bay Area schools in January, she has two on-campus interviews in February, and in early March she receives a job offer at a private girls' school south of San Francisco. The teaching assignment is perfect: two sections of English and two sections of math.

In her hiring conversation on the phone, Janet Blake, the new head, explains her vision for the school by saying that not a single alum is currently a CEO, and that it is her goal to change that. The girls need to be groomed for leadership, and a strong female math teacher can be one piece of the puzzle in moving the school in that direction. Allison is too excited about the job offer to think much about this remark.

When Allison calls Meagan with the good news, they both cry. The one year interruption in their relationship will end. "I never want us to be apart, ever again," Meagan says.

"We never will," Allison says. "Never."

The day after graduation at Allison's school, Meagan flies to Portland and they drive to Berkeley together, stopping for a couple of days at the Shakespeare festival in Ashland, Oregon. They had originally planned three days, but they can't wait to get to Berkeley and settle in to their new home. They feel that Berkeley—together—is where they are supposed to be.

Part Six

San Quentin

In the spring of 2002, the year Allison meets Starburst at math camp, James is transferred from Tehachapi to San Quentin. He is thirty-one. The annual calculation of his classification points—based on time served, conduct record, and work history—qualifies him for a lower security level prison. He doesn't care that much—prison is prison—but at least it won't be so baking hot in the summer. As the van pulls away from Tehachapi, James looks out the window and thinks about Lonny, Mister B, Dwight the shot caller, Flo in the kitchen, and BZ now out on parole. He feels a tinge of sadness, as if he's going to miss them.

There are two inmates on this van ride, James and a middle-aged brother named Habeeb. Once they are on the freeway, Habeeb asks, "Aren't you the young brother they call Shakespeare? Writes things for people?"

James says that he is.

"You must be jacked to get to San Quentin then," Habeeb says.

James shrugs. "Don't know much about it."

"I got two cousins there. San Quentin has lots of programs," Habeeb says. "Yoga, Shakespeare acting, all kinds of self-help. College classes, even. Good for someone like you."

San Quentin is notorious for what it used to be—a violent maximum-security prison housing infamous murderers and revolutionaries. Older guys—and even some younger ones—can point out the spot in front of the gate where guards killed author and revolutionary George Jackson in a 1971 escape attempt. But things have changed. Though one of its cellblocks still houses the six hundred men on California's death row, the rest of the San Quentin population is medium security. While physically decrepit, San

Quentin offers such a wealth of programs provided by non-profit groups that the prison has become a poster child for rehabilitation efforts.

When James steps off of the prison van that afternoon, the smell of the bay brings back a flood of memories. He remembers Mama coming home from work, Spike chasing his ball in the park, Einstein making commentary outside the corner store, Keesha taking him to the beach on the day he first saw the ocean. If only Mama were still living, she could visit him much more easily here.

When the guard unlocks the cell, he says to James, "This is Williams."

James steps in and nods to an older Black man, thin with gray stubble on his chin and jaw, lying on the lower bunk, propped up on one elbow reading a comic book. Ignoring James, Williams says to the guard, "Man, why you give me some young buck? They don't pay me to babysit."

The guard says, "Have fun, gentlemen," and closes the cell door with a clang. Williams turns the page of his comic book and without looking up says, "Clean the toilet and basin after you use them, don't step on my bunk when you get up onto yours, and don't mess with any my stuff, especially my TV."

Before his work assignment is processed, James spends entire afternoons on the yard. In his first days, he finds himself sorry he left Tehachapi. Everything here seems older and dirtier. The concrete is cracked, the metal is rusted, the paint is peeling. The cells are small—two inmates share a space ten feet long and five feet wide with two bunk beds, basin and toilet at the end. It's like living in a bathroom.

Though the yard seems racially divided, James does notice a mixed-race basketball game, and at one of the tables a Black guy and an Asian guy are playing chess. At another table, Blacks,

Whites, and an Asian are playing Dungeons and Dragons. None of this would have happened at Tehachapi. Anyone race-mixing without his shot caller's permission would have been in deep shit. James will learn that there are no shot-callers here.

Mount Tamalpais is only five miles from the prison grounds, and it can be seen from anywhere on the yard. James is mesmerized by the view. During his high school years from certain parts of Oakland, he could glimpse the outline of Mt. Tam far in the distance. It looked as far away as the moon, belonging to another world. Here it seems just beyond his reach. Supposedly, a Miwok legend viewed the range of hills as a giant girl sleeping on her back, the highest hill her breast. James sees the resemblance and feels inspired by her presence.

The view of Mt. Tam changes according to the weather and the time of day. Sometimes the peak rises above a low layer of fog that glistens like cake icing in the sun. At other times the fog is higher, revealing the base of the mountain while hiding its peak in a gray ceiling. On hazy days, the mountain looks ghostly in a faint mist. When it's clear, the early morning sun lights the mountain slopes in a warm orange glow, and near sunset they turn pinkish and then a mournful purple as dusk falls. The mountain stands in a majestic beauty, powerful, self-contained, needing nothing, wanting nothing.

Williams

James feels stress whenever he's in his cell. Williams seems angry with him for being there. James is careful not to bother him, and by the second week Williams begins to say a few words. Eventually Williams asks him a few questions—where's he from, what prison was he in last—and James answers and then asks Williams the same question in return. That seems the best way to proceed. Williams is from Oakland, and he came here after ten years at New Folsom.

"What you in for?" Williams asks.

"Murder," James says.

Williams shakes his head.

When James asks, Williams says he's in for burglaries. He was caught when he fell through the skylight of an electronics store. His garage was filled with stolen goods that tied him to a string of thefts.

"Broke my leg in the fall," he says. "Doctors didn't fix it right. Hurts me bad when it rains."

One afternoon Williams offers James a cookie from a bag he purchased at the canteen. James takes one and thanks him.

James gets assigned to the kitchen, the morning shift just like at Tehachapi, for thirty-cents an hour. It makes him feel lonely that Flo is not here.

Peace Day

After the second fight in a month, a mixed-race group of inmates discusses having a Peace Day. They call themselves a committee and present their idea to the Warden. To the surprise of everyone, the Warden agrees. All the races agree. Some of the guards like the idea, while others think it will compromise security, a demonstration that the Warden is too liberal.

Peace Day is months in the planning. Musicians and community leaders agree to come in from the outside. A TV station sends a reporter and a camera crew. Inmates gather on the yard to listen to the music, hear the speakers. There is a Native American peace dance and chanting. Plastic wrist bracelets imprinted with the word *peace* are handed out. Holly Near visits the prison and gives a performance, leading the men on the yard in song,

> *We are gentle, imprisoned people,*
> *And we are singing, singing for our lives.*

James joins in while he gazes at the mystical woman of Tamalpais Mountain. He imagines the mountain-woman stirring from her sleep and then sitting up, looking down on the yard.

A chaplain leads a prayer, and at noon there is a moment of silence for those who have died in prison violence. Some inmates wipe their eyes. Guards watch nervously from the edges. Though it has been rumored that groups will start fights, that does not happen. Williams walks up to James and says, "This is all right."

Dreads

James' hair is getting long, about four inches, natural. He has avoided the prison barber since the day the barber fumbled the electric clippers and accidentally cut a wedge out of James' hair down to the scalp. He likes the look of dreads, and he wonders if a new look would help his spirits. The numbness that set in after Mama's death has never left him.

One day he asks a brother with good dreads how he does it.

"You can try to do it yourself, but I go to the Hair Professor. In C Block. He does it right."

When James approaches the Hair Professor on the yard, he peers into James' hair and lightly tugs it with his fingers. "You got good hair for dreads," he says. "Best it be at least six inches, so give it another two or three months, and then come see me. Twenty dollars, including quality oil."

The Hair Professor does dreads out of his cell, a small business thriving in the leeway the COs allow. Three months later, James visits him and comes away with dreads and good mahogany beads. The next day he starts to grow a beard. The dreads lengthen, and the beard fills in. He studies his face in his stainless-steel mirror. He likes the look, but he is struck by the deep sadness in his eyes.

A Found Bullet

A 9mm bullet is found on the yard. The prison is locked down, and a search begins—every common area and every cell. The prison administration assumes an inmate has a contraband gun or is constructing one. A zip gun that fires a single bullet can be made from materials smuggled from the machine shop. Inmate word on the yard is that the bullet was planted by a guard, either to generate overtime pay from the prison-wide search or to punish the prisoners for Peace Day. James believes that either of the two theories could be true.

When searching the cells, the guards sometimes dump the inmates' possessions into a heap on the floor; at other times, the disruption is minimal. It depends on which guard is doing the search and whether he wants to get back at a particular inmate. James and Williams' cell is roughed over, but not trashed.

The search lasts two weeks and yields many forms of contraband—marijuana, meth, crack, heroin, tranquilizers, jars of pruno, porn magazines, cell phones, shives, tobacco cigarettes, tattooing equipment, prescription pain killers, hand-printed betting slips, candy not sold in the canteen, incense, White supremacist propaganda, and cash. No firearm, homemade or otherwise, is found. The origin of the bullet remains unknown.

Lonny's Drawing

James writes a short letter to Lonny at Tehachapi. A month later Lonny sends one back. James hasn't received a piece of mail since Mama died, and it feels good to sit on the yard and open an envelope, even if the letter has already been read by the prison censors.

> *Dear James,*
>
> *It is Lonny. I red your leter. San Cwentin sound better then here. Maybe some day I change to there. Take GED agin but fail. Try agin. Guy on yard aks me where Shaxpeer? I tell him. I make picture of sky give you. Girlfren not writ sence two months.*
>
> *Your fren,*
>
> *Lonny*

From the envelope James unfolds a pencil drawing of the sky above Tehachapi, the clouds mournful and sublime. Though the drawing is in black pencil, in his mind James fills in shades of orange and deep purple above black razor wire. So Lonny, too, saw the sky—really saw it. That night James tapes the drawing to the wall above his bunk.

The Punching Bag

Two cellblocks are on quarantine for an intestinal virus outbreak, so the yard is sparsely populated. James runs ten laps on the track and then does push-ups, pull-ups, dips, and crunches. Since his high school days when he cared for Big Mike's dogs, his determination to be fit has never wavered.

James walks over to the punching bag, something he has never used, not wanting to suggest he's ready for a fight. He assumes a boxer's stance and looks into the shiny black surface of the bag gleaming in the sun. He sees his own reflection. His fists pummel the bag, faster and harder. Suddenly, the face reflected in the shiny vinyl is not his own but Black Snake's. His fist slams against the face with a crack. He feels the crunch of Black Snake's nose, hears the thud of Black Snake's head hitting the ground and the clank of the gun striking the asphalt. He sees his right hand grab the gun and shove it into Black Snake's mouth. He hears a strangled gag and then a loud explosion. The gun jolts three times. Black Snake's mouth fills with blood and overflows. A pattern of gray brain splatter and white bone bits glisten on the asphalt. The ground moves and he feels dizzy. Is it an earthquake?

"You finished?"

James turns. Dazed. Gasping for breath. "What?"

"You finished here?" It's a White guy who wants to use the bag.

"Oh. Yeah," James answers. He staggers to the fence by the baseball diamond, a volcanic rumbling in his stomach. The ground spins. He grabs the chain link with his trembling fingers and leans over, vomiting into the weeds. He sinks to his knees.

A CO approaches.

"You need to go to medical?"

James half turns, leaning against the fence. “No, sir.” He wipes his mouth with the back of his hand. “I’m okay.”

“You don’t look okay,” the CO says. He walks away.

That night James lies on his bunk, earplugs muting the sounds of the cellblock noise. How had he not remembered the bits of brain and skull? The glistening brain chunks are gray and have the gelatinous consistency of pudding. The bone fragments look like broken pieces of an off-white plate that smashed on the asphalt. Is this image a true memory or one manufactured in his mind?

To calm himself, he tries to imagine a happy scene. He thinks of Spike, but he sees him bleeding from three bullet holes in his side. He remembers passing the baseball with Pops in the park, but in his mental picture, Pops winces with back pain when throws the ball. Mama brings to mind the sadness of her death. He feels bereft of good images.

During his sleep James grinds his teeth so hard that the next morning his jaw is sore.

527

James has been considering a self-help group he heard about on the yard, and seeing Black Snake's face reflected in the punching bag gives him the push he needs. The only requirement is a willingness to openly discuss his crime. The group is called CAPE—Changing Anger to Positive Emotions.

At the first meeting, thirty inmates plus three graduates of the program and two outside facilitators sit in a circle of chairs in a room in the education building. One of the outside facilitators is an Asian woman with spikey hair who wears purple-framed glasses. Her name is Lark. The other is Fidel, a huge Hispanic guy with shoulder-length black hair. He wears black slacks and a black T-shirt. They go around the circle, and each inmate states his name and how many years he's been incarcerated. Lark writes down the numbers and adds them up. The group is named for the total number of years served: 527.

One of the graduates of the program offers a testimony. He is Big Chuck, a dark-skinned Black man with a full beard. He rises from his chair, looks around at the group, and says, "I shot and killed my wife. In my year doing CAPE, I had to confront not just my crime, but I had to dig back in my life to understand why I did my crime. I grew up seeing my father and my uncles abuse women. I had to learn how that toxic masculinity infected me—because I let it—and led me to do violence against my wife. I learned this: hurt people hurt people. The hardest part was to see and to say that I had been hurt. I didn't want to admit that. I had been hurt by the things I saw. We look backwards so we can move forwards. That's what this program is about."

Lark folds her hands in a prayerful gesture and thanks him.

Fidel thanks him.

The 527 tribe meets once a week. Some of the men remain wary. It's hard for them to unearth their buried feelings, to share their pain, to hear the feelings of others. *Feelings* is a hurt zone, and they don't want to go there. They don't know how to express feelings in words. Shouts or groans would be easier. Or just hitting something. Which is how some of them ended up in prison. James thinks about hitting the punching bag. He thinks about shooting Black Snake.

Lark asks the group members about their emotions as if they are physical pains. "Where do you feel it?" she asks, tapping her chest. "What does it feel like?"

One member answers that he feels it in his throat. Another says his stomach, like a tight knot. The facilitators have in their tool chest yoga poses, breathing exercises, meditation techniques, visualizations. Inmates are asked to see themselves committing their crimes. "Don't run away from your feelings," Fidel says. "You have to sit in the fire with it. Yes, it hurts, but you have to do it. Let the fire burn away what needs to be burned away."

Lark talks about trigger moments—the instant in which anger bubbles up like the lava of a volcano and explodes. Fidel says that most crimes are expressions of anger.

"Think about your crime," Lark says. "How much time elapsed between the anger and acting out?"

They go around the room. Most times are short: an hour, a day, ten minutes, two seconds.

James has been thinking about this since the day of his punching bag experience on the yard. "Five seconds," he says.

Lark nods and says, "Will you tell us about those five seconds and what surrounded them? This is what we all need to understand. What happened between the moment of rage and the moment of acting out? Or, for some of you, between the moment of craving and the moment of giving in to alcohol or drugs."

James describes the incident—the shooting of Spike, knocking Black Snake to the ground, then jamming the gun in his mouth and pulling the trigger three times. There's a mantra around the prison when guys talk about their crimes: *I made bad choices.* James has no memory of a choice. It is as if his mind went blank and his body acted on its own. But that's not possible. A body cannot act on its own.

Fidel asks where it started. James tells about the times Black Snake stole his money, pushed him into his locker and gave him a fat lip, broke his watch, jerked his ear. James says, "It wasn't the money, or the broken watch. It was the humiliation. He robbed me of my dignity. And then he did it to Spike. If he'd just killed Spike, I don't think I would have shot him. When he laughed and insulted Spike for shitting himself, I went off."

"What was it about that? If he said the dog was ugly, would you have reacted the same way?" Fidel asks.

"No, I don't think so. But he made fun of Spike's vulnerability, mocked him for shitting himself while he was dying. He made fun of his weakness. That's what I hated."

Fidel says, "That anger, do you feel it now?"

"Yes," James says.

"Where?"

"In my whole body. But especially my hands. They're shaking right now. I still want to kill the motherfucker. I want to rip his fucking face off." After a beat he adds, "I'm glad I shot him. I'm glad I blew his head off."

"It's good you're opening up, Brother. Thank you. Sit in the fire with these feelings. You're digging deep. But you're just beginning. You have a lot of work ahead."

The weeks pass. James likes it all. He's been hungry for this kind of communication—truthful and deep—since he first moved to Oakland. Now that he is expressing himself, the numbness afflicting him since Mama's death begins to ease. He wants to tell Mama and Pops that he's feeling better. Or at least feeling more alive. He wants to tell them that they should not worry about him anymore.

Fondoolah

Fondoolah is a term James hears from the brothers at San Quentin. It means to elevate something, to add style. Someone says it's a Cajun word. Someone else says Rasta. One inmate, talented with needle and thread, re-tailors his prison blues into a sleek fit. He has an iron and shoe polish in his cell and he never walks across the yard without a razor-sharp crease in his blue pants and a mirrored shine on his shoes. He's a walking lesson that no matter how grim, the world through which a man moves can always be enhanced in some way. Guys see him and think, *Fondoolah*.

Another inmate decorates his cell walls with murals. He uses panels made from cardboard boxes that he draws on with colored chalk. Walking past his cell, one would think he has a picture window looking onto a meadow of cows in the Swiss Alps.

James remembers Oakland, those who wore fancy styles, gold neck chains, and big rings. At the time, James disliked their style; it was materialistic and crass. Bling. They were Felix Mitchell wannabees. They were part of the evil that killed Pops. He realizes now that his contempt for them lacked understanding. It lacked generosity. They were adding style. Better Fondoolah than death.

Get Busy

One day in the 527 group, a younger guy, Jamal, talks about how for his whole life he felt deep inside himself something that he kept hidden.

Lark does not ask what the feeling was. She asks where it was.

"In my stomach," Jamal says, pressing his fist to his midsection. "From the time I was a little kid. When one of the other boys trampled an old lady's flowers just to be doing it. Or threw a rock at a kitten. I didn't want that shit to happen, but I went along. Later on, when we broke into a candy machine or stole from somebody's house, I felt sick in my stomach. But the more I felt it, the more I tried to be hard, to be gangsta. I did bad things to prove I was bad." He starts to sob. "It tore me up."

Fidel says, "Thank you, brother, for showing us the way. You're sitting in the fire—as we all must. This is what we're trying to get back to. No one is born armed and dangerous. We're trying to reach that core of goodness we all had before we got fucked up. It's still in there. Some call it God. Some say Allah. Some say Jah. Some say human nature. We just have to find it."

On a wet, winter day the members of 527 walk across the yard in a hard rain to be here. They sit in a circle. Under the lights in the room, raindrops glisten on their shoulders and on their hats. Their shoes leave puddles on the concrete floor. Fidel says, "If you took someone's life, stand up please."

Chairs squeak. About half of the men in the circle, James among them, stand.

"Thank you. Sit back down, please."

He slowly walks back and forth and then stops.

"These words are for you who took a life. What's the worst

thing about death? It's the end of possibility. When you're alive, no matter how shitty things may be, there's always tomorrow. But death is the end. No more tomorrows."

Fidel pauses, looking down at the floor.

"The person you killed might have been an innocent victim. Wow. Hang your head for that, brothers. Or they might have been the most vicious gang banger around, and maybe you believe they deserved to die. But if they had lived, they might have turned themselves around. They never got the chance. You killed that chance, brothers. Whether they were innocent or vicious, you ended their possibility. You have to sit in the fire with that."

He pauses, looks down and then up. "I know it's hard, and I know it hurts. I know it because I took a life, too."

The silence in the room is absolute. James watches Fidel.

"We stole their possibility. But we've still got ours. That means we're carrying the responsibility for two lives of possibility—ours and theirs. We've got to do good in the world for both ourselves and our victim. That's a great burden. But it's also an opportunity. We can't just sit here and feel the crushing weight of burden. We have to pick up any chance we can find. We have to get busy."

James walks back to his cell remembering his boyhood feeling that since Mama could have no more children, he had to become something for his unborn siblings as well. Now he can add Black Snake to his duty. It's the kind of weight that might crush a person, but as he walks toward his cell block, what he feels is challenged.

His Own Story

When James listens to the guys in Tribe 527, he compares their stories to his own. James grew up with fewer troubles than anyone in his tribe. A White guy was given the nickname "Pig Face" by his father. A Hispanic guy was whipped with an electrical cord by his own mother. A Black guy from Arkansas saw three White racists drag his cousin behind their pickup truck; his body parts were found the next morning being eaten by vultures along a stretch of gravel road. Many did not have fathers and some did not have mothers, raised instead by grandmothers, aunts, or cousins. Some lived in foster homes. Many had unemployed, addicted, or incarcerated parents. Some had relatives in gangs, and many joined gangs themselves. They dropped out of school. Some went hungry or lived on the streets as kids. A Cambodian fled the Khmer Rouge with his family when he was five, and when his father was caught and decapitated, he continued running with his mother. One of the White guys says, "We was White trash in my town. Everybody thought of me like that." A Hispanic inmate says, "Nobody told me how I was supposed to be. I had to figure it out by myself and I got it all wrong."

James feels shamed. By contrast, he had a safe and comfortable life until he was thirteen. His parents took care of him and taught him right from wrong. Even after Pops' death, he and his mother managed okay in a rough part of Oakland. She loved him. She had a secure job. They sat at the kitchen table together every night and ate a good meal. James wore clean clothes. For over three years he was blessed with the friendship of a great dog. As a Black teenager, he was able to find summer jobs. He graduated high school with good grades and was about to start college. All that, and in less than a minute, he fucked up his life. By that measure, he is the worst failure in the group.

When he tells this to the tribe, Fidel says, "Everyone's journey is different. One person will have the hardest journey with the most pain. Another person's journey is less hard. Everything you said is true—others had it worse. But our suffering is not a contest. Everyone's pain is priceless. It doesn't matter if the pain is level ten or level one. What matters is not your journey backward but your journey forward. What matters is your journey to who you're going to be."

The 527 group doesn't work for everyone. As the months pass, their number falls. A few stop showing up. One night a White guy named Judd blows up during a meeting and shouts, "I don't want to sit in no fucking fire. I've lived my whole goddamned life in a fire. This is bullshit. I am out of here." He picks up his chair, slams it to the floor, and stalks out. The metallic bang echoes outside the room, and a CO appears in the door. Fidel says, "No problem, officer. Just some emotion coming out. It's all good."

When their one-year graduation date is a month away, only eighteen of the original thirty remain. James has found the group inspiring. This is what church should be like. But he knows that while eighteen have graduated in this year's class, the prison population is over four thousand.

Their assignment for the next meeting is to write a letter to their victim. James writes at the top left of the page, "Black Snake," and under it today's date, "June 9, 2012."

A week later, the rest of the page remains blank.

College

When James first entered Tehachapi, he thought constantly about his eventual parole, but after a year or two he pushed it out of his mind. In the 527 tribe, there is so much talk about looking forward that he is once again thinking about parole. He should come up in eight years, 2020, so he's three-fourths there. The work done in 527 makes him feel that he's served out whatever years he owed. He needs to make something of his possibility as well as Black Snake's possibility—which he took away. He's turned a corner and now he wants to resume his life. He's overdue to leave.

There is a two-year college program at San Quentin, and knowing it will strengthen his parole application, James enrolls. It will also give him another chance at college work that he blew over twenty years ago. The classes meet in the education building, and in his first semester he takes English 101. Inside the classroom, he almost forgets he's in prison. Without the distractions of high school kids misbehaving, the classroom has a sense of purpose. Though he has loved reading during the years he's been in prison, and his list now totals 385 books, it's an added dimension to discuss literature with others, to consider the teacher's comments, and to write his own interpretations.

Though he read *The Odyssey* when he was at Tehachapi, it takes on new meaning now. While Odysseus is heroic for his courage and his skill with weapons, what James admires most about him is the power of his mind—his craftiness and his self-control. James argues this in a paper he writes, citing as examples Odysseus' tying his men to the bellies of rams to escape the Cyclopes' cave and plugging his men's ears with beeswax so they can't hear the Sirens. He loves the scene where Athena chides him for always being the trickster, never dropping his guard. Odysseus would have been well equipped to survive in prison. James feels him a kindred spirit. The instructor tells them that the Greek term describing Odysseus is *polytropos*, a word with a double meaning: much turned and much turning. James in his life has been much turned. He needs to become someone who does the turning. That means making parole.

In his third year of the college program, James takes a class in memoir writing. He paints word pictures of Pops dancing to Motown records, Spike tilting his head to sounds in the building, seeing the ocean for the first time with Keesha. Eventually he writes of the day he shot Black Snake. There's a new tutor, a high school teacher from Berkeley named Allison. When he shows her his piece about shooting Black Snake, she tears up about Spike. She doesn't think James is a monster. She looks at him like he's a human being.

James meets with Allison every week. She's slim and plain-looking, married to a woman. She's good at pointing out ways to improve his writing, but more than that, she seems to really take in what he writes. He feels at ease with her. She's on his mind when he writes his memoir pieces. He feels he is writing them for her to read.

The instructors in the program are great, most of them grad students at Berkeley or retired teachers. But they teach twenty students. What he loves about Allison is that they meet one-on-one, so whatever she says, she says solely to him, and whatever he says, he says to wholly to her.

Part Seven

Lockers

When Allison walks in the door, Meagan is squeezing limes for margaritas. After a relaxing summer in Berkeley, this is their first day of faculty meetings, Meagan in her school in San Francisco and Allison in her new girls' school on the peninsula.

Allison gives Meagan a hug from behind and asks, "Was your day as bad as mine?"

"However bad yours was," Meagan says, "mine was worse. The new thing this year is that the administrators—none of whom teach, of course—are speaking a new language. I call it *edu-babble.* We have a new academic dean who reads all the latest books. Naomi. Who the hell names their kid Naomi?"

Allison says, "The weirdest part of my day was not in the meetings."

"Ice or no ice?" Meagan asks.

"No ice."

"What was the weirdest part?" Meagan asks.

"The sixth graders got their locker assignments, and there was a flurry of activity—not from the girls, but from their mothers decorating their lockers."

"Like welcome signs or something?"

"No. They were decorating the insides of the lockers. With very high-end contact paper. The kind we couldn't afford for our kitchen cabinets. They had brought yardsticks and scissors. One mother dropped an f-bomb because she mis-measured and had to start over. Some had patterned paper for the sides and back of the lockers and a complimentary solid color for the shelves. They were giving the side-eye to the other mothers and trying to make theirs the best. I don't even know what word I'm looking for, but is that just weird or what?"

"Helicopter parent," Megan says.

"Worse. Helicopters just hover and watch. This was doing-for. I felt like an anthropologist observing some exotic culture."

"You were," Meagan says, passing her a margarita. "Where were the girls?"

"A few were watching. The others were off somewhere."

"These mothers don't work?"

"That's the other thing. I heard one of them say she had to get back to her office for a meeting."

Meagan says, "I have to get the sociology right here. Is this because it's California, or rich people, or the weird times we're in. Or all three?"

"Don't know," Allison says. "But I'm in some kind of shock."

They sit at the kitchen table and clink their glasses. Meagan takes a sip of her margarita and smacks her lips.

"Tell me about Naomi," Allison says.

"Oh, Jesus," Meagan begins. "It was a PowerPoint, of course, and she had made this conceptual map, as she called it. Different sized circles in a variety of colors with lines connecting them. Both the circles and the lines were labeled."

Meagan pulls an index card from her pocket. "To amuse myself, I wrote down her buzzwords: metrics, interface, move the needle, lean in, deliverables, value-added, deep dive, empower, experiential, visionaries. And get this: we're no longer teachers. We're facilitators of learning."

"How were the teachers reacting?"

"A lot of the younger faculty were lapping it up. Some of the veterans, too. *The kiss-ass caucus*, I wrote on my card. But others seemed to be voting no with their faces. I saw some subtle eye rolls. Slightly furrowed brows. My favorite was Mr. Robertson, the old not-a-team-player English teacher, whose face became so still I thought he had turned to stone."

"You were really noticing all of this," Allison laughs.

"It was more interesting than watching the PowerPoint. You know what else I noticed? There are some darn good teachers there, and from listening to students last year, I kind of know who they are. There was a high correlation between being one of the master teachers and having a stink-face during Naomi's presentation."

Allison sips her margarita and says, "Those words you wrote down—what's weird is I'm hearing them at my new school. Some today, in fact. Is there some vast conspiracy among private schools creating this stuff?"

"Oh, and afterwards, we broke up into groups and wrote specific ideas about how we would implement the colored circle terms in our teaching—sorry, in our facilitation of learning. We wrote ideas on Post-It notes and stuck them on the walls. Then we milled around and read everyone's notes. During that part I looked out the window and saw Mr. Robertson getting into his car. I'm developing a new appreciation for cranky old men."

Special Admits

Allison's mantra is that every student can succeed—especially in math, where some girls have strong doubts about their abilities. By the end of the first semester, three out of her thirty freshman math students are testing her belief. All three of them fail the semester exam and one scores twenty percent. This is a mystery to be solved.

Allison walks to the admin office and looks at their files. Two have very low scores on the math aptitude section of the entrance exam, and one has no record of taking the exam at all—strange for a school so selective it accepts only forty-percent of its applicants. That night, Allison searches the parents of the three students on the internet and finds that all are CEOs, one of them on the *Forbes* list of wealthiest Americans.

The next day at lunch she walks out of the cafeteria with one of the older teachers, Alice Jones, who is a member of the admissions committee. Allison mentions the test scores of the three students and asks whether wealth plays a role in admissions.

"Ah," Alice says. "The dirty little secret of private schools. Colleges, too, of course."

"Really?" Allison says.

"In the admissions committee, there are a few applicants that we don't vote on. Don't even discuss their applications. They're called 'institutional admits.' The number seems to increase year by year. This past year there were seven. For a class of sixty."

"People don't know about this?" Allison asks.

"It's not something we put on the website. Besides, people don't want to know."

"What if the students can't pass?"

"They'll pass. It may take a team of tutors and expensive

psychologists stipulating that they need special accommodations on tests, but they will pass. They will pass, they will be admitted to good colleges, and they will earn diplomas. Well—receive diplomas."

Allison is flabbergasted, and it must show.

"If they're in trouble, just tell the dean. He'll take care of it."

Sorority News

Once a year Allison receives a newsletter from her sorority at Purdue. She ignores the appeal for money and scans the alumnae news. This year an item catches her eye. Mary Henderson, a girl one class below her, has announced her marriage to Laura Smith of Louisville. Their wedding was held in Stowe, Vermont. At first Allison wonders if it's a misprint, but then she remembers reading that gay marriage is legal in Vermont.

Though Allison did not know Mary well, she remembers no hints that Mary was gay. Mary was a French major and took her junior year abroad, so she would have been away when Allison was a senior. While Allison feels happy for Mary, she is disturbed by the empty shell of a missed opportunity. She wonders if Mary felt as alone in the house as she had, surrounded by talk—about clothes, dating, birth control, and the psychology of college boys—that assumed everyone in their sorority house was straight. She can't remember if Mary had ever dated. There were about fifty girls in the house. How many of them were gay? Maybe she and Mary were the only two. Maybe there were more. What would the world be like, Allison wonders, if they all knew one another's true stories? She regrets that she didn't simply tell hers—what better way to invite the stories of others? She feels a wistful wish that she could turn back the clock and relive her college years as an out-lesbian.

The Wedding

After the passage of Prop 8 bans gay marriage in California, the issue bounces around in the courts and legislature until the final victory of same-sex marriage in California in 2013. Two years later, in June of 2015, the Supreme Court legalizes same-sex marriage in all fifty states.

Along the way, Allison and Meagan participate in some marches and rallies. They sign petitions. When the issue is finally settled in favor of gay marriage, it is Allison who says, "I want to be married."

Meagan responds, "Oh, Alli. We're already married in our hearts, so let's make it official. Rings and a cake and all the rest."

They want their wedding to be intimate: the four parents, Meagan's brothers and two best friends from college, and Gene. Each invites a couple of colleagues from their schools.

In California, anyone can be certified as a one-time wedding officiant, so Allison and Meagan choose Gene. They write their own ceremony, pieces of prose and poetry expressing what they feel about life, love, and one another.

On a sunny July afternoon, Allison and Meagan are married in their back yard. A clean, cool wind blows in from the bay. They both wear simple dresses from J. Crew, each holding a bouquet of violets. Their cake is chocolate. Allison feels like a circle has been completed.

Rupa

Walking from school to the commuter train one afternoon, Allison sees one of her students sitting on the bench at a bus stop. It is Rupa, a student in her freshman English class. Allison is struck by Rupa's aura of solitude, as melancholy as an Edward Hopper painting. Allison starts to call out and wave, but she doesn't want to disturb the tableau.

Rupa is a scholarship student, the daughter of an immigrant mother, her father not around. She has bowl-cut hair, and a look that is half waif and half tomboy. She rarely speaks in class, and when Allison gently calls on her, she seems to shrink into herself. It's not hard to see that she feels out of place. It's not that the other students are cold or standoffish, but they don't hide their ski vacations, their trips abroad, the expensive cars that shuttle them to school, their perfectly straight teeth, the glint of good fortune in their eyes. They would not, for example, be found waiting alone for a bus.

This is Rupa's first year in a private school, and her writing is uneven. But between her comma splices and her disjoined paragraphs are flashes of soulful insights into a novel or a poem, and Allison highlights these with praise.

Allison boards the train still carrying the image of Rupa alone on the bench. As an introvert herself, Allison is drawn to loners, and she feels for Rupa. She wants her to grow.

The Stumble

On the day that Allison introduces some Emily Dickinson poems to her freshman class, Rupa springs to life as if a switch has been flipped. Rupa volunteers to read "I'm Nobody" aloud, and in the discussion she shows a kinship for the Dickinson poems. Allison credits Emily Dickinson and the soulful solitude from which she writes.

One morning before class, Allison is writing on the board when a student bursts into her room and says, "Rupa OD'ed. Can you come?"

Allison grabs her bag and follows the student to the restroom where Rupa is sitting on the floor, her teeth clenched and her fists pressed to her chest. She has snorted meth and fears she might have overdosed. Her face is flushed and she is hyperventilating. Allison pulls out her phone and calls 911. She sends the student to the driveway to wait for the paramedics. She kneels beside Rupa and holds her hand. When they hear the siren, Rupa says she's scared. Allison rubs her back between her shoulder blades and tries to reassure her.

Two paramedics enter and set their case on the bathroom floor. They listen to Rupa's heart and check her blood pressure. The paramedic asks what she took, and she tells him it was a line of meth but that she didn't drip.

"Bigger line than usual?" he asks.

"I'm not sure," she says. "Maybe."

"We have to transport you," he tells her.

Dave Block, the dean of students, arrives as they're strapping Rupa onto the gurney. Rupa looks at Allison and asks her to come.

"That okay?" Allison asks the paramedic. He nods.

In the ambulance, the paramedic starts an IV. The monitor shows that her pulse is 140.

"Am I in trouble?" Rupa asks in a muffled voice, the oxygen mask over her face.

"No," Allison smiles. "The new policy, remember? Your friend came to ask for help. You won't be in trouble."

The policy was adopted at the beginning of the school year after an in-service day on combatting student drug abuse. Head of school Janet Blake announced that the school would adopt the package of recommendations, consistent with the *We Do It All* theme on the school website. One of the recommendations was a school pledge than any student who comes forward for herself or another student to ask for help with drugs will be immune from disciplinary action.

Allison waits outside the emergency room until a physician appears and says that Rupa will be fine. She had a moderate overdose likely compounded by a panic attack. Rupa's mother arrives, an Indian woman with kind but frightened eyes. She is wearing a green sari. Allison says some reassuring words to her and then calls a cab.

Back at school, Allison taps lightly on Janet's glass door. Janet waves her in, and by the time Allison closes the door Janet is standing at her desk, spitting the question, "Do you know they've already heard about this over at the Thomas School?"

Allison remains silent, trying to grasp what she just heard.

"I've already talked to the police," Janet fumes. "For God's sake, I hope they don't tell the news media it was meth." Meaning, apparently, that meth suggests the ghetto and the trailer park. Upper-class cocaine would have been preferable.

"I thought you might want to know how Rupa is," Allison says evenly. "She's going to be okay."

Janet looks at her blankly. Then there creeps into her face the suspicion that Allison is judging her—her!—who heads the school.

"I have a class to teach," Allison says, and leaves the office.

Their hatred for one another is permanent.

At home Meagan listens to Allison's story and says, "Here's a riddle. What's the difference between a for-profit and a non-profit institution?"

"I don't know," Allison says.

"There isn't any!" Meagan shouts. "And it's driving me crazy. On the surface everything is the high ideals of education, but you dig deeper and it's all about money. And appearance—which translates into money. My school's as bad as yours."

Rupa enters a juvenile halfway house for a month, after which no charges will appear on her record. Allison visits her twice a week after school, making sure she keeps up with her reading and writing assignments.

"Meth gave me a real boost," Rupa confides to Allison on the second visit. "I felt energized. For the first time all year, I felt confident to talk in class." She looks down. "Of course, I know now that drugs are a dead-end street." She presses her lips together and then looks at Allison and says, "When I get back, I hope I can be a better student the natural way."

The care Allison feels for Rupa swells in her chest.

Snookered

The week before Rupa's release from the halfway house, Allison is called into Janet's office. Dave Block is also there.

Janet says, "Dave and I had a conference with Rupa and her mother and we agreed it would be better for Rupa to transfer. She will start public school next week."

Allison is flabbergasted. "I just saw her two days ago. She was looking forward to coming back."

Janet shakes her head. "Public school is better for her."

"Why is it better?" Allison asks.

Janet looks at her with feigned patience. "It will be a better fit, Allison."

"I don't agree. She was progressing here."

"By taking meth on school grounds?" Janet asks, her eyebrows arched.

"There's an old proverb," Allison says. "Sometimes a stumble prevents a fall. This was Rupa's stumble. I think she's on the right track now."

"She's lucky she didn't get sent to juvenile detention for a year," Janet says. "Besides, if this is the way she pays us back for her scholarship, she shouldn't be here anyway."

Allison says, "What about the school policy of no disciplinary action if students ask for help? Her friend came to me that morning. She asked for help. And now Rupa's being expelled."

Janet looks to Dave, as if to cue him.

"She wasn't expelled," Dave says.

"What do you call it?" Allison asks loudly.

"She was counseled out," Dave says, raising his chin.

"Sounds like a euphemism for expulsion," Allison says.

“Hold on, now,” Dave says.

“It’s better for Rupa,” Janet says. “That’s how she feels. Her mother, too.”

If it’s what Rupa and her mother want, there’s nothing more Allison can say. The meeting ends.

The next week, Allison stops by Rupa’s apartment to deliver some graded papers. It’s a long two-story building that looks like a motel. They sit in aluminum lawn chairs on the small balcony, the hum of freeway traffic audible from half a block away. Rupa has started in the public school and hit the ground running, doing homework and learning other students’ names. “The homework is a lot easier,” she tells Allison, “but I wish I could have stayed.”

“But you wanted to go to the public school, right?” Allison asks.

“Not really,” Rupa replies.

“I thought it was your choice,” Allison says.

Rupa shakes her head. “They pushed me out the door. Even Mom asked if I could stay.”

“And they said no?”

“Ms. Blake said it wasn’t a good idea.”

“I’m really sorry, Rupa.”

Rupa squints and says, “Yeah, I think I could have made it there. You know, getting back on the horse after I fell off.”

By the time she gets home, Allison is livid.

“Janet Blake fucking lied to me,” she tells Meagan, slamming her books on the kitchen table. “The head of the goddamned school told me a deliberate lie. I’d like to shoot her.”

“Didn’t she know you’d talk to Rupa?” Meagan asks.

“Probably not. *She* never talks to students. Why would she believe anyone else does?”

“That’s really shitty,” Meagan says.

"As my dad would say, I got snookered. I should have put up a fight that day in her office. It was stupid of me not to see what was happening. I really let Rupa down. My mission is to help people by being courageous and smart. I had a chance to fight for her and I blew it. I was cowardly and dumb."

Meagan puts her arms around Allison in a gentle hug.

"Nancy Drew would be ashamed of me," Allison says.

The next time Allison sees Janet on campus, she turns her head. She feels that if she has to look at her, she might spit in her eye. Allison's sense of her own failure does not fade. It lodges in her chest like a hot coal of shame.

Her Father's Shame

During her spring break, Allison flies to Indianapolis to visit her parents. At the end of the week, Allison tags along with her dad to the supermarket. It's going to be Allison's last night, and he wants to broil steaks on his grill. In the parking lot they see Harriet Morton, her mother's friend of many years, who hurries over to greet them. She is wearing a pants suit the color of raspberry sorbet and a white turtleneck. Her mode of relating to others is to gush.

"Why hello, Cliff. And your very lovely daughter Allison, who I haven't seen in the longest time. California, right?"

"Hello, Mrs. Morton," Allison says, smiling politely. "Yes, Berkeley." Harriet Morton shakes Allison's hand and instead of letting it go, she holds Allison's fingers up for display and says, dropping her chin in mock coyness, "And what's this?" She brushes Allison's gold band with her thumb. "Are you married?"

From her dad Allison hears a nervous staccato laugh, and she replies, "Yes, last July."

"My goodness. Who's the lucky man?" Harriet says, a teasing lilt in her voice.

Allison smiles softly and opens her mouth to say it's a lucky woman, but before she can utter the first word, her dad interrupts, "A boy she met at Purdue, Harriet. Good to see you. We have to run."

With his hand on her elbow, he steers Allison in the direction of their car, leaving Harriet standing in front of the store.

Her dad wrinkles his nose and says, "People like her—it's just best to, you know...Harriet likes to gab. We'd be there all day. Your mother needs these groceries."

He picks up the pace of his walk, but hers slows. He looks

back, his face red. He knows he's been caught.

As he pulls out of the parking lot, he mistakes the windshield wiper lever for the turn signal. The windshield is sprayed with wiper fluid.

In the car Allison's silence is stony, and he adds, "I accept it, of course, but you never know about other people."

It is a betrayal. If he were truly accepting, he would not only defend Allison but shout from the rooftops: *My daughter is a lesbian and has a wife, and if you don't like it, go fuck yourself.*

That evening, the terrible scene replays in her mind: her father blurting out that she's married a guy from college, cowering before Harriet Morton and all she represents. Or possibly represents. For all they knew, Harriet might have overflowed with congratulations. Allison feels sick—sick that her father is so weak, so lacking in courage, so lacking in heart. It's not just that he didn't stand up for the cause; it's that he did not stand up for her. She will never forget this day.

On Sunday, he drives her out to the airport. Allison can't wait to be back in Meagan's arms. Halfway there, he clears his throat and says, "I'm sorry about that business with Harriet Morton. I didn't handle that well."

She looks out the window and says, "Don't worry about it." She doesn't mean it, and she doesn't try to animate her voice to convince him that she does. At the airport, her goodbye hug is short and stiff.

From her old bedroom Allison has slipped into her tote one of the Nancy Drew novels, and she opens it on the plane. Aspects are familiar. Nancy Drew's friend George, the tomboy with a boy's name, is solidly butch. Bess is ultra-feminine and fearful, prone to spraining her ankle when danger is present. Nancy herself transcends any role with her smarts, her courage, and her determination. Crooks, kidnappers, and forgers cannot deter her. She exudes a subtle but strong sense of authority. She's also gay, no doubt about it. Allison smiles to herself for the first time today.

Still, the writing is formulaic and the Nancy Drew on the pages is less than the Nancy Drew in Allison's memory. Her young self must have supplied the missing parts, as if in reading those novels, she was also creating them. Nancy Drew was an outline, like a figure in a coloring book, and Allison used mental crayons to fill her in. Allison must have been Nancy Drew even before she read the books.

A New Turn

One night at the beginning of the next school year, Allison is standing at a faculty party, holding a glass of white wine, watching from across the room as three of her colleagues try to ingratiate themselves with Janet. Christina, a new colleague in the English department, approaches Allison and introduces her boyfriend Todd.

"You look so relaxed and confident," Christina says to Allison. "I feel really awkward."

"It's a ruse," Allison says. "I was just calculating how soon I could slip away without seeming rude."

Christina and Todd laugh. When Allison asks Todd about himself, he says he's a PhD candidate at Berkeley, and he's teaching a class at San Quentin prison. Allison cocks her head. There's no pay, but he finds it rewarding.

"I feel like it's keeping me sane while I write my dissertation," he says.

"Going into a prison to stay sane," Christina laughs. "That says something about dissertation writing."

Allison wants to hear more about it, so he describes what it's like. He says you need at least a master's degree to teach a class. "But they also need tutors," he says. "You don't need an advanced degree for that. You just go in one evening a week for two hours."

When she gets home, Allison visits the website, Meagan looking over her shoulder, and signs up for the next volunteer orientation. They need tutors in both math and writing. Her application is accepted, and she is scheduled to begin the first week in October.

The Gulls of San Quentin

On a cool evening, Allison enters San Quentin Prison as a volunteer tutor in the college program. She has submitted her driver's license number for security clearance, and her name is now on a list at the gate. She is wearing closed-toe shoes and modest clothing of black, white, khaki, purple, or red (blue, green, orange, and yellow being prohibited). Her pockets are empty of money, metal, cell phones, food or drink, chewing gum, spiral bound notebooks, maps of any kind, or hardback books. Car keys, watches, and underwire bras are allowed. With five other volunteers, she shows her ID to the guard, who checks her name against the clearance list. She signs the entry ledger and has her wrist marked with a UV stamp. A second guard sweeps her body with a metal-detecting wand. A guard in a bullet-proof plexiglass booth hits a switch, opening the door of steel bars. She enters the sally port, and behind her the first door closes and locks with a sharp bang. She and the others show the guard in the booth their IDs. The second door pops open and the group walks onto the prison grounds. One of the volunteers jokes that it is easier to leave the prison than to enter it.

Leaving *is* easier. The volunteers walk to the gate, hold up IDs, pass through the two gates of the sally port, sign out, flash their IDs to the gate guard, and show their wrists under the UV lamp. They walk down a sidewalk, administrative buildings to their left and San Francisco Bay to their right. At the outer gate they again hold up IDs and the guard waves them through.

On this first visit, Allison wonders how an inmate might escape. It is her first time in a prison, and the question engages her problem-solver mind. When she walks across the prison grounds and sees the forty-foot walls, the spirals of razor wire, and the imposing guard towers, she muses that there are only two ways to escape without being shot, and both were used by Odysseus. One is by disguise (the beggar in the palace) and the other is by hiding (Odysseus' men clinging to the bellies of the giant sheep to escape the Cyclopes' cave). She does not know that she will one day devise an escape plan. She does not know that she will put the plan into action. For now, it is just a thought experiment, a challenge for a woman whose childhood heroine was the girl sleuth.

The group reaches the education building, a structure that looks like a metal barn. There are four tutors, two in math and science and two in English. A grid is drawn on the whiteboard and inmates sign up for twenty-minute slots. Allison lists herself under both English and math. Her first tutee is a middle-aged man named James, dark brown skin, dreadlocks, a do-rag, and a beard. He wears glasses with black frames.

He sits down and says, "You're new."

She nods. "First night."

"Nervous?" he asks, raising his eyebrows.

She considers. "A little. Just because it's new."

"We're harmless," he says. "Me—I'm in for felony jaywalking."

"And misdemeanor lying," she adds.

He laughs softly and points a finger at her. "Good one. You're quick." Then he says, opening his notebook, "You help with math and writing both?"

She nods.

"A jack of all trades," he says.

"Jill of all trades," she answers.

He chuckles. "I knew it. Another Berkeley feminist."

"We're taking over the world," she says.

He smiles and says, "The world needs it."

She sees his notebook. "What are you working on?" she asks.

He takes a deep breath. "This is for my writing class. Personal memoir. I need someone to read it and tell me what they think. Our teacher says there's ultimately one question in writing: *Does it work?* I want to know if this works."

See puts out her hand. There is something quietly thoughtful about him, and she likes it.

He says, "Of course, this might be fiction. I'm not saying." He hands her three handwritten pages.

"It's memoir or it's fiction," she says. "It can't be both."

He nods. "Then I confess. It's memoir."

> *The End of Spike*
>
> *When I was in high school, I had a dog named Spike. He meant a lot to me. He had been through hell, and I hadn't been doing too great myself. I loved him, and he loved me. Some people think dogs and people can't love each other, but I know better.*
>
> *One foggy day Spike and me were in the park. We saw this kid named Black Snake. More like he saw us. He was back from juvie, which is prison for people too young to go to prison. Black Snake and I had history. Before he got sent up, he had bullied me bad. The last time I saw him, he tried to rob me. Spike was with me and bit him hard on the hand. He didn't rob me that day! That was three years earlier.*
>
> *He comes out of the fog like a ghost and sees us. He looks at Spike and says, "I remember him." Out of nowhere he pulls a gun. Pop-pop-pop. Spike yelps and falls over, blood running from three holes in*

his side. His legs jerk like he's trying to run away. It must have hurt so bad. I try to put my hands over the holes, but the blood keeps coming. Spike whimpers and he looks at me like he's saying something. I think he's saying, "I'm sorry." That doesn't make any sense, but that's what I felt he was saying—sorry I'm going to leave you. He was thinking more about me than himself. Maybe that's what love is. He whimpers some more and then he groans. I kiss his big face because I know he's going. He licks me twice and then the light in his eyes fades out. My dog is gone.

I look up. Black Snake has watched him die. He has a sneer on his face. Then he says, "Dumb dog shit himself." It was true, it came out as he was dying. Black Snake says, "He's dead meat now."

I think if he hadn't mocked and insulted Spike, things might have gone a different way. But here's what went down. I stood and walked toward him. He raised the gun and pointed it at me. In that moment I had no fear. My dog was dead. I didn't care if I got shot or not.

My fist flew out and hit him hard on the nose. I didn't even plan it. My fist just went. He fell backward and hit the ground. The gun bounced on the asphalt. I grabbed it and jumped on Black Snake's chest. I shoved the gun in his mouth. He choked and I started pulling the trigger. There were three loud shots and then just clicks. Blood poured from the back of his head and filled his mouth.

I stood up. No one was around. I walked away, like

> *I was suddenly in a dream. I felt like I had stepped off a cliff. All that was left was to fall.*

After she finishes reading, Allison stares at the page. She reaches into her pocket for a tissue and dabs her eyes.

"It works," she says.

"I never wrote anything that made someone cry," James says.

Allison clears her throat. "What's weird—what *scares* me a little bit—is that I'm not crying for Black Snake. I'm crying for Spike."

"Yeah," James says. "Same for me. To this day."

A New Commitment

When Allison arrives home after her first night of tutoring, Meagan wants to hear all about it. They brew mint tea and sit at the kitchen table.

"It was the most amazing thing," Allison begins. "The two hours went by like ten minutes." She tells Meagan about the six men she tutored, and she saves the story about James until the last.

The next day at school Allison's memories from the tutoring session replay in her mind. The men in study hall wearing their prison blues are a diverse lot. They range from their twenties to their seventies. They are Black, Asian, Brown, and White. Clutching their notebooks and pencils, they seem by turns hungry and reluctant, some limited and others oozing potential, but they all are richly, simply, themselves. Most vividly, she remembers James. He seems soulful. In some way she does not understand, she feels that they were meant to meet.

By contrast, her school and everyone in it seem anemic and half alive, as if they are photos with the color saturation dialed down. Her nights of prison tutoring become the highlight of her weeks.

One of Allison's regular tutees is an old White man who has mentioned his seminary training, though he never became a priest. He is a good writer with an Irish last name and a round, pink face with crinkles at the corners of his eyes. His hair is thick and snow white. He has a beaten-down look, and though he says he's been in for ten years, he looks like he's still at a loss to understand how he ended up here. Allison wonders if he's in for child molesting.

Overcome by curiosity, she does an internet search of his name. "Oh my God," she shouts. Meagan walks over to her desk and rests her chin on the top of Allison's head. "This sweet little white-haired man walked into a court room with a loaded gun and fired three shots at a pro-abortion judge."

"What happened?" Meagan asks.

Allison keeps reading. "He missed."

James signs up for one of Allison's tutoring slots nearly every week. Week by week, she reads his memoir pieces. She reads about the death of Pops, Felix Mitchell's funeral in Oakland, James' job with Big Mike's dogs, arriving at Tehachapi, his mother's death, his role as a writing helper for other inmates. After every reading, Allison can't wait to summarize the latest installment for Meagan, who looks forward to the weekly updates.

Allison tutors the next semester and the summer as well. James and Allison grow comfortable with one another, develop a repartee. She can tell he trusts her. He knows she has a wife, grew up in Indiana, and teaches at a private school. When she reads his pages, she sees what he sees, feels what he feels. She responds to what he has written. James has told her that he comes up for parole in five years, and she is optimistic that it will be granted.

Allison frequently tutors Richard, a slim, middle-aged Black man enlivened with bubbling energy. She helps him mostly in geometry.

One evening he tells her, "You know, at this place I'm basically cattle. Been here twenty-four years. They might as well put a hot iron right here," and he presses his fist to his forehead, "and brand me SQ. Guards tell me what to do and when to do it. Line up for this and for that. Chow, showers, mail call, get in line. Like cattle. You feel me? Guard tells me to drop my pants, bend over, and spread my butt cheeks—excuse me for saying that—I got to do it or I get a write-up. Then I come in here, to these classes..." He pauses and leans back in his chair, nods around the room and folds his arms across his chest. "I read the smartest people that ever lived. Plato, Hemingway, history, geometry. Big ideas that stretch my head. Novels that jump inside me. I get asked for my opinion. My opinion! Like it matters what I think. These people with degrees from famous colleges come in here and treat me like I am a person—a *person*, not a criminal. I may be in class only four hours a week, but it reminds me I'm a human being. It really does."

Allison believes in the organization and its mission. She develops a reputation as a dedicated and helpful tutor. At the end of every term, guys ask if she's coming back. She senses that buried deep in every inmate is a fear that the volunteers will not return, the programs will fold, their visitors will stop coming. It's part of a larger dread that the world will forget about them. Life is on the outside. What's on the inside is something else.

Allison assures them that she will be back.

Part Eight

Hamlet

In 2019, James signs up for the Shakespeare program at the prison. He's never acted nor even read Shakespeare, but the mere name *Shakespeare* has the allure of buried treasure. Since it's been his nickname since high school, maybe this is his destiny.

One foggy night in June, the fifteen inmates who have signed up sit in a circle and listen to the two leaders talk about *Hamlet*, the play they will perform in December. The director is Bunny, a petite, wiry White woman with short gray hair, glasses with oversized red frames, and a big voice. Kip, her assistant, is a young, flamboyant Black man wearing a bright yellow scarf around his neck. They give each member a copy of the script, a shortened version of the original. "It's the essential third," Bunny says. "If we do the whole play, it lasts six hours." She recites a summary of the plot.

In his cell James studies the script. At first it reads like muddy water in which there are submerged jewels, barely visible. With each reading, the water becomes less muddy, the jewels more visibly luminous. Sensing Hamlet's deep loneliness, James knows that's the character he wants to play.

He begins memorizing lines, reciting them to himself or to others on the yard. The weird language feels like something he knew long ago and forgot. The more he recites it, the more familiar it feels. On a foggy, windy evening, James says to Williams in their cell, "The air bites shrewdly."

"The air do what?"

"It is a nipping and eager air," James answers.

Williams shakes his head., "Man, you gone *way* off the deep end."

"Fie upon it," James says.

Williams pretends to yell for medical. "Man down. Needs to go to the looney bin."

A few minutes later Williams asks, "You like that Shakespeare?"

"Yeah," James says.

"That's good you do that. Better yourself. Not like so many these young punks doing the same shit got them here in the first place."

When the group learns that some of them will play women's parts, there is nervous chuckling. Kip tells them that it was done in Shakespeare's time when women were not allowed to be actors on the stage. He says, "If you're going to be in the theater, gentlemen, you have to expand your horizons." Then he adds, "And yes, I'm gay."

When a couple of the men read the lines of Ophelia or Gertrude, Bunny allows the overdramatization and the jokes. She seems to know that it will pass, and eventually it does.

When James takes a crack at the soliloquy, "What a rogue and peasant slave," Bunny claps her hands to stop him. She says with dramatic flair, "This above all. Don't *act* Hamlet. *Be* Hamlet. Search your life for times when you have felt what he is feeling. Use that." She asks if he understands.

"I'm not sure," James says. "What is he feeling?"

Pointing her forefinger at him, she says, "Have you ever felt like a coward? Or have you always been a man of courage? Think." She strokes her chin with her thumb and forefinger.

Remembering how he was bullied by Black Snake, he says, "I've lacked courage. Definitely."

She snaps her fingers and points at him again. "Forget Shakespeare for a minute. Here—" She reaches for her notebook and tears out a blank page. "Go sit over there and write a short speech beating up on yourself for being a coward."

While she's helping someone else to pronounce the words, James writes a few sentences and brings Bunny the paper. She reads what he has written and says, "No good. It's bland. Do it again. Put feeling into it, for Chrissakes. You're angry at yourself. You're disgusted. Use foul language. Call yourself a motherfucker. You're a convicted felon. Talk like one. And James—let yourself go back to that time. Don't just remember it. Relive it."

She hands him the paper. Several guys have been listening. They've never heard a White lady talk like her. Though she has raked James over the coals, something about the way she has done it makes him feel elated.

"My mother named me Bunny hoping I'd be soft," she tells them in her vibrant voice. "Nice try, Mom."

When he brings her a new version, she nods and says, "Now act it. Read from the page if you need to." When he finishes, she tells him to do it again. With more feeling. He reads again, looking up from the page more often. "Better," she says. "But still not good enough. Do it again."

By the fifth time, James is feeling rage at his fourteen-year-old self for allowing Black Snake to humiliate him so. "You little pussy," he rages. "You should have grabbed Black Snake's hand and broken his fucking fingers!"

"Okay," Bunny nods, her eyes bright. "Now take those same feelings from James and give them to Hamlet. With Hamlet's language. Because you *are* Hamlet now. Hamlet, you didn't wimp out to the neighborhood bully—you did something worse. You failed to punish the son of a bitch who poured poison into your father's ear." She hands him the script and says, "Start here and stop after 'O Vengeance.'"

She makes him do it five times. His throat is raw. He's panting like he's run five miles.

Bunny says, "So Hamlet, you have worked yourself into a frenzy." She pauses and lowers her voice. "Suddenly you realize this frenzy is all bullshit. The only thing that matters is action, and you're just spouting words. It's an abrupt about-face. A total change in emotion, from raging frenzy to quiet disgust. These abrupt changes are an actor's ultimate challenge. Start with 'Why, what an ass I am.'"

The more he reads, the more he feels he really *is* Hamlet speaking this strange language.

As everyone files out of the classroom at the end of the session, Kip brushes past James, raises his eyebrows, and whispers, "If she's hard on you, it means she believes you have potential."

Three evenings a week James hurries to the education building with his script, now filled with notes in the margins, underlined words needing stress, slashes indicating where to pause. The numbness that plagued him after Mama's death has passed. In early July, Kip posts the cast list. James gets the part of Hamlet. A Hispanic guy named Miguel is Horatio, Big Chuck is Claudius, and Habeeb—who transferred to San Quentin on the van with James—plays the ghost. A slim White guy named Jack is Ophelia, and a Black guy named Leroy plays Gertrude. An older White guy plays Polonius, and others in the group play guards. Everyone has a part.

Sometimes Bunny and Kip lead the cast in a discussion of how the play relates to life as they have known it. The guys recognize Rosencrantz and Guildenstern as snitches. Ophelia and Gertrude fail to be down broads. King Claudius murders King Hamlet in a pussy way; they don't like the use of poison. They can't get behind Hamlet; he's a wimp. James tries to defend him, but the other cast members aren't buying it. "Why can't he just kill the motherfucker?" Big Chuck wants to know.

"Yes," Bunny shouts, "that's why play has confounded audiences for 500 years. Why can't he? He doesn't know and we don't know. But still we ask and wonder. That's Shakespeare's genius."

Bunny tells them they are actors and must conform to the ways of the theater. They say "break a leg," not "good luck." Before rehearsals they remove their watches and neckwear. They stretch and do weird facial exercises. They sing nonsense rhymes. They chant. One evening Kip leads them in the hokey pokey. Bunny shouts, "Loosen up, God damnit!"

Kip works with them on blocking the scenes. "The audience wants to see your face, not your butt. And don't stand like trees," he tells them. "Move, gentlemen, move. Dance as you speak. Pace. Lean. Let your hands become birds at the end of a tether. You can be still when you're in your cells. On stage, move like the wind, bounce like a ball, go this way and that."

The first read-throughs are terrible. The language ties them in knots, and they stumble and falter through their lines. They forget. They start talking too early or too late. They step on one another's lines. No one in the cast, including James, believes they can pull it off.

But no day is as bad as the day before. Weeks pass. Summer becomes autumn. Rehearsals move to the chapel, where the three performances will be held. It is now dusk when they begin. They can get through their lines with minimal prompting, but there is something stiff and artificial in their delivery that bleeds the play of its life. On some nights Bunny and Kip work individually with the actors while the others listen. Bunny works with Big Chuck on Claudius' chapel scene. Built like a linebacker, he's so heavy and musclebound that it's hard for him to bend his knees to kneel.

Bunny says, "This little trick of Hamlet's means King Claudius watches a version of his own crime. He's alone now, about to pray, but he's not even sure he can, so he talks to himself aloud. A soliloquy."

Big Chuck winces from the pain in his knees, and he begins.

> O, my offense is rank, it smells to heaven;
> It hath the primal eldest curse upon't.
> A brother's murder.

Big Chuck's voice cracks just perceptibly on the word *brother*, and James realizes it's because he killed another Black man. Claudius and Big Chuck merge.

Two weeks before the production, Bunny gathers the cast into a circle before rehearsal and says, "I feel like a coach talking to a team that expects to lose. You're all wearing hangdog looks." As if the building's on fire, she yells, "Snap out of it!" She puts her hands on her hips. "What's the worst thing that can happen? You screw up. Even if opening night is worse than our worst rehearsal, so what? It means you took on one of the hardest plays in the world, a play that most directors never had the balls to do, and you didn't win a Tony. Big fucking deal." The cast members grin. She looks at them, waits a beat, and says in a serious tone, "You had the guts to try." She lowers her voice and says, "In the process, you grew." She points to herself and raises her voice. "I know you did because I saw it."

She waves her arms. "So have fun. And by the way, I believe in you."

Kip adds, "We both do."

The speech helps. The run-throughs get better. One afternoon James sees Habeeb walking along the wall intoning,

> I am thy father's spirit,
> Doomed for a certain term to walk the night
> And for the day confined to fast in fires

Till the foul crimes done in my days of nature
Are burnt and purged away.

Bunny is right. They have grown. The play has given them something to become. Like the 527 group, they have dug deep—Habeeb speaks as one who has crimes in his past, Big Chuck as Claudius has in fact killed a man, and James was a coward for too long.

James is realizing that literature is not merely a story of Odysseus or Gatsby or Bigger Thomas; it's an invitation to see reflections of oneself—as Hamlet says, a mirror held up to nature. James works hard, pacing the yard with the script, practicing his lines, learning to bring more of himself to the part. In his mind's eye, he watches a Sacramento drug dealer pour poison into his father's ear. As much as all occasions informed against James, he should have thrown a brick through the glass carriage carrying Felix Mitchell's body and told people to rise up against the bling-crazed thugs terrorizing their own communities. He should have shouted on the streets that something was rotten in the city of Oakland. He should have led a movement to gain what the community lacked—good schools, good jobs, good housing, and police who serve and protect.

Parts of the play mingle with his memories. In James' mouth, "To be or not to be" is to kill Black Snake or not, as if the act were in front of him, not behind him. When Hamlet says the deaths of Rosencrantz and Guildenstern are "not near my conscience," James knows this is his attitude toward Black Snake. When at last kills he King Claudius in Act V, he imagines making a drug lord swallow his own poison.

The Curtain Rises

When Bunny learns that some corrections officers have raised security concerns about outside guests at the *Hamlet* performances, she marches into the Warden's office with an invitation to attend the performance. She tells him she's invited a state senator and some county officials. Next month she is attending a dinner where the Governor will be present, and she intends to tell him about the production. She will see to it that in press coverage, the Warden is credited for supporting the rehabilitative effects of theater. Nothing comes of the guards' objections.

On opening night, the audience consists of other inmates. There is no curtain, so the actors sit towards the side of the first pew. Barnardo walks to the front, wheels around, and shouts, "Who's there?" James is so nervous he can barely breathe. But with his first lines, a strange calm moves over him. He feels the transcendent pleasure of being someone else.

At the first appearance of Jack and Leroy in their wigs as Ophelia and Gertrude, there are catcalls, but they die down. Kip has to prompt the actors a few times, but there are no major snafus. The audience grasps the plot and is drawn into the drama. At the end, the applause and the shouts are enthusiastic, heartfelt, and long.

On the final night of the production, the audience includes cast members' relatives, some program volunteers including Allison, donors to the Shakespeare program, the politicians that Bunny promised, and the Warden himself. The chapel is full and the air is charged. Eight COs stand against the back wall.

On this night, like the previous nights, there are some sour notes, but they are minor. Jack as Ophelia still speaks in a stiff, halting cadence as if he's a kid just learning to read. The older White guy playing Polonius soars into overdramatized, lilting sentences that make the audience uneasy. But otherwise, the cast is more relaxed as they inhabit their roles like it's their own skin. In James' performance, Hamlet's torment comes alive.

Before the production, because his mother is going to be there, Miguel asks Bunny if he may say his final line twice, once in English and again in Spanish. She says he may.

In their shortened version of the play, Hamlet's last words are his request to Horatio,

> In this harsh world draw thy breath in pain
> To tell my story.

Then Miguel as Horatio says,

> Now cracks a noble heart. Good night, sweet prince,
> And flights of angels sing thee to thy rest.

For his mother, he repeats this final line in Spanish.

> Y que coros de ángeles os canten en vuestro descanso.

There is a collective gasp from the audience just before they stand and burst into applause. The cast members stand at the front of the chapel and take their bows, then again joined by Bunny and Kip, both of whom wipe tears from their eyes. The standing ovation is long.

As everyone mingles, the excited guests gush with congratulations and praise, and the cast basks in the attention. Allison tells James that he was wonderful. He wishes that Mama could have seen it. Big Chuck asks the Warden if there's any chance they could take the show on the road. Bunny and Kip work the crowd, deflecting all of the praise of themselves onto the cast. Fifteen minutes have been allotted for socializing after the performance ends, and then the COs clear the chapel.

The guests are escorted to the gate. The cast members change back into their blues and cross the yard to their cellblocks. They chatter with excitement, though James is quiet with feeling. They are prisoners heading back to their cells, but they have also become something more, and they know it.

The Light at the End of the Tunnel

The days following the *Hamlet* production are bittersweet. With a sense of accomplishment, James bobs like a cork on the water, but the return to everyday prison life is a letdown. The ancient Greeks believed that the swan, silent during its life, sang a beautiful song just before its death. James feels that his Hamlet performance was the swan song of his twenty-nine years in prison. It's time for the death of James the inmate and his rebirth as a free man. All of his energy now focuses on making parole.

James' hearing is scheduled for February of 2020. He solicits letters of support for his efforts in the Shakespeare program, the college program, and the 527 tribe. He writes his personal statement and focuses on what he wants to do after prison, the principles by which he intends to live. He's sure he can get a job in a restaurant kitchen to start. His memories of Oakland are not good, so maybe he'll try Sacramento or Berkeley. He would like to get a dog. He might shave his beard and cut his dreads for a new look. He'll buy clothes—nothing fancy, just something other than the prison blues. Simple and basic, not Fondoolah. He'll eat healthy food. He will visit Mama's grave. He will find ways to bring some good into the world. He feels like a boy counting the weeks until Christmas.

When James tells Allison about his hearing date, they have known one another for five years. She is excited for him and shares his optimism. She and Meagan brainstorm ways they can help him establish himself once he's out. Meagan looks forward to meeting him.

On a Friday evening a week before his parole hearing, Allison and Meagan snuggle on their couch with pizza, red wine, brownies, and a movie.

"King of Masks," Allison says aloud as she looks at the DVD case. "Good reviews?"

Meagan nods. "A recommendation from Mr. Robertson. He said poignant and sweet."

"Then why are you frowning?"

Meagan massages her brow and says, "I had a disturbing conversation with Charlotte—you know, the biology teacher—at lunch today."

"Disturbing how?"

"You know that new virus in the news?"

"Yeah, Coronavirus."

"Charlotte says it's the real deal. The nightmare pathogen everyone's been fearing for decades."

"Why does she think that?"

"I don't know. But she seemed sure. She said all the signs are there. And she's not a hysterical person. She says it could be the next plague."

The Prisoner's Dilemma

In the days leading up to his parole hearing, James feels increasingly nervous. Electricity buzzes through his body. He has imaginary conversations with the parole board, rehearses what he's going to say. Twenty-nine years with no write-ups, a good work record, and successful participation in programs should count for a lot. It seems a natural progression: maximum security Tehachapi, medium security San Quentin, and then parole. His rational mind tells him that parole is very likely, but his rational mind cannot calm his doubts and fears.

On the day of the hearing, a CO walks him past the chapel and into a hallway outside the hearing room. He sits on a wooden bench holding his packet of documents in his lap. He feels rivulets of sweat run down his sides. This will be the second most consequential day of his life; the first was the day he shot Black Snake. He hasn't felt this nervous since he appeared before the judge for his plea agreement.

He remembers the TV coverage of the OJ trial. Every day Simpson wore a pressed suit, a crisp shirt, and a handsome tie. A puppy dog look of innocence on his face. James wishes he could dress like that. He worries that his baggy prison uniform sends the message that a felon is what he is and San Quentin is where he belongs. He wonders if he should have cut his dreads.

Feeling bound up by nerves, he closes his eyes and takes slow deep breaths, like Kip taught them to do in theater. Trying to think of something peaceful, he imagines the ocean, the waves spreading white froth across the hard sand while the gulls caw overhead. When he's paroled, a visit to the ocean will be near the top of his list.

He is called into the hearing room. He takes a chair facing two parole board commissioners, one man and one woman, seated at a heavy wooden table facing him. There are no VNOKs—victims or next of kin—here to witness or testify. That's a relief. He'd hate to hear from Black Snake's mother.

The first part of the hearing is devoted to pre-conviction factors, aspects of James' life or environment that may have led to his crime. James explains that the move from their nice street in Sacramento to a rough neighborhood in Oakland was hard, but that he and his mom managed. They had a good relationship, and he has good memories of living with his mom and their dog in the apartment. He avoided trouble in high school and graduated with good grades. He was just starting college classes when he was arrested.

The man says, "It looks like you've been in some worthwhile programs. You have favorable letters from your teachers in the college program. You were apparently a star in the production of *Hamlet*," he says, looking up at James with a smile.

"Thank you, sir."

"In prison, you haven't done AA or NA. Why not?"

"I never did alcohol or drugs."

"You're telling me you were a teen in Oakland in the eighties and never did alcohol or drugs?"

"That's correct. I probably had a beer three or four times, but never even finished the can. I didn't like the taste." James chuckles. "I was kind of a nerd."

The man does not smile back. "Three or four times is not really 'never,' is it?"

"Almost never," James responds.

"Did you drink one of those half cans on the days of your crimes?"

"No, sir." James wonders if they are trying to rattle him.

The woman remarks that the murder was committed two weeks before his high school graduation.

"Yes, ma'am," he answers.

"And when you were arrested, you had actually started college?"

"Yes, ma'am. By a couple of days."

"What did you do that summer?"

"I worked two jobs. McDonald's and a supermarket."

"It seems the murder didn't bother you much."

This one catches James off guard. His face burns.

"I thought about it," James offers.

She raises her eyebrows and says flatly, "You thought about it."

"Yes, ma'am."

"Walked in your graduation ceremony, did you?"

"Yes, ma'am."

"Did you go to your prom?"

James hesitates. "Yes, ma'am."

"Was that after the murder?"

"Yes, ma'am."

"How long after?"

"About a week," James says.

She frowns. "Did you have a good time at prom?"

James is nonplussed. "It was okay."

The man looks squarely at James and says, "Why did you kill him?"

James takes a deep breath and recounts how Black Snake shot Spike and then pointed the gun at James. With this, James wades into the quicksand known as the prisoner's dilemma. California policy states that admission of guilt is not a precondition for parole. That's the theory. In practice, parole boards operate on the assumption that the conviction was true and just, and the prisoner who does not exhibit full accountability and remorse has not fulfilled the suitability requirements for parole.

The man lifts a paper from his folder. "If that were true, you would have been charged with voluntary manslaughter. At most. But you were charged with first-degree murder and you pled guilty."

"Yes, I did plead guilty to that. My lawyer recommended I take the plea deal so I wouldn't receive 'life without' and get sent to someplace violent like Pelican Bay."

"Mr. Fields, you have to understand that our responsibility is to judge your suitability for parole. We can't re-adjudicate your trial. We have to accept your conviction as the truth."

James nods.

The man says, "You do not deny that you murdered Marvin Mitchell."

"No, sir. I do not deny that. I am guilty of that crime. I am very sorry for it."

"You were carrying your gun in the park."

"No, sir. It was Black Snake's gun. He pulled—"

"You knew him by his gang name?"

"I don't think it was a gang name. It's just what everyone called him. A nickname."

"Back to the gun," the man says.

"Yes, sir. He—Marvin Mitchell—pulled out a gun and shot my dog. He pointed the gun at me. Then I hit him, and the gun fell to the ground. I picked it up and shot him. But it was his gun."

"There's nothing about a dog in the police report."

"I know. But it happened."

The man holds a paper. "You shoved the gun into his mouth and shot him three times, blowing his brains out?"

The silence in the room feels like it weighs a ton. A CO is standing against the wall, and James hears his shoes creak as he shifts his weight.

James swallows. "Yes, sir. I did."

"Let's back up. Why did he walk up and shoot your dog?"

"He remembered Spike—that was my dog's name—from three years before. Spike bit him when he tried to rob me."

"You had an ongoing feud with Marvin Mitchell?"

"He had robbed me several times."

"Did you resist when he robbed you?"

"Not very much. He was bigger. And tougher. I had never faced anything like that in Sacramento."

"According to the police report, you kept a diary in which you wrote of killing the victim long before your crime."

"I didn't really mean it. I just wrote it."

"It certainly seems like you meant it. You did it," the man says. "You don't deny that you wrote that?"

"No, sir. I do not deny that." James wants to explain the journal entry, but he doesn't know how.

"Mr. Fields, some of what you are saying about the dog and the gun are not in the police report. If you tell us thirty years later than it happened a different way, we have no way to relitigate your trial—or your plea agreement. But I have to tell you,"—and here he pauses and raises his index finger—"even if we accept your account today, which contradicts the plea agreement, the questions raised about your suitability for parole are significant. You harbored resentment of this boy for several years and then one day you murdered him in a particularly heinous fashion, sticking a gun in his mouth and pulling the trigger"—he stops to shuffle through his papers—"pulling the trigger three times. According to the coroner's report, his head basically exploded. The fact that you were a good student makes it more disturbing. Inside this person who made good grades and held steady jobs, there was someone capable of sticking a gun in a boy's mouth and blowing his brains out. And then walking calmly away."

"And a few days later dancing at the prom," the woman adds.

James feels pinpricks in his face. His mouth and throat have gone dry. He swallows several times.

The woman speaks again. "Why did you shoot him in that way? Why didn't you just shoot him in the chest? Why did you stick the gun in his mouth?"

"That's just the way it happened."

In a flat voice, she repeats his words. "That's just the way it happened."

"Yes, ma'am." He wonders if he can ask for a drink of water.

"Mr. Fields, with all due respect, earthquakes *happen*. Murders are deliberate, intentional acts committed by one person against another."

James tries to answer. When he starts to speak, he makes a sound like the croak of a bird.

"Excuse me?" she says. "I couldn't hear you."

"Yes, ma'am. I know they happen."

This is the opposite of what he had meant to say, and she seizes on it. "I don't believe you understood me. I said murders do *not* simply happen. They are intentional acts."

James tries to produce some spit in his mouth. "Yes, ma'am. Intentional acts."

Each of the parole officials has a water bottle. James wishes he had brought one, too. No one told him.

The man asks, "You wrote in your personal statement that you think you might get a dog if you are paroled?"

"Yes, sir. I would like to have a dog," James answers hoarsely, relieved at the change of subject.

"What if someone harms the dog?" the man asks. "How do we know you won't blow that person's head off?"

James' mind empties. He can't think of a thing to say.

The hearing is over after an hour. Sometimes they last as long as three.

James is led back into the hallway where he slumps onto the bench. He knows he has lost. He hopes it's a one-year denial so he can try again next year.

In fifteen minutes, he is called back into the hearing room. As soon as he sits down, the man says, "Mr. Fields, we find you unsuitable for parole at this time, and we are giving you a ten-year denial." He continues talking, referring to accountability and suitability factors and the heinous nature of the crime, but James can't hear because of the roaring noise in his ears.

Worry

Meagan comes in the back door while Allison is making salad. She dumps her bag and her books onto a chair.

"God, I hate faculty meetings. We have them because the administration thinks we ought to have them, and they fill them up with nothing. Edu-babble and corporate speak. Metrics, value added. Data-driven. What are we, a freaking Google offshoot? It's like eating an air sandwich for two freaking hours and pretending you love the taste."

Allison laughs. "I bet ours are worse. Even though your descriptions are funnier than mine."

"Bet," Meagan says, slapping Allison's palm with hers. Meagan picks a piece of carrot from the salad bowl and pops it in her mouth. "I'll make the sauce," she says.

"I'm nervous about going in tomorrow evening," Allison says. "James' parole hearing was yesterday. 'Nervous' is an understatement, by the way."

Meagan begins chopping onions and mushrooms for a spaghetti sauce. She lays chicken sausages in a pan to sauté.

"When does he find out?" Meagan asks.

"He knows already. They tell them right after the hearing."

"Yikes. He's got a really good chance, though, right?"

Allison says, "*You never know*—that's the phrase they all use when parole board decisions get talked about."

"He has to get it," Meagan says. "He sounds like a model prisoner."

Bad News

When Allison walks into study hall the next evening, she writes the sign-up times on the whiteboard. She writes in James' name for the first slot even though he's not there yet. The inmates start filing in, but she doesn't see James. A couple of minutes past the start time, he walks in the door, looks at the whiteboard and then spots Allison. He walks to her table and sits hard in the chair. He looks at her and shakes his head. She looks back, horrified.

"Ten-year denial," he says.

"Jesus Christ," she whispers. "Ten years? Why?"

He tells her about the hearing, the catch-22 of not being able to tell the truth of what happened. In a way that frightens her, he looks as if the very life has drained from him. She would feel better if he were enraged. Her eyes glisten with tears, and he gives her a tight-lipped smile when he notices.

At the end of the evening, Allison erases the sign-up list from the board. James pauses beside her and says, "I don't think I've ever told you this, but I really appreciate everything you've done for me. I really do. You read every one of my memoir pieces. What is it—five years? It's meant a lot." Then he glides away.

She is moved, and then she panics. Something in the way he said it suggests a finality that frightens her. She hurries to catch up with him, but count has cleared and he is already gone.

The Lure of the Fifth Tier

James lies in his bunk thinking. Williams is snoring below him. He listens to the usual prison sounds—a key in a lock, a CO's boot-steps echoing on the concrete, inmates moaning in their sleep, an occasional angry word shouted to no one but heard by all. The roar of flushing toilets. This will be the soundtrack for the rest of his life.

He thinks about Allison, how she teared up. Not since Mama died has anyone fully felt what he felt. The guys who heard about his denial got on board with his anger and his disgust, but they didn't feel his feelings. There's too much pain in prison. Anyone who starts feeling the pain of others will collapse under the weight.

For thirty years he has survived within the fortress of his self, fending off forces that lie in wait. Now the enemy has tunneled inside, sapping his determination, his hope, his strength. Even his mind feels defeated. Nothing is left but surrender.

Lying here, his hands behind his head, he has an epiphany: the only way out is to jump from the fifth tier of the next cell block. It does not seem like an idea coming from inside his head, but from some over-voice stating what cannot be denied. Maybe it's the voice of God. It is said on the yard that hope is the one thing they can never take from you. James does not know whether hope has been taken or by whom, but he knows that hope is gone. He recalls Hamlet's words:

> How weary, stale, flat, and unprofitable
> Seem to me all the uses of this world.

He drifts toward sleep thinking that death is *devoutly to be wished.* The possibility of parole was the thin cord holding him up.

Now that it has broken, he does not want to continue life in prison. The only way out of this unbearable life is death. He wonders if there is an afterlife. Maybe he will be reunited with Spike.

Denied

James awakens the next morning with the will to take his final act. A night of sleep has changed nothing. This is not like the numbness he felt following Mama's passing. This is death. He has no life left inside. All that remains is to pull his body into that realm of endless sleep.

He uses the 527 group as an excuse at the guard station and secures a pass to West Block. He will make his way up to the fifth tier cat walk and jump to the concrete floor five levels below. It's been done before. The trick is to make sure you don't land on your feet unless you want spend the rest of your life paralyzed, lying in a bed with tubes running in and out of you. If your head or torso hits first, you'll splatter like a watermelon. It's a surer method than trying to use a cord or a belt in his cell. Were Mama alive, he would not do this because of the pain it would cause her. But no one will be seriously grieved by his death. It will save the taxpayers money. He will place his palms against his chest and fall gently forward. He will whisper, "I'm coming, Spike."

At first, he thinks he should take some time, at least look at the sky one last time. Say goodbye to the world. Write a note to Allison. Donate his savings account to some charity. He hasn't the energy. It's all he can do to put one foot in front of the other. He thinks, *To hell with it all. Let's just do this.* He's walking through a tunnel leading to his own end. He can only move forward.

He walks over to West Block feeling strangely ethereal, as if he's already left this world. He shows his pass to the gate guard, who looks at it and shakes his head. COs do that sometimes, deny an inmate something that the rules state he should have. James starts to argue, his voice shaking. He shouts and raises his arms—or the guard claims he did—and is told he'll be issued a 115 write-up for threatening behavior toward a CO. Unsuitability points for his next parole hearing. Even ten years from now, they'll bring it up. They'll say it shows he's still a danger.

Back in his cell, he examines the electrical cord to Williams' TV. It's too short. He feels so deflated that he doesn't go to chow. Suicide was his last hope, and even that has been stripped away. Despair coats his mouth. He longs to cry but can't. His history teacher said that in the nineteenth century, Native Americans who were captured and imprisoned willed themselves to die. He wonders if that's really true. He wonders how they did it.

Time's Up

When James slumps into his chair at the study hall table, Allison says, "You don't look so good."

James shrugs. No way is he going to tell her about his plan to jump from the fifth tier. Then he does. He doesn't know why he tells her. It just spills out.

She looks at him with the deepest care. He drops his head, removes his glasses, and presses the heels of his hands against his eyes.

"Sorry," he says. "All my hopes were riding on parole. I know I'll never get out of here."

For something to do, he flips some pages in his geometry book.

Allison stares fiercely into her lap. There is a very long silence. What is going on in her mind he cannot fathom.

She raises her head. The look of determination on her face is one he has never seen before.

"Listen to me," she says.

James waits.

She says, "This new virus. You've seen it on the news, right?"

He nods.

"Well, it's the real deal. My school announced that it's closing down after tomorrow. My wife's school closed today. Businesses are closing. People are mobbing the supermarkets to stock up. The word among the tutors is that the prison will close to outsiders, probably this week. So I'm not going to be around to talk you out of killing yourself."

She leans forward and locks eyes with him. "Listen to me. I know how you can get out." Her face turns bright red. At first he thinks she'll write to the governor requesting a pardon. In an intense whisper she says, "I know how you can escape."

He leans back and raises one eyebrow in mock surprise, reacting to what she said as the joke it's got to be.

"You've been watching too many *Mission Impossible* movies," he says.

"I'm serious. Trust me. I have it figured out. It will work. But you've got to hold on. They're going to close down the prison and I may not get back in here for weeks. Maybe months. You have to wait. Do you hear me? I swear to Christ, James, if you kill yourself, I'll dig up your grave with my bare hands and feed your body to the fucking fishes."

He chuckles. This is the first time he's ever heard her swear. Her passion and her care breathe life into his dead flesh.

"Will you promise me that one thing? Promise you'll wait. Promise me now or I'll hit you over the head with this chair. James? Will you?"

She waits. He is moved.

"I promise," he says.

Part Nine

Allison's Plan

The rumors prove true. Two days after Allison's conversation with James, San Quentin goes into quarantine and the prison is closed to visitors and volunteers. Miraculously, there are no Covid cases in the prison. In the ensuing weeks, Allison's school starts online classes. Meagan's school does the same. There is no internet in the prison, so the college program temporarily disappears, as do all of the programs staffed by outside volunteers.

"This is spooky-weird," Meagan says. "It's like they've dropped the neutron bomb."

They are sitting at the kitchen table after dinner sipping cups of white tea.

Allison nods.

Meagan watches her. "What?" she asks. "You're looking very, very Allison at this moment."

"I'm going to get James out."

"How? Write the parole board or something?"

Allison shakes her head, then stares at the wall and says, "He has to escape. I know how."

Meagan's mouth opens slightly and her eyes go wide. Then she says, "Tell me you're joking."

Allison shakes her head again.

"It's impossible."

"I've got it figured out. Well, a lot of it. There are still a few problems to solve."

"He'll get killed. You both will."

"No violence involved. It's not a break-out. A walk-out. An exodus."

"Am I allowed to ask how? Or should I just schedule an

appointment for your psychiatric evaluation?"

Allison leans forward and puts her elbows on the table. She describes the plan, step by step.

"It won't work," Meagan says.

"It will work," Allison answers, leaning back.

"When did you get this idea?"

"That's the funny thing. It started the first night I went in, before I'd even met James. Deep down inside, I knew I'd have to get someone out of there."

Megan stands up. "Okay, the escape idea is crazy enough, but this clairvoyant shit is freaking me out."

"I don't know if clairvoyant is the right word. More like destiny."

Still standing, Meagan waves her hands in the air. Her face is flushed. "Oh, now I feel better. It's only your destiny to bust a convicted murderer out of San Quentin. I'm relieved."

Allison smiles in spite of herself. "Very funny. Can I just explain?"

Allison says that she knows James. She has read all his memoir pieces. She is sure he is a good person, that he's been in prison much longer than is justified, and aiding his return to life on the outside is simply being helpful. It's something Nancy Drew would do.

"Nancy Drew was a character in novels. She wasn't real."

"She was real to me."

"How can you be sure it will work? How can you say there's no risk?"

"Oh, there's definitely risk. If I didn't admit that, *then* you should be worried. But I'll do everything I can to minimize the risk. The probability of failure can approach zero, but it can never be zero."

"I think I'm going to faint," Meagan says.

"Wait on that. The plan can't go forward until this crazy pandemic ends."

Meagan says, "I married a madwoman."

The first few weeks of the pandemic are something of a novelty, like a series of snow days back in the Midwest. Then Allison and Meagan begin to feel the strain of teaching on-line, masking up to buy groceries, and confining their lives to their house and the hiking trails in the Berkeley hills. Their hearts ache at the stories of people dying alone in ICU wards. Allison worries about James.

"The freeways are wonderfully empty," Meagan moans, "but there's nowhere to go."

The school year ends, and seniors graduate in online ceremonies. The world feels broken and unreal.

Death Invades San Quentin

At San Quentin, weeks pass without a single case of Covid. "We're the safest place around," the inmates joke. "Rich people will start robbing liquor stores just to get in here and be safe from the pandemic."

In May the CDCR transfers 120 older inmates from Chino to San Quentin. It is reported that they have been tested, but some become sick as soon as they arrive. COVID spreads like a wildfire through the cellblocks. The prison goes into lockdown. The case count hits one hundred, five hundred, a thousand. By June there are two thousand cases, half of the inmate population. The furniture factory is used as a sick ward. A hospital tent is erected on the yard. The worst cases are taken by ambulance to hospitals. One man dies, then a second.

Williams has had a headache and a cough for three days. One morning he rises from his bunk and falls to the floor, gasping like he's drowning. James presses his face to the bars of the cell and yells "man down." The guards summon the medical volunteers, who wheel Williams away on a gurney. In a weak voice Williams tells James not to let anyone take his TV.

Two days later James develops fever and chills, a cough, loss of taste and smell. He is so weak he can barely sit up. A nurse in full PPE comes by his cell and administers a test. She checks his oxygen level, and either it's not bad enough to send him to the hospital tent or the hospital tent is simply full. His temperature is 103. She leaves him with aspirin and tells him to stay hydrated. His head feels like it's being squeezed in a vise and his skull is cracking. His scalp hurts to be touched, and his skin is so sensitive that his clothes scrape like sandpaper. Rumors pass from cell to cell—the death toll is rising, someone saw body bags being loaded into a truck, the virus has invaded the prison water supply.

James has delirious dreams in which he sits on a prison bus with murderers who say the destination is hell. He is shivering and says he thought hell was hot. What about the fires? They tell him it's a myth and that hell is cold and dark. He awakes in his bunk, his teeth chattering but his forehead as hot as an iron. He shivers so violently he wonders if he's having a convulsion. He thinks, *Hurry up, virus. Do your work. I'm not breaking my promise to Allison if I die of Covid.*

Early one morning his fever breaks and he wakes up so drenched in sweat that he thinks he's peed his bunk. Leaning against the tiny basin, he stares into the metal mirror and touches his fingertips to his gaunt, dark brown face. He looks like a man of eighty. The inmate delivering his breakfast tray tells him that Williams died in the hospital tent.

The food on James' breakfast tray has no taste, and he's not especially hungry, but he makes himself eat half of it. He looks at Williams' belongings: Afro comb, toothbrush, deodorant. Photos of his two grown daughters in LA. A green and yellow baseball cap. Two packages of trail mix from the canteen. A miniature checkers set. His stack of comic books. The tiny TV.

In the coming weeks, James' cough gradually diminishes, and the smells of prison slowly return—the chow halls, the distinctive disinfectant, the pungent state-issued soap, the salt air that blows in from the bay. The smells remind him of when he first arrived. When the lockdown is modified so that he gets to leave his cell, he takes his first shower in four weeks, washing away layers of fever-induced sweat. He walks outside and sits on the asphalt in the morning sun, mentally alert but as physically frail as a newborn kitten. He cinches up his belt to its last hole, so much weight has he lost. He studies his hands, his fingers looking like twigs on a tree. He marvels that he's still alive. It is late August. He sees a golden California poppy growing near the fence and remembers the day he was arrested. He feels a strange calm, and it occurs to him that feeling so close to death has purged his desire to die. It perplexes him now that he felt so determined to get to the fifth tier.

In the coming weeks, James' vitality grows, and with it his conviction that he must leave the prison. Remembering the advice that inmates survive by living one day at a time, he tries not to think about his next parole hearing, ten years away. Besides, his recent write-up for aggressive behavior toward a CO all but guarantees another denial.

He keeps remembering that uncanny conversation he had with Allison the last time he saw her. He is rational enough to know the idea is crazy—a thirty-something school teacher believes she can help him escape. As if anyone tries to escape San Quentin and lives to tell the story. How absurd. How utterly impossible. And yet, he cannot forget what he felt from her that night, the determination in her voice, the force of her steely will.

The Ringing Phone

One morning in August, Allison is awakened by her ringing phone. When she pulls it from her purse and answers, her mother tells her that her dad has been admitted to the hospital with Covid. He had been sick for several days, but yesterday when he was in his basement workshop he had trouble breathing and was too weak to make it up the steps. She called an ambulance and he was admitted to the ICU. She is not allowed in his hospital room.

That night Allison searches the internet for assurances that he will recover. After all, he's only sixty and has no preexisting conditions. When she finds cases of healthy adults, some younger than him, dying from the virus, she logs off of her computer.

The next afternoon her mother calls from the hospital. Her dad wants to hear her voice. He's been intubated, so he can't talk, but he has a whiteboard tablet and a marker. A few minutes later their phones connect for a video chat, and a nurse in full protective gear holds the phone above his head. Allison hardly recognizes the patient with a breathing apparatus strapped to his face, a hospital gown, and a plastic hair cap. His skin looks like parchment. IVs run into his arm, and monitors and medical devices surround his bed. He looks like he's been locked in a space capsule. Allison struggles to keep her voice from cracking as she assures him he'll be okay. He lifts his hand in a gesture she can't interpret. The nurse pulls the phone back to reveal he is writing on the whiteboard tablet. The nurse tilts it to face the phone's lens. At first Allison can't make out the letters because they are backwards, but she finally makes out what he has written: *how ventilator works—genius!*

She says, "That's great, Dad. I know it will help you."

She waits to see if he writes anything else, but he makes a small wave and his eyes close. She says, "I love you, Dad." She doesn't know whether he heard her.

He lies very still and the image swivels to the nurse in a face shield who says he's fallen asleep. Allison feels frightened and powerless. After dinner, Meagan holds her while Allison tells the story of the rocket he helped her build in high school.

The next morning, he dies.

Allison's impulse is to fly home, but her mom insists that she not. They can't even hold a funeral, and the planes and airports are not safe. Nothing can be done. Her father's death makes her fear all the more for James.

Lonny's Ocean

As the pandemic enters its second year, a vaccine is rolled out and made available to inmates. One afternoon James sits on the asphalt and leans against the concrete wall. The air is cool and the sun warm. The basketball thumps on the court, the gulls caw overhead. The word on the yard is that programs will resume in a few months. James wonders how Allison has been, whether she will come back, what she meant when she said she could help him get out.

Something catches his eye. A fluffy gray mouse runs along the fence in bursts of scamper and stop, scamper and stop. James wonders if they crawl into the prison from the surrounding fields or whether they've bred inside for generations. He's heard that a man in North Block has several as pets. Out of nowhere a blur of blue feathers dives to the mouse. A jay stands on the asphalt, the mouse jerking it its yellow beak. The jay drops the mouse and stabs at it, breaking open the hairless stomach. In a series of quick pecks, tilting up its beak to swallow, the jay eats the mouse even as it struggles in its death throes. The jay tips its head, a bead of an eye on James. As quickly as it landed, it flies away.

Back at Tehachapi, James and Lonny had a philosophical talk one night in their cell. Lonny had returned from five days in the hole for mouthing off to a CO. "It's like the ocean," he said. "Big fish eat the little fish, little ones eat littler ones, all the way down to the minnows. I'm a big whale, can't be bossed around."

"How come you ended up in the hole, then?" James asked.

"Whales got enemies, too," he said. "White sharks. They circle around, waiting to attack." He laughed bitterly. "Motherfucking white sharks put me in here in the first place. It's a mean ocean we live in."

James remembers his high school chemistry course, and he wonders. If the world is made up of atoms and molecules, obedient only to the laws of science, where is meaning? Where is goodness? Where is love? Hamlet called man the quintessence of dust. Are people more than hydrocarbon molecules, more than a jay or a mouse? Are we just machines that happen to bleed? The virus that made James sick and took Williams to his death was no more evil than the jay. It just did what viruses do. Was Black Snake just another jay, trying to make of James a mouse?

He remembers a conversation at chow one evening when an inmate named Earl told how he had come up for parole but skipped his hearing because he didn't want to leave prison. He explained that there was nothing for him on the outside. His parents were dead, his wife had divorced him long ago, and the so-called free world was brutal—scarce jobs, high prices, no housing, people hating ex-cons. In prison he had three meals a day, a roof over his head, and medical care. He had a job in the furniture factory and he could watch TV in his cell. What was the point in leaving? To sleep cold and hungry under a freeway? James got up from the table that evening thinking it was the most deflating conversation he had ever heard—a life without goals.

Still alive after Covid, James cannot accept that there's nothing to life but survival and that people are no more than fishes in Lonny's ocean. The universe has to be more than blind atoms. George Washington Carver was neither mouse nor jay—he lived to help people, and that's what James must do. But to do it, to become something more than his molecules, he has to get out of prison.

After the Quarantine

Allison and Meagan resume teaching in September, still in an online format. In late December, the first vaccine is rolled out, starting with medical workers and the elderly. As teachers, Allision and Meagan receive their shots in February. By summer, the programs at San Quentin resume, though inmates and volunteers are required to wear masks. James signs up for the college astronomy course. It will satisfy a requirement for his AA degree. For over a year he has been awaiting Allison's return.

During the first week of class he goes to evening study hall so he can sit at a table and read the assignment. But mostly he wants to see Allison. On many occasions he wished he had her address and could write her. He now wonders if her talk about escaping was even serious or just a trick to lure him away from a suicide attempt. Some of the volunteers are still concerned about Covid and stay away from the prison. He fears Allison may be one of them.

When he spots Allison at Wednesday study hall, he feels relieved and elated. He signs up for her time slot.

"God," she says. "How have you been?"

He tells her about having Covid and how it ended his suicidal thoughts. She tells him about her and Meagan being shut up in their small house and teaching online, one computer in their spare bedroom and the other on the kitchen table. She tells him her father died. He says he's sorry. From reading his memoir pieces, she knows about the deaths of his own father and mother, and she feels that his sympathy for her is real. Their N-95 masks mean that each sees only the other's eyes, and it makes their interaction feel all the more intense. They are both aware of the elephant in the room, but it is Allison who brings it up.

"You remember the last conversation we had?" she says.

"Most definitely."

She looks around—they're the only ones at the long wooden table—and then she turns his astronomy book around so it looks like she's helping him.

She tells him that during the pandemic she researched every escape attempt at San Quentin, and they fall into two categories—forceful and sneaky. Forceful always fails, often with injury or death to the inmate. Most of the sneaky ones fail, and those that succeed usually result in recapture. James is certain she is about to tell him that escape is impossible.

"Those people didn't plan well enough," Allison says. "They ended up on the highway in their prison blues trying to carjack someone. Sometimes they didn't even make it out because they told someone what they were planning. A big lesson there. Words are like water. They leak."

James rubs his chin through his mask.

"In my research I found that the few people who made it out used ram's belly plans."

"They used what?" James asks.

"Remember how Odysseus got his men out of the Cyclops' cave?"

"Oh, yeah. He tied them under the bellies of the giant sheep."

"At San Quentin one man attached himself to the underside of a delivery truck and was killed when he fell off on the freeway. Another hid in a giant fan that was made in the metal shop and shipped out in a truck. He made it, but he was recaptured years later. Which means we need not just an escape plan but also a plan for life-after-escape. I've got good ideas for that."

James' glasses are fogging up so he presses his mask more tightly to his face.

"We're going to do it a different way. Remember how Odysseus walked into his palace and no one knew who he was?"

James nods. "Except his old dog. Argos."

"Right. That's how you're getting out. It's never been done. At least, I don't think it has."

Then she explains, step by step, how he can walk out of San Quentin. He challenges her on every point, and against every objection she has answers.

He says he can't let her do it. If it goes wrong, he gets sent to the hole or maybe to a higher security prison—where he's been before. But if she gets caught, it ruins her life.

She says, "Your risk is your decision. My risk is my decision." Her voice is determined and absolute.

"The escape is not the first issue," she says. "The first issue is, do you want to do this? Now it's my turn to play devil's advocate. There are worse places to be than San Quentin—"

James throws his head back and rolls his eyes. Another inmate walks past their table and Allison waits until he passes to continue.

"I know that I've never been a prisoner here—or anywhere—so maybe I have no right to say this. But you are fairly safe here. You have food and shelter. You can take classes and act in Shakespeare plays. All things considered, is it worth the risk to leave? Because no plan, no matter how many safeguards, is risk-free. The *Challenger* blew up. A nuclear power plant in Japan melted down. You need to think about this. You might get parole in ten years, or fifteen, but if you get caught attempting to escape, you'll never get out."

"Actually, I do understand what you're saying," he says, adjusting his mask. "I would be the first to admit that good things have happened for me, especially up here at San Quentin. Like you say. In some way—I can't believe I'm saying this—it's easy. Three meals a day and a roof over my head. I've even heard one or two guys in here say they don't want out—for just that reason. But for me, the time has come for a change. It really has. I'm fifty. Like everyone, I only have one life, and I need to move to a new phase. I can't even explain it, but since recovering from Covid—and from wanting to die—I've come to realize that I have to get out. *Have* to. A necessity."

Looking at him, she says, "Today is June 28. Think some more. Give me your final answer next week. If your answer is yes, D-day will be in October. Most of what I have to finish planning is your life after you leave here—the part that most people ignore. You don't want to live the rest of your life looking over your shoulder. And don't be stupid enough to mention this to anybody."

"This is some new kind of you," he says.

"Call me Pallas Athena," she says.

"What's the 'Pallas' mean? I forget."

"A childhood friend she accidentally killed with a spear," she says.

"Oh, great," he says.

To Be or Not To Be

James sits on the yard, his back against the wall and his face lifted into the mild morning sun. Mount Tamalpais appears both close enough to touch and as far away as a dream. Allison will be here tomorrow evening and he will tell her yes or no. This will be his moment of "to be or not to be." He is still unsure.

In the past week, his strong determination to get out has been outstripped by his realization that the plan is batshit crazy. A school teacher who's spent her adult life in the classroom is going to coach his escape from San Quentin Prison. For thirty years James has listened to men tell stories of how they ended up in prison because they ignored a voice—inner or outer—that said, "No. Bad idea. Don't even think about it." And now he's on the verge of doing exactly that. The warning signs are there: the monumental audacity of the plan, the improbability that it will work, and Allison's lack of experience outside of books. He imagines the guys on the yard slapping their knees and laughing. *He tried to just walk out. Because a schoolteacher said so. And he thought it would work.* He can almost laugh at it himself.

The consequences of failure would be bad for both of them. She would be prosecuted, and he would be transferred to a higher security prison with his chances of parole shrinking from slim to nothing. It all adds up to saying no. The realization settles over him like weariness unto death.

He was his parents' only child. The other kids they wanted were never born, never had a chance at life. James carries all they might have become in himself. Of course, he can be a good person in prison, and for thirty years he's done that—avoiding trouble, educating himself, helping guys write. But with every fiber of his being, he wants out of the cage. For however many years he has left on earth, he wants to follow the example of George Washington Carver. He wants to live in a way that would have made Mama and Pops proud. In high school he wrote—and believed—that he should remain true to himself. He believes it still.

He gazes at the shadowed slope of Mount Tam, its peak hidden in a gathering of clouds. He remembers that when Horatio warned Hamlet against what his mind disliked, Hamlet replied, "The readiness is all."

James has his answer.

A Flat Tire on a Rainy Night

When Allison returns home after receiving the go-ahead from James, she sits beside Meagan on the couch and tells her that they are going forward with the escape plan. Meagan listens in silence, anger rising in her face.

"I don't like it," Meagan says. "Jesus, Alli. If you get caught, you go to jail, lose your job, and probably we can't ever adopt a kid. It ruins everything. You're risking the life we planned together." Her eyes glisten with tears. "And all for a guy who blew a kid's head off," Meagan adds, raising her voice. Hot tears spill down her cheeks. "You must have ice in your veins."

It is this last comment that enrages Allison. She hates being told she's all head and no heart. She looks into her lap and counts slow, deep breaths to five. It's not enough so she counts off five more. Then she looks up at Meagan.

"What I have in my veins is love for you," she says, her voice cracking. "And for us. For our marriage. But I have to do this. I *have* to."

She reaches out and takes Meagan's hands in hers. "When he was eighteen, someone shot his dog and laughed about it. He snapped. I might have done the same thing. *You* might have done the same thing. After thirty years the parole board wouldn't even consider what really happened that day. They'll never let him out. It's unfair and it's wrong. Besides, if you do something once—whether cheat, or steal, or even murder—how long are you a cheater, a thief, or a murderer? Forever?"

"Okay, but even if it's a good cause, what about *us*?"

"We'll still be us."

"Not if you're in jail."

"Actually, we will. We'll write letters and you'll visit me and be there at the gate the day I get released."

"You're freaking me out." Then she puts her hand on her forehead and says, "God, I think I'm going to throw up."

"Seriously?"

"Yes."

Allison runs to the kitchen and returns with a lemon wedge. "Suck on this," she says.

"Why, for god's sake."

"To keep you from throwing up."

Meagan holds the lemon to her lips.

"It's sour," she says, making a face.

"It's a lemon," Allison says.

"I hate that you're always the rational one."

"Okay, it's a banana."

Meagan breaks into laughter and then tears fill her eyes. She says, "If I didn't love you so much, I'd strangle you."

Allison smiles. She picks up Meagan's free hand. "I'm not going to get caught. I'm really not."

"I just want us to be on the same team," Meagan says. "I love you."

"I love you more. And we *are* on the same team, just playing different positions. There can't be two shortstops."

Meagan does an exaggerated facepalm.

"Seriously, though. I'm need your support in this."

"So why do you have to do this?" Meagan says. "Explain it to me. And don't mention Nancy Drew."

Allison takes another deep breath.

"It's like seeing someone with a flat tire on a lonesome road. A rainy night. You can stop and help them, or you can keep right on going. It just so happens I know how to change the tire. The stranded driver doesn't have a jack, but I do. I happen to *like* changing tires. It's my destiny. So, I'm going to stop and help. If I drove past, I would betray who I truly am. Simple as that."

Meagan nods.

"Rupa was in the flat tire position a couple of years ago and I failed her. I'm not going to fail again. And if anyone says I have a White savior complex I'm going scratch out their eyeballs."

They look into one another's eyes.

"Plus," Allison continues, "think about us. Coming out wasn't that difficult. We never got fired or denied jobs. And after an exasperating delay, we were able to get married. And why? Because people before us fought hard, risked a lot, and paid big prices. What was hard for others made it easy for us. They stopped in the rain for us in ways we didn't even realize. There isn't anyone alive that hasn't been saved by others who came before. It's the human way. Or should be."

Meagan places her palms against the sides of her face. "When is this going to happen?"

"October 12."

"Jesus. You have it all planned, even the date?"

"Not *all* planned. I still have a lot to do. Did your nausea pass?"

"Yes," Meagan says. "The banana helped."

Allison bursts out laughing, and then they embrace and their tears flow. They blow their noses. Meagan takes a very deep breath and says, "Okay, wife. Till death do us part. I'll visit you in prison."

"The sentence is only one year."

"Of course, you've looked it up."

The Private Detective

Allison rides BART over to San Francisco and walks ten blocks to the office of a private detective she read about. She has made an appointment.

She leaves on her N-95 mask. He isn't wearing one. She tells him she is a fiction writer working on her second novel. She pulls from her tote a paperback detective novel she bought at the used bookstore for fifty cents and waves it in front of his face.

"This is my first novel," she says. "I know I don't look like Russ Steele, but that's my pen name. At present, detective novels written by females don't sell as well. I hope that changes."

He glances at the cover and then raises his eyebrows as she lifts from her tote a fifth of single barrel scotch and places it on his desk.

"A token of my appreciation for your time. I just have a couple of questions."

"If I can't answer them, do I still get the scotch?"

She laughs lightly. "All I ask is that you do your best."

"Fire away," he says, leaning back in his swivel chair and lacing his fingers together in front of his chest.

"In my next novel, a convicted bank robber escapes from prison. I've got that part written. He needs to create a new identity. Can that be done?"

"To a degree. These days, you can find places on the internet that for a hundred and fifty dollars will send you a driver's license for any state in the country, and it looks so authentic, hologram and all, that a cop pulling you over won't know it's fake."

"These places can operate?"

"They're offshore, mostly in Asia. You don't even have to

access the dark web. Do an internet search for *fake ID* and you'll find dozens. It's as easy as ordering a box of fortune cookies." He smiles. "There are even some stateside ones for people who want to buy American."

"The government can't stop them?" Allison asks.

He shakes his head. "Too many. And we have no jurisdiction to knock on doors in China. Besides, the toothpaste is already out of the tube. Half the college kids in America have one of these IDs for getting into bars, and a bunch of Chinese geeks are rich. Supply and demand."

He shrugs. "Of course, if a cop runs a check, which they always do when they stop you, then you're screwed."

"What about a new identity, something that's foolproof."

"Foolproof is a high bar. Since 9/11 there is more computerized cross-checking by government agencies. The key is a good seed document."

"What's that?"

"A seed document is a single document that isn't a fake, that won't ring alarm bells if it's checked. It's your seed, and it makes other things grow. Let's say you have a birth certificate, the best kind of seed document. You can use it to get a driver's license, then a passport, credit cards, the whole nine yards. Then you're a new person, the person named on the birth certificate."

"How can someone get a seed document?"

"That's the tough part. When it's done, it's usually through a person working in some documents office—birth certificates, say. Some of those people are on the dark web, but so are the scam artists. Finding a good seed document—you'd have to be a real sleuth to do that."

He doesn't notice Allison's faint smile.

"So your character escapes from prison?"

Allison nods.

"Escapees are easy to catch," he says with a wave of his hand. "They all make the same mistakes. They go to their old neighborhood, they contact family and friends, they commit the same crimes, they get pulled over for driving drunk. Mostly they talk too much."

"What if he doesn't do those things?"

"Then he's got a chance. Of course, he's got to find a way around the fingerprint problem."

"Which is?"

"When a person is arrested, his fingerprints go into a national database. In California now, they scan your thumbprint when you get a driver's license. Not to mention criminal background checks for some jobs."

"There's no way around that?"

"There's one." He leans forward, places his elbows on his desk. "I went to a presentation on this at a security conference. Last month, in Vegas. There are 3D printers that can make finger gloves you slip on that have fake fingerprints. The technology was originally developed to test fingerprint scanners—you know, the kind they have in airports now—to make sure they couldn't be fooled. Pretty soon bad guys figured out another use for the gloves."

"Anybody with a 3D printer can make one?"

"Not anybody. First, the person really has to know what they're doing. Takes a high level of expertise. And second, bargain 3D printers can't do it. It takes one of the real high-end models."

Allison nods. "Thank you so much," she says. "You've been very helpful."

He nods at the bottle of scotch. "Want to sample that with me?"

"No, thanks," Allison says cheerfully. "It's all yours."

After she leaves his office, she walks to a place that sells the UV stamps that clubs use to mark patrons for re-entry. She requests a stamp saying *San Quentin*. She could have ordered it online, but she doesn't want to leave a trail. Very often Nancy Drew saved herself by planning for contingencies. In the shop Allison chooses a font like the one she has observed at the prison gate. She pays cash and tells the clerk it's for a theme party, though he doesn't seem to care. She feels safer that her face is mostly concealed behind her N-95 mask. When she leaves, she uses her phone to look up 3D printing services. At home she signs up for a VPN and downloads a TOR browser to access the dark web.

Seed Document

In late July, Meagan and Allison drive to Reno where they meet a woman at a parking lot in the Freight House District. Meagan stays in the car while Allison and the woman walk a path along the Truckee River. The woman, perhaps in her fifties, looks like an office secretary—permed gray hair, a mint-green pants suit, and a white purse. She's wearing a blue surgical mask. Allison has on her black N-95.

When no one is around, the woman says, "Sorry, Babe, but I have to pat you down."

She rubs her hands up and down Allison's blue jeaned legs. She presses the back of Allison's head, looks inside her mask. She pats her back and sides. She looks down the front of Allison's blouse.

"You're keeping your girlish figure," the woman says.

"Thanks," Allison says. "You thought I might be armed?"

"Wired."

"Ah."

"You're sure this is a boyfriend on the wrong side of the law? I don't deal with foreigners or terrorists."

"Cross my heart," Allison says.

The woman laughs. "I haven't heard anyone say that in years."

They sit on a bench under a tree beside the river.

"Here's the deal," the woman begins. "It's a real birth certificate, not a fraud document. Legit. Anyone runs it, it comes up clean. Your friend can use it to get a driver's license, a social security card, even a passport. The name is James Allen Greene and he would be forty-six, born in Nevada, race African-American, sex male. He died—by drowning—when he was twelve, but there was no death certificate. No driver's license, no social, no arrest record.

Totally clean. It's as good as they get. Five thousand cash."

Allison hesitates. The woman has a truck stop waitress toughness about her. No nonsense.

"You're being straight with me?" Allison asks.

"Honey, I could be a fraud, just like your butcher could sell you dog meat. But when you've got a business, whether it's above ground or underground, you screw people and it will come back to bite you in the ass. So, the hamburger you'll buy at the store today comes from a cow, not a dog, and what you're getting from me is not a shit document. Now, I've put a *People* magazine beside you. When I pick it up in 30 seconds and the money is in it, I will put the document in the magazine and walk back to the parking lot. You wait five minutes."

When Allison returns to the car, Meagan says, "I was worried. The woman left five minutes ago. Did everything go okay?"

"Yes, but it worries me that this is so much fun."

"I know one thing," Meagan says. "If we have a daughter, she's not allowed to read Nancy Drew."

Meagan's Epiphanies

When Meagan walks in the house, she lies on her back, spread-eagle on the living room rug, and groans, "Make margaritas. Quick."

Meagan's school brought in consultants who put on an all-day anti-racism workshop.

Allison kneels beside her and pecks light kisses on her cheeks, chin, nose, eyelids, forehead, and lips.

"I was going to say just shoot me, but I do like those kisses," Meagan says.

"Good faculty workshop?" Allison asks playfully. She reaches for Meagan's hands and pulls her up. They walk into the kitchen.

"I had two epiphanies today," Meagan says.

"What?" Allison asks, slicing limes.

"Our administration gives zero fucks about racism. But they care about appearances, and today's workshop is a great story for the newsletter and the website."

"Same with my school, for sure," Allison sighs. "What was the other epiphany?"

"That wasn't one of the epiphanies. That was just a basic recognition."

"What were the epiphanies?" She measures out tequila.

"These consultants. What they advertise as anti-racism isn't really about improvements in the lives of Black people. It's about Whites feeling morally validated. Woker than thou. I saw some of that at Madison, for sure, but nothing as bad as what I saw today. We did a thing in the morning where we wrote on a piece of paper our confessions—they really used that word—as to our racism. It was a masochism contest. 'I'm realizing so much about my own racism,' someone at my table said. With pride. That and crocodile tears about White skin privilege. Workshops are the new baptism."

Allison nods. "I agree with your epiphany."

"Those two summers when I worked with teen girls in Milwaukee. I came away with a sense of what was needed there—and probably every American city. For the Black girls, the Brown girls, a few White hillbilly girls from Kentucky. I thought about them today while everyone was speaking masochistic moral-babble. I made a list."

Meagan pulls her phone from her breast pocket and reads.

"Meagan's big six. Jobs that pay a living wage. Decent housing. Police that serve and protect—not oppress and abuse. Good schools. Health care, including contraception and treatment programs for substance abuse. A nice physical environment—you know, rec centers and parks and trees along the streets. If you want to help people, focus on those things, not your own woke consciousness."

Allison puts chips and salsa on the table, kisses Meagan lightly on the lips, and hands her a margarita. She says, "I think you're totally right. Every time I hear our administration trying to advertise their commitment to diversity, I think, 'If you really cared about underserved students, you wouldn't have expelled Rupa. Spare me your bullshit.'"

"Honey, this is a great freaking margarita," Meagan says.

"What was the second epiphany?"

"The second epiphany is that I really feel proud of what you're doing with James, even if it's giving me a nervous breakdown."

Allison clinks her glass to Meagan's. "I'm glad you're on board. It means everything to me. Really."

"I'm totally on board. I just hope to hell it works."

"It has to work. I'm channeling the girl sleuth."

Walking Out

One evening in early October, Allison enters the education building and nods to the CO, who is listening to a baseball playoff game on his radio and eating a burrito. She unlocks the padlock on the metal cabinet—right to 16, left one full turn and stop at 21, right to 6—and removes an empty plastic box, which she carries into the staff-only restroom down the hall. Inside, she removes her oversized khaki men's trench coat, purchased the week before at Goodwill. She takes out the man's suit, hat, and shirt that are folded against her stomach under her black turtleneck. From the two deep pockets in her trench coat she removes men's dress shoes, size 9, black socks, a rubber stamp and UV ink pad, gold rimmed glasses, and a necktie with a Windsor knot, ready for James to slip over his neck and adjust. She neatly folds the clothes and lays them in the box. She places a black N-95 mask on top of the shirt, and a black fedora on top of that. She exists the restroom and carries the box to the B building, unlocks the cabinet, and pushes the box to the rear of the bottom shelf. With a black marker, she uses her left hand to print on the box in block letters: *Drama.* There is a miniscule risk that someone—it would have to be a teacher or tutor—would open the box, not believe it's for drama, and report it to someone, but nothing in the box implicates her or James. She walks into study hall and writes her times on the board. James signs up for the second slot, 6:20-6:40.

When he sits down in front of Allison and opens his astronomy book, she says in a low voice, "A week from tonight. Tell me the six steps."

He says, "Don't forget our agreement. If this blows up, you don't know a thing. I take the fall. Totally. Alone."

She turns his book and points to a diagram on one of its pages. "Agreed. But it won't blow up. The six steps?"

He recites them perfectly.

"I have a driver's license for you to use. It's safer with you than in the box. Take good care of it this week and don't forget it."

"Where is it?" he asks.

"Tucked into your book. Page 100."

James breaks into a wide smile. "Remind me never to play three-card monte with you."

"I don't even know what that is."

James looks at her. "You sure I won't be on the run forever?"

"That is the hardest part, but we have a very good plan. It's all set up. You're sure you're okay with a shave and a haircut? It didn't work out too well for Samson."

"It's fine," he says, pulling at one of his dreads. "I've been thinking about changing that anyway."

On the day of the exodus, October 12, 2022, Allison and James have one thing in common. For each, the world seems in sharp focus. Allison sees that one of her prep school students has neglected to button her uniform skirt, that the damp leaves are too heavy to move ahead of the maintenance man's blower on the front lawn. James will remember that he ate pancakes at breakfast chow, that he and Habeeb—Hamlet's ghost—exchanged fist bumps on the yard.

James takes a late afternoon shower, waiting his turn in the line of naked men. He feels too nervous to eat, so he waits in his cell for the gate to the education building to open, rehearsing the details of the plan. Before he leaves, he arranges his laundry in mounds under the blanket on his bunk so that during the guards' informal walk-through, it will look like he's sleeping. It helps that he has never been assigned a new cellie. Covid has kept new prisoner intake low.

When James walks into study hall at 7:15, Allison is tutoring a student in pre-algebra. James sits at the next table, pretending to read his astronomy book. They exchange glances only once. She tugs her right earlobe and he does the same. The gesture confirms that nothing has happened to require aborting the plan. It's a go.

When the CO enters study hall for count, he calls out names, and each inmate answers with the last two digits of his prison number. When the CO says "Fields," James answers, "Eighty-five." Half an hour later, count clears. Every inmate in the prison has been accounted for. Allison has blocked out her last two time slots, so she's helping her last tutee of the evening. James walks out of study hall and down the hall into the dark, empty classroom where

Allison has placed the plastic box on the floor. These are the riskiest minutes of the plan. He strips off his blues and stuffs them in the box. He dresses in the shirt and suit, tightens and adjusts the tie, puts on the socks and shoes. Everything fits, and his confidence rises. He replaces his black frame glasses with the gold frame glasses. The prescription feels identical. He slips the California driver's license into his pants pocket. He inks the stamp and presses it to the inside of his left wrist. He slips on the black N-95 mask, and pushes his dreads under his do-rag. He adjusts the fedora on his head. He walks from the room. His chin is up and his chest his out, his stride confident. When he passes the study hall, one inmate glances through the doorway at the man in the suit.

Allison walks to the empty classroom. She imagines her dad reminding her to take her time and get everything right. She lifts James' prison blues from the box, folds them flat, tucks them under her turtleneck, and slips on her trench coat. She drops his old glasses and the UV stamp into her pocket. She tells one of the tutors she's leaving early because of a sore throat, and she walks from the education building, staying a few hundred feet behind James as they cross the yard. They are both wearing black N-95 masks, this tall Black professor in his suit and fedora and the White tutor who looks pregnant in her oversized khaki trench coat. He helps maintain his calm by silently humming Curtis Mayfield, "People Get Ready." Walking past the spotlights shining from the top of the wall, Allison and James cast elongated shadows on the asphalt, like two characters in a noir film. Allison is pleased to note James' slow confident strides. It helps to calm her. She walks past the chapel, remembering the night of the Hamlet performance.

She sees James enter the door to the sally port. Beneath her trench coat and James' folded prison blues, her heart is pounding. She hears the lock to the first door clang open and then shut. He will now be showing his ID to the CO in the booth. Waiting for the sound of the second door, she counts off seconds, fear rising in her throat. Then she hears the clang of the opening door, followed by its reverberating bang. James has closed it too hard. She approaches the door and sees through two sets of bars James holding his left wrist under the UV light. Her skin prickles with exultant joy.

The UV lamp is exactly where James expected, and he passes his wrist under the bulb. *San Quentin* glows in silvery block letters. The guard nods. James steps to the ledger. His back to the guard, James runs his finger down the names, lifts the pen, and wiggles it above the page. He walks out into the night air. He looks to the right, awed by the lights twinkling across the bay.

He hears the gate clang behind him, and he knows it is Allison, but he doesn't turn. He walks at a measured pace to the final station, waves his ID at the guard sitting in the kiosk, and walks through the gate. Stifling his impulse to shout and break into a sprint, he walks at a moderate pace down the main street of San Quentin Village.

In two minutes, headlights approach from behind and a car slows. He opens the back door and lies down on the back seat so that his figure will not show in any of the traffic cameras on the bridge. Allison's plan has been designed to avoid glitches, the likely as well as the unlikely. From his position on the back seat he says, "I heard your description so many times, I felt like I had done it before. The guards, the UV lamp, the ledger. Just another day leaving the prison."

"That was the plan," she says.

First Stop

Meagan is peeping through the blinds on the front window when Allison drives up. When Allison and James enter, Meagan gives James a wide smile and offers her hand, "Hamlet, I presume."

James laughs and shakes her hand. He removes his fedora. Meagan and Allison hug tightly.

"Shit," Meagan says. "I was a nervous wreck."

"It's harder to be the one waiting," Allison says.

"What about you?" Meagan asks James.

"I was real nervous until I walked out onto the yard. Then I felt like I was dreaming. I still do. I got nervous again in the car. Kept listening for sirens."

Allison says, "They won't know you're gone until morning count."

"A real house," James says, looking around. "No bars."

"Welcome to the outside world," Allison says.

"Oh, man," James says, "what do I smell?"

Meagan says, "I didn't know if you'd be hungry, but in case you are, I made some food. Plus, it gave me something to do."

"Maybe in a minute. I'd like a glass of water, if you don't mind."

Allison motions to the rocking chair and he sits. "A real chair," he says. He bounces his knees, looks around the room. "I like your place. Everything looks so...soft."

Meagan returns from the kitchen with a tall glass of water. He drinks and says, "Even the water tastes better."

Allison asks how he's feeling.

He shakes his head. "Dazed. Exhilarated. Happy. Surreal. Scared. Guilty. All those things at one time. If my head explodes, you'll know why."

"Why guilty?" Allison asks.

James looks at her. "The risk you two saints are taking. On my behalf."

"We already had this conversation," Allison says.

"If you giving me orders counts as a conversation, I guess we did."

"She does that to you, too?" Meagan asks.

Allison mock-slaps her on the arm, and then says, "No guilt allowed. Guilt traps you in the past. We're about the future. We do things."

James says, "I hope I'm allowed to say thanks, but *thanks* does not even cover it. When I think of the right word, I'll say it."

They move into the kitchen. Meagan serves barbequed chicken legs and thighs, thick-cut French fries baked in the oven, and Caesar salad. When they sit down at the table, they all join hands. "We're not religious," Meagan says, "but we want to offer thanks. Just to send up there to the gods or whatever. Like a weather balloon."

"Amen to that," says James. "Weather balloons of thanks. To Pallas Athena."

James starts eating. At his first bites, something awakens. He feels like it's the first real food he's eaten in thirty-one years.

Allison asks if he'd like a beer. Or a glass of wine.

He shakes his head. "I tried beer a couple of times in high school, but I didn't like the taste. Think I'll focus on a clean-living lifestyle."

When they finish, James says, "That was *so* good." His voice cracks and he tears up. He shakes his head. Allison squeezes his hand. She realizes it's the first time she's ever touched him.

Haircut

The next morning Allison calls in sick and drives James to his savings and loan. She parks two blocks away. The branch opens at 9:00 and James walks in at 9:02 wearing his suit and tie and his black N-95 mask. Allison waits in the car. Morning count in the prison will have been completed and they are no doubt trying to locate James Fields. The kitchen supervisor would have reported that he didn't show up for work.

Both the teller and the manager look at James' fake driver's license—in his name—and approve the cash withdrawal of eighteen thousand dollars, all but two hundred of the balance. He tells them that he's buying a used car this morning. They ask what kind. He says it's a late-model Honda. The manager says he can't go wrong with a Honda. On the way out, James whispers, "Thank you, Mama."

When they arrive back home, Allison pulls a chair into the middle of the kitchen and spreads newspaper on the floor. First with scissors, and then with electric clippers, she takes him from dreadlocks to a quarter-inch of hair. She moves the clippers with the precision of a surgeon.

"Where did you learn this?" James asks.

"Watched videos on the internet."

After Allison clips his beard, she sends him to the bathroom with a new razor and a can of shaving cream. The shaving completed, he studies himself in the mirror and likes what he sees. On his head he has more gray than he realized. The dreads had kept it hidden.

Allison asks him to handle his prison ID and his glasses and then drop them in a large manila envelope. Tomorrow she will take the envelope to her lockbox at the bank.

Early that evening, Allison, Meagan, and James watch a short segment on the local news about the escape. It shows James' prison photo and says prison officials aren't sure how he escaped. He was doing time for murder and should be considered dangerous. The thirty-second segment makes them all nervous. Allison switches off the TV.

Allison says, "You could be in a room full of people watching that news segment and not one of them would recognize you. Having a haircut and no beard changes your whole face. And the different glasses. You also look thinner."

"I *am* thinner. When they took that photo, I had come from working in the kitchen at Tehachapi and I'd porked up a little bit. Then last year, I got on the Covid weight-loss program, free of charge. Never gained it back."

Allison says, "When they start their investigation, they may find out about your bank withdrawal, but if they retrieve a bank video, it's you in dreads, a beard, and a N-95 mask."

The Fugitive Task Force

Three days later, James is safe in a studio apartment in Sacramento. A Bay Area news story reports that prison officials speculate he may have escaped on an early morning garbage truck—in which case he could be dead, crushed by the compacting mechanism. Two cadaver dogs have been working the dump. They show his prison photo again, and then the story disappears from the news. Allison returns to the prison on her usual tutoring night. On the way in, one of the other tutors asks if she heard about James. Allison replies that she saw it on the news and hopes he wasn't killed in the garbage truck. Neither inmates, guards, or other tutors give her suspicious looks.

The following week, as expected, Allison receives a call from an investigator for the CDCR. He makes an appointment for the next afternoon when she gets home from school. James has been in his Sacramento apartment a week by this time, and all traces of him have been mopped and vacuumed from their house. His prison blues were dropped into a dumpster on the far side of Berkeley.

Allison feels a bit shaken when the clean-cut young man in a coat and tie rings the doorbell and flashes a badge identifying him as a member of the Fugitive Apprehension Team. The name sounds formidable. Maintaining her cordial cool, she invites him inside.

The man opens a small note pad and states that James Fields was last seen in study hall on the night he disappeared. Allison volunteers that she saw the news story on TV.

Did she see Mr. Fields that night? She doesn't think so. He may have been there, but she's pretty focused on who she's helping. She's sure she did not tutor him that night.

Did anyone walk out with her that night? No, she left early because she was getting a sore throat. She walked out alone. Allison senses that the investigators think it possible romantic feelings could have induced a volunteer to help James escape, and sure enough, the man seems less interested in her after Meagan walks in from the kitchen and Allison introduces her as her wife. Meagan offers to make tea or coffee, but the officer declines.

How well did Allison know Mr. Fields?

She's tutored him going back several years.

Did they talk about things other than his lessons?

No.

Did he ever mention family or friends?

No.

Had he acted different lately?

No.

Did he work with any tutor more than others?

Not that she's aware of. Allison explains the sign-up system on the whiteboard—it's pretty random.

Does Allison know which inmates Mr. Fields hung out with?

No.

Does Mr. Fields know where she lives or works?

No.

Has anyone such as a family member contacted her about Mr. Fields?

No.

Does Allison know he was in for murder?

Not until she heard it on the news.

How long has she been tutoring at the prison?

Six years, minus a year and a half during the pandemic.

Did she tutor Mr. Fields on the night of his escape?

No. (Are repeated questions part of a strategy?)

Did Mr. Fields ever give her anything to carry out of the prison, such as a letter to mail?

No. Allison adds, "We all value the program and are careful to obey the rules."

"Does he know where you live?" (Another repeated question.) Allison shakes her head.

"But he knows your name."

"Just my first name."

He stands up and hands Allison his card in case she thinks of something.

After he leaves, Meagan says, "I listened through the door. You were scary-masterful."

That night Allison looks up the Fugitive Task Force on the internet. Their special training is in executing warrants and battering down doors. There is nothing to suggest they are a match for the girl sleuth.

A New Life

James' escape date was October 12. By December he has a valid social security card, a new bank account, and a credit card, all in the name of his new identity, James Greene, four years younger. He likes that he has the same first name. The fake driver's license he used to withdraw his savings has been burned. On his kitchen table, he spreads out the ID cards to be placed in a new billfold he has bought himself. It feels more like the resumption of his old identity, the person he was before the shooting dropped him into a thirty-year hole. It's like awakening from a long bad dream.

At his strong insistence, he has reimbursed Allison for her expenses, all the way down to the UV ink pad. It is what he wants to do, and what Mama and Pops would have wanted him to do. He starts temporary work in the kitchen of a Black-owned barbeque restaurant in Sacramento, and he's been accepted to a six-month veterinary assistant program that begins at UC-Davis in January.

His studio apartment is not far from Sacramento State University. He can walk to the campus and to a nice park along the Sacramento River. He no longer pauses breathlessly when a car passes or when he hears someone near his door. He no longer feels a pang of fear when he senses someone looking at this face. He takes pleasure sitting at his kitchen table and looking out the window at the sky above the rooftops and trees. He allows the sights to fill his eyes. He hears every sound, especially ones like the wind in the trees or birds chirping in the morning. He takes slow, deep breaths and thinks, *I am here.*

He realizes things about prison he didn't fully grasp when he was there. Only now does it register that he didn't have a good night's sleep for three decades. He can hardly believe how refreshed he now feels in the morning. He marvels at his new freedom of space. He can leave his apartment at any time, board any bus, or walk in any direction as far as he likes. He begins an adult driving class, having never learned as a teen, and the car feels as miraculously powerful and free as a spaceship.

He savors taking showers alone, unseen by anyone else. He loves having soap that's not the industrial-smelling prison issue. Most of the smells in prison were bad. He loves being able to hum a tune without anyone hearing him. He loves to shop at the supermarket. He notices colors. In prison, the range of hues was limited—the dark asphalt, the ocher walls, the dull blue uniforms, the dark muted grays and browns of the cell blocks, the olive green uniforms of the COs. What does one even call the color of steel bars? Out here, he delights in the colors of flowers, clothing, cars, items in store windows. One day he passes a yard sale and pays a dollar for a Tibetan prayer flag for its vibrant red and orange. He hangs it in his small kitchen.

There are moments when petty demands seem great. One Sunday he feels paralyzed trying to decide what to do. He finally walks to a park and reads, ironically something he could have done in prison, except here he sits not on the asphalt but on a bench under a tree. After a while he moves to the grass, something else he missed in prison.

James is flooded by vivid memories from the years leading up to his arrest. The emotions that come with the memories—whether happiness or fear or grief—seem stronger than they were when he had the actual experiences years ago. It's as if his emotions, dormant during his prison years, have been set free. His eyes fill with tears when he remembers Pops taking him to the park, or Mama cooking good dinners, or Spike's unflagging loyalty and love. He wishes he could show Mom and Pops his apartment, tell them that he's okay.

Mommies-To-Be

The week after the Fugitive Apprehension Team officer interviews Allison, she and Meagan solidify their plan. They will become mommies. Allison will carry the baby, and Gene has agreed to be the father. They will use artificial insemination. They may have a second in a couple of years, that one in Meagan's baby oven.

"If the kid inherits Gene's looks," Meagan says, "we'll have to keep it locked up, male or female."

Gene is touched and excited. He makes several visits to the fertility clinic in Berkeley, and after the last one, Allison and Meagan have him over for dinner. He is the only person who has heard—or ever will hear—the story of James, and he asks how he is doing.

"Very well," Allison says. "Everything has gone according to plan."

"Speaking of plans," Gene says. "When do my little swimmers go to work?"

"I love your word choice," Meagan says. "More poetic than *intrauterine insemination.*" She lifts her glass and says, "Here's to little swimmers."

Allison and Meagan clink glasses with Gene, who says, with mock drama, "The things I do for you!"

"Actually," Allison says, smiling her brightest smile, "there's one more thing."

A Probable Death

Gene rides his red Pinarello bike onto the bike lane of the Bay Bridge. It is a bright, crisp day in late December, and there are whitecaps on the bay. He carries in this jacket pocket the envelope that had been in Allison's lockbox at the bank. He stops his bike in a spot not covered by bridge traffic cameras—Allison has done the recon—and without touching the items, he empties onto the sidewalk James' old black-rimmed glasses and his prison ID card. He takes out his phone and dials 911. In his best frantic voice, he tells the dispatcher that he just saw someone jump from the bridge. The first CHP car arrives in ten minutes.

"He was jogging a couple hundred feet ahead of me," Gene tells the officer. "I saw him bend down and put something on the sidewalk, and then he vaulted the railing and was gone. An African-American man with dreadlocks and a beard. I couldn't believe what I was seeing. It was horrifying."

The officer picks up the glasses and the ID card. He peers over the railing.

"As soon as I got off my bike, I looked over," Gene says, "but I couldn't see anything."

The officer takes a pair of binoculars from his car and scans the water. He calls in a report and writes down Gene's contact information.

The next morning a five-inch story appears on an inside page of the *San Francisco Chronicle*. The jumper, presumed dead, is believed to be an inmate who escaped from San Quentin Prison in October. A bicyclist witnessed the jump. Though the Golden Gate Bridge averages twenty suicides a year, the Bay Bridge has only five. Mental health advocates have argued that the new span's railing, only fifty-five inches high, is too low. The actual number of suicides is likely higher than the official count due to jumps that go unwitnessed and bodies that are never recovered.

The next week Gene receives a call from the coroner's office. He goes in and signs an affidavit as to what he witnessed on the bridge. In ninety days, a death certificate is issued for James Fields, age fifty-one, address unknown. Cause of death: probable suicide by drowning.

For Allison, the symbolism is perfect. The man society had made of James is dead. The man James can now make of himself is born.

New Jobs

It's not through a sudden epiphany but rather a gradual drift of mind that Allison and Meagan conclude the private school world is not for them. After completing a program to earn her teaching credential, Meagan accepts a job at the public high school in Berkeley. Allison leaves her school to be a full-time mommy for a couple of years. The faculty throws her a baby shower. When she tells Janet Blake of her resignation, Janet's show of regret is unconvincing.

It is a tradition that at the end-of-year faculty luncheon, the school head presents people who are leaving with a book as a gift, accompanied by a few words of thanks. When Allison's turn arrives, she accepts the book and the two sentences of thanks. Smiling with cordiality, she gently pulls the mic from Janet's hand and says, "I have loved my students and my faculty colleagues here, and I thank you for making these first years of my teaching career really wonderful."

People smile.

Allison takes a breath. "As long ago as Socrates, there has been tension in education between the quest for truth and goodness on the one hand, and the tactics for getting ahead on the other. The former is real education. The latter is something else. The responsibility for keeping our school on the road to real education lies in the hands of the people here," she says, sweeping the room with her eyes. "I wish you success."

She lays the mic on the table, and after a moment, Janet picks it up, smiling like a frozen corpse.

Visiting Davis

On a hot Saturday in September, Meagan and Allison drive to Davis. Allison is six months pregnant and showing a considerable baby bump. It has been eleven months since James left San Quentin. He works as a veterinary assistant in the vet school hospital at UC-Davis, the 6:00 AM to 2:00 PM shift. He rents a one-bedroom bungalow at the edge of town. It has a fenced-in back yard, and he has gone to the local shelter and adopted a female pit bull he's named Hope.

Allison and Meagan meet him after his shift for a late lunch.

"Oh my God," Allison says when she sees him in his scrubs, "you're wearing blue again."

"Yeah," he chuckles, "but it's a lighter shade."

Meagan and Allison order BLTs. James chooses egg salad. He's become a vegetarian. He tells them that at the clinic he is known as the dog whisperer. "Animals seem comfortable with me. Especially the pitties," he says. "They trust me. My supervisor says I have the gift." Next year he will start a program to become a veterinary technician.

Allison asks, "Do people ever ask, you know, the story of your life?"

"Not much. This is the West Coast. People aren't much interested in where you're from. I tell them I moved from Chicago. I complain about the weather there, like Pops always did."

They exchange news. James finished adult driver's training and got his license. He successfully used the thumb glove for his print; the DMV woman was looking at her computer screen and didn't notice.

"We wanted to come see you now," Allison said, "because in

three months we'll be unable to carry on a conversation that isn't about breast feeding and diapers."

"Still tutor at the prison?" James asks.

"Oh, yes," Allison says. "Word spread about the suicide of James Fields. It kind of freaked me out to hear it."

"They all believed it?"

"Good question. You remember Habeeb?"

"Of course. Hamlet's ghost. We transferred up from Tehachapi at the same time. On the same van, in fact."

"Well, I was looking at his face in study hall when someone mentioned the suicide, and he smiled. It definitely wasn't a smile about the suicide. *Maybe* it was a smile of remembering good old James, but I don't think so. I felt—don't ask me why—that it was a smile that meant, I don't believe for a minute that he's dead."

James smiles and says, "I'd love to write him. Him and a couple of others, but I can't take the risk."

"No," Allison says, "Definitely not."

James says, "Sometimes I have dreams where I go back to San Quentin. Most of the dreams are kind of peaceful. I look around, shake hands with everyone. What's also strange is when I think back on San Quentin—in my waking mind—it doesn't make me cringe. I thank God I'm out, but at times I feel a kind of nostalgia for it."

"That makes sense, though," Meagan says. "It was a part of you. How could you regret yourself?"

"I still wonder why you did it," James says. The look on his face is softly inquisitive.

The waiter brings their sandwiches, and Allison waits until he has left the table.

"It goes way back," she begins. "Somewhere deep in my little girl self, I decided that Nancy Drew was what I wanted to become.

She had good radar for people who could use her help, and she showed up to give it. She was a problem solver. That's what I wanted to be. Algebra problems, what a poem means, how to escape from prison—they're all puzzles to be solved. There's that line from Wordsworth, *The child is the father of the man.* Correct it for the gendered language, of course, but it's true. That young girl wanting to be Nancy Drew was my parent."

Allison continues, "A few years ago one of my students needed someone to speak for her. No one really heard her true story—because they didn't try—just like no one in the criminal justice system heard yours. I didn't think fast enough or act fast enough. I failed her, and my failure tore a hole in the moral fabric of my little universe. Though I could never sew that one up, I needed to sew up another one, in some future time, to make up for it."

James and Meagan watch her and listen.

"That wasn't the only hole in the fabric. My dad tore one. He could have stood up for me, but he didn't. The actual incident was trivial, a silly moment in a supermarket parking lot, but it mattered. A lot. He needed to just say a few words, and he failed. When I see a tear like that, I want to sew it up. To make up for Dad's failing, for my own, for anybody's. Like picking up a piece of litter, even if you're not the one who dropped it. You pick it up to be a good citizen in the human nation."

James looks at Meagan and says, "You married a beautiful woman." As he says it, he is aware that Pops once said something similar about Mama.

Bee Sting

One day after work, James walks into the park with a novel and heads for his favorite bench. He sees a woman kneeling beside her dog, a whining Golden Doodle, trying to look at the front paw that he's licking furiously. James notices the clover and a few bees. He walks over.

"This just happen?" he asks.

"Yes," she says, looking up at James. "Suddenly he came up limping." She says it in a way that suggests she's open to receiving help.

"What's his name?" James asks, kneeling.

"Doodle," she answers. "Not original, I know."

James smiles at her. She looks Blasian, in her forties, and she's wearing pink scrubs. James rubs the dog's chest and uses his name in a soothing voice. He gently rolls the dog on its side and the dog submits, licking James' hand. Squinting, James gently spreads the pads of the dog's paw.

"Ah," James says. He reaches for his keys with his Swiss army knife attached. He pulls out the tiny tweezer and gently lifts something from the dog's paw. He spreads it on the nail of his index finger and shows it to the woman. It is the tiny stinger from a bee.

She wraps two fingers and a thumb around James' index finger. "Oh my God," she says. Her touch goes straight to his heart.

"See that tiny blob of viscous matter?" James says. "That's the venom sac. Looks like I got it."

James gives a head rub to Doodle, who bounds off with no limp.

"Are you a bee expert?" she asks.

"Vet assistant. My name is James."

"Felicia," she says. "It's nice to meet you."

They stand. She looks at James and nods toward the end of the park, "See those kids with the lemonade stand? Can I treat you to a lemonade?"

James smiles. "I would love that."

She calls Doodle over and clips on his leash.

Her Dad

Being pregnant, Allison finds herself thinking a lot about her dad. He would focus on the medical angle of fertility technology. He would call it amazing, which it is.

Her act of planning James' escape would shock him, and he would say you can't break laws like that. But he would be proud of the step-by-step thinking she employed, the way she thought about the contingencies, how she measured twice and cut once. If she tried to explain that helping James escape was a truer kind of justice, he could not hear it.

She has made peace with his clumsy betrayal of her that day in the parking lot. She wonders if he remembered it, if it gnawed at him. When she looks at the spice cabinet on their kitchen wall, it reminds her that people love in the way they can, even if it isn't the way we might wish.

She feels warm and grateful that when she was a girl, he taught her what he knew—how to use tools, how electricity works, how to approach a goal like making the rocket that will fly the highest. How to solve problems step by step. He never believed there were limits on what a girl can do.

The Cemetery

On the internet, which James is learning to navigate on his new laptop, he locates the gravesites of his mother and Black Snake at the cemetery in Oakland. One Monday in October, a year to the week after his prison exodus, he drives there. The grounds are quiet except for an occasional twittering of birds. A warm breeze rustles the dry leaves on the trees. No matter how loud or violent the city, the cemetery is always a place of peace.

He finds Mama's marker, a small stone with her name and the dates of her birth and death. Looking at the dates, he realizes that he's now outlived her by a year, something he does not deserve. He squats, and then leans forward, his knees pressing into the earth. Her marker is plain—a small granite stone dulled with a film of dirt, surrounded by uncut grass. He is carrying a water bottle in his pants pocket, and he uncaps it and pours water over the stone. He pulls out his shirt tail and shines the stone clean. He should have brought flowers.

Because it's October, the light is different, a touch softer, casting shadows mournful and long. How Mama must have loved him, how she must have worried about the streets he had to navigate, how proud she must have been about his good grades, and how his crime and his incarceration must have broken her heart. When he remembers the Air Jordans she got him for Christmas, tears roll freely down his cheeks. He thinks of the long bus rides and overnights in the motel she endured to visit him at Tehachapi.

He leans forward on his knees and presses his lips to the stone. He places his palms on its smooth, cool surface.

"I'll be back, Mama," he says. "I'll be back."

He thinks of skipping Black Snake's grave, but he has driven here, so he might as well go through with it. When he finds it, James looks down at the stone marker, his hands in his pockets. In his mind, he watches the killing as if it were yesterday. The emotions of that infinite moment—the rage at Black Snake, the grief at losing Spike—return, and James realizes his legs are shaking. To remember this event is to relive it. Now and forever. He looks up at the blue sky and takes some deep breaths.

He looks at the name etched in the stone: Marvin Reginald Mitchel. He speaks in a low voice.

"You know, Black Snake, I came here thinking I might make some kind of peace with you, once and for all. Say I was sorry. Forgive you and ask you to forgive me. At San Quentin I was in this self-help group called CAPE, and my final task was to write you a letter. I never did, so maybe this is it."

James looks down.

"I wish I knew your story, what made you such a poisonous snake, like your name, what made you so mean and heartless you'd kill a dog and then laugh at it. My 527 tribe had this saying: *hurt people hurt people*. I saw guys who had done some terrible things move in a better direction. It was like they were on the ground wrestling with the devil. Some of them were winning. As Fidel said, I robbed you of the chance to ever struggle to be better, and I'm sorry I did that. If I could relive that moment, I wouldn't shoot you. I'd just sit there with Spike's body, holding your gun, and watch you walk away. That's what I should have done. When I killed you, I took away your chance. And it didn't help Spike at all. What I did was wrong. It's on me, and I know it. I'm sorry, man."

James looks across the cemetery, stones of all shapes and sizes set on the rolling green slopes, all swimming in his tear-filled eyes. The leaves on the trees are turning yellow and brown. They will fall, and then the winter rains will come, and after that, spring.

"For me, I've got things to make up for. I've got to do the good I can do, and I've got to do the good you might have done. I'll never do some big heroic deed. That would be the easy way out. I will just pay it forward in small change, a little at a time. Not causing hurt. Helping sick and injured dogs. Being nice to people who cross my path. Breathing in the beauty of the world. All those things I'm going to do for Mom and Pops, for the guys back at the prison, for Allison, and for myself. I'll do it for you, too. I'm not saying it's enough. But it's all I've got."

After James leaves the cemetery, he stops at an art store in north Oakland. He finds a deluxe set of colored pencils and asks that it be shipped. He pays in cash and gives the clerk an index card on which he has written Lonny's address at Tehachapi.

Book Group Discussion Questions

1. Which character did you like best? Which character did you most identify with? (These two questions may have the same answer, but not necessarily.)
2. This a braided novel, following two very different characters whose paths don't cross until well past the halfway point of the story. What did you think of this aspect of the novel? Did you like it?
3. Did any of the scenes move you to tears? To outrage?
4. What scene do you think will remain the longest and the most vivid in your memory?
5. The prologue reveals that an escape attempt will be made. As you read the book, did you have a feeling as to whether the attempt would succeed? What made you feel that way?
6. Literature was important to both James and Allison. James sustained himself by reading novels through his thirty years in prison, and performing *Hamlet* was important to him. Allison became a literature major (and teacher), and her childhood love of Nancy Drew novels shaped her life's mission. How important—if at all—has literature been to you?
7. When we see contemporary prisons depicted in both movies and novels, often they are rife with violent inmates, abusive guards, and corrupt prison officials. By contrast, the two prisons depicted in this novel are much less dysfunctional. Do you feel that this book was painting a more truthful depiction of prison?
8. Allison does one thing (plan a prison escape) which

would seem "out of character" to almost everyone who knows her. James acts similarly "out of character" when he shoots Black Snake. Are these actions indeed out of character, or are they in fact consistent with the characters of Allison and James?

9. How has James changed by the end of the book? How has Allison changed?
10. Did James achieve redemption for his crime? If so, how was it achieved? Was the prison system an aid or a hindrance?
11. Did you ultimately find this novel uplifting or depressing?

Author Interview

Readers' Circle: How did you get the idea for this novel?

Bill Smoot: Back in 2013, I started teaching in the college program at San Quentin Prison. Walking into the prison in those early days of volunteering, I found myself gazing up at the high walls and wondering how someone might escape. My experience was very much like Allison's on her first visit to the prison. Then, as fiction writers are wont to do, I began to imagine an escape plan. I wondered. Who would be escaping, and why? What was that person's backstory? The story began to take form.

RC: Why did you decide to compose the novel as a series of very short chapters?

BS: One way to tell the story of a life—or two lives in this case—is to create select scenes, stringing them together like bits in a mosaic. I started writing this novel in that way—the death of James' father, the day they leave their little house in Sacramento, his first encounter with Black Snake. I liked the way it was going, so I made that my storytelling mode. It's not original, so I was partly going to school on other writers. Joyce Oates has done it, and Anthony Doerr does it in *All the Light We Cannot See*, a novel I really love.

RC: How did you create the character of Allison?

BS: In my first imaginings, the character who would help an inmate escape was some version of myself. But I knew that wasn't right, so "myself" was just a placeholder until the right character came along—and she did! I don't want to sound too woo-woo here, but I don't create characters in a deliberate and rational way. Instead, I ease my mind into a receptive mode and wait for the character to appear. Allison arrived, first as a young girl, watching her father in his basement workshop. Then she read Nancy Drew, came of age, and her life continued to unfold in my imagination.

RC: And how did James come about?

BS: Like Allison, he just arrived, first as a boy of twelve, and then he grew up. It occurred to me that among the archetypes of young males, one is the Good Boy—who wants to listen and learn, to do the right thing, to obey the rules. That's James. Good Boys become choir boys and Eagle Scouts. They often pay a price from their peers, especially the Bad Boys. At San Quentin, I have recognized a few of my students as former Good Boys. The character of James is in part a composite of them. As a child, I myself was a Good Boy, so that made James easier to write.

RC: A Good Boy commits a murder?

BS: At the moment Spike is killed, James ceases to be a Good Boy and becomes an Avenger. It both continues and destroys his essence as a Good Boy. Like so many definitive moments in life, it is a great and painful contradiction.

RC: Allison is radically different than James, and yet they collaborate on a prison escape.

BS: In terms of demographics, yes, James and Allison are polar opposites: straight-gay, Black-White, male-female, under-served Oakland-suburban Indianapolis. But in another way, they're the same person: introverted, watchful, a little nerdy and shy. For each, their isolation gives them a kind of freedom to grow and develop, unshaped by forces of conformity. Each is mission-driven. James wants to follow in the footsteps of George Washington Carver, and Allison wants to be Nancy Drew.

Of course, there are other differences. Even as a child, Allison was not a Good Girl. I think of her as the classic Huntress—independent and determined. Which she carries into adulthood.

RC: You've been teaching college classes at San Quentin for a decade and a half. Are any characters in the novel based on your students?

BS: Not based on, but snippets and details observed in the prison show up in the novel. Like many writers, I'm a bit of a voyeur by nature. I look and listen with great interest and care. Some of what enters my eyes and ears flows out the tip of my pen, usually in altered form.

RC: In the past few years, many have argued strongly that a White author should not create a Black character, especially a point-of-view Black character.

BS: Oh, yes. Many publishers, editors, and agents won't touch such works. I have followed the controversy and read the writing on both sides of the issue, which is difficult and complex. At the end of the day, my own feeling is that an important function of fiction, both reading it and writing it, is to help us understand one another. Success is partial—at best. It's hard enough to understand ourselves, let alone someone else, especially those whose life experiences are very different than our own. But we have to try, especially given the current state of our world. I am inspired by works—whether poetry, film, or fiction—that tackle the challenge of building empathy and understanding. Just last week, I screened for my San Quentin film class the Barry Jenkins film, *Moonlight*. It had tough guys in tears. Barry Jenkins is not gay, but he had the courage to make the film about a gay man. And it worked—because he's empathic, his film is empathic, and his viewers are moved toward empathy and care.

Whether in my novel I have failed or succeeded in creating fully human characters—Black, lesbian, felons—is a question for each reader to answer. All I know is that for me, James and Allison are fully human. No stereotype loves its dog the way James loves Spike.

In my other works of fiction, I have created point-of-view characters far outside my demographic: children, females, and gays. Even ghosts. I recently published a short story from the point of view of a coyote. If the coyote caucus wants to cancel me, so be it.

RC: What do you hope your reader takes from this novel?

BS: Like any novel, *San Quentin Exodus* is a bit of a Rorschach. Perhaps some will see there some moment of recognition, or empathy, or inspiration. That would be my hope.

Beyond that, since a large part of the novel takes place within prison walls, I hope that readers will become aware—or be reminded—that incarcerated people are as fully human, deep, troubled, and complex as only humans can be. They have hearts. For fourteen years, it has been my privilege to teach them works of literature, film, and philosophy. Whatever I have given, I have received back in greater measure. Truly. That is why this novel is dedicated to them.

Acknowledgments

A complete list of people to whom I owe thanks for their role in the creation of this novel would include almost every person I have known. For brevity's sake, I give special thanks to the following. For reading and providing helpful feedback on early drafts, I am grateful to Lori Ostlund, Angela Pneuman, Jack Metzgar, and Lynn Brown. I am grateful to Jenna Mattern, Kate Tourison, Chase Lawson, and Kevin Atticks at Apprentice House Press, and to Jessie Glenn and the good folks at Mindbuck Media.

For immeasurable inspiration, I thank all of the men I have taught in Mount Tamalpais College at San Quentin Prison. I am thankful for my dog Artemis and her loving fidelity.

For everything, I am so very grateful for my parents, Helen Rozan Smoot and William R. Smoot. Though they have long departed this earth, I should like to feel that I am always writing for them.

About the Author

Bill Smoot grew up in Maysville, Kentucky. He received a BA in philosophy at Purdue University and his PhD in philosophy at Northwestern. A life-long teacher, for the past fourteen years he has taught in the college program at San Quentin Prison.

His short stories have appeared in such periodicals as *Ninth Letter*, *Crab Orchard Review, Barely South Review*, *Crab Creek Review*, *Narrative*, and *Literary Review*. His non-fiction book, *Conversations with Great Teachers,* was published by Indiana University Press.

Apprentice House Press is the country's only campus-based, student-staffed book publishing company. Directed by professors and industry professionals, it is a nonprofit activity of the Communication Department at Loyola University Maryland.

Using state-of-the-art technology and an experiential learning model of education, Apprentice House publishes books in untraditional ways.This dual responsibility as publishers and educators creates an unprecedented collaborative environment among faculty and students, while teaching tomorrow's editors, designers, and marketers.

Eclectic and provocative, Apprentice House titles intend to entertain as well as spark dialogue on a variety of topics. Financial contributions to sustain the press's work are welcomed. Contributions are tax deductible to the fullest extent allowed by the IRS.

To learn more about Apprentice House books or to obtain submission guidelines, please visit www.apprenticehouse.com.

Apprentice House Press
Communication Department
Loyola University Maryland
4501 N. Charles Street
Baltimore, MD 21210
Ph: 410-617-5265
info@apprenticehouse.com • www.apprenticehouse.com

www.ingramcontent.com/pod-product-compliance
Lightning Source LLC
LaVergne TN
LVHW010559100826
845148LV00014B/2777

* 9 7 8 1 6 2 7 2 0 6 7 2 3 *